BLUE MARBLE

LOVE BEARS ALL THINGS

A Novel

RAY WHITE

BLUE MARBLE

Chapter One

Colorado, November 1906

"F ATHER," LEVI NUDGED. "FATHER, we're here."

"Wha… What?"

Levi tapped my shoulder again. "We're here, Father. Wake up. End of the line."

"Where are we?"

"Don't know. The conductor said this was the last stop and all passengers without round-trip tickets must exit the train. Guess we got to get off." Levi was already digging bags from under the honey-varnished benches. Two steamer trunks still sat in the baggage car. It was practically everything we owned.

"Father, come on. We gotta go." Levi's eyes rose to the conductor in the aisle.

The train puffed out the last of its steam and went quiet. Everyone had disembarked. I squinted through the soot-stained window. A warm sunny day, even for November, like always in Colorado. That is, if we were still in Colorado. I guessed so from the brass plaque above my head reading, Crystal River & San Juan Railway. That was Colorado, right? West side of the Rockies? Probably.

A warm sun went to work on what remained of a bad headache and bad memories. Even with smiling people gathering outside my

1

window I felt no desire to leave the bench.

Where I could avoid actual contact with any human being.

Anywhere. Ever again.

I scowled at cheerful families greeting travelers in groups and pairs, milling, happy and welcoming. A dismissive puff escaped my lips at the shouts and hugs, gasps at the long and dangerous trip into the mountains, and assurances of an uneventful trip. Elation and more hugs. Glad to be together again. Bags were lifted and knots of folks turned to locate carriages and motorcars for the final leg home. Within minutes the ritual ended, leaving the loading dock quiet and empty. Just like the little train, resting at the end of the line.

Nobody came for Levi and me.

Because nobody knew where we were, and that was fine by me.

"Father, I know you miss…" He stopped. "So do I, but–"

"I just want to sit here." And cry. But I didn't tell Levi that.

"We can't, Father. We don't have round-trip tickets. The conductor said all passengers without round trip tickets…"

He noticed my lip.

"Hmm, Micah and Caleb," I muttered, still breathing on the window.

"They're going to be all right, Father. Now come on. We got to go."

"Okay. You take the bags, son," I said, forcing my eyes forward, still unsure if I could face the thought of what this place meant. The pain of starting over. The grinding nothingness. The freefall into some unknown but certain destruction.

Just enough space had been hacked out of the Ponderosa pines for a depot shack and platform at the end of the tracks. Little curls of smoke from morning fires sifted through boughs that practically touched the ground from years of weighty snows. Deeper into the Ponderosa's lay a tidy little town in a steeply sloped valley with woods practically crushing in. In the distance a swift creek, or river as they call them in Colorado flowed west from the mountains. Tributaries fell in from distant elevations south and east. The gentle water, a flock of honking geese, and a slight breeze mingled into pleasing rhythms. At least it wasn't ugly.

"Got everything?" Levi asked.

I screwed my bravery on. "Let's have a look, son."

Our first communication with locals came from a sign posted at the end of the depot platform. It read, "NO CREEKERS." A peace-officer patrolled the plankway with a 12-gauge double-hammer, observing every passing person.

"Hello, Sheriff," I said, stepping up with a hand. I had brightened up enough to take in the fresh sights of a new place. "Nice town. Nice little—"

The stoic man squared off and gripped the scattergun. He clearly had no interest in exchanging pleasantries or discussing the bucolic qualities of his little mountain town. I guessed he was a man of duty. Square jaw, tight shirt, lean muscle. The type to do a job. I'd seen plenty like him.

"What's this, NO CREEKERS?" I asked lightly.

The mountain-raised man's voice was trained to convince. "Means what it says. Don't abide no Cripple Creekers. No professional instigators or seditionists. No drifters, drovers, gamblers, or union men. If you got any dealings with the Western Federation of Miners, you git right back on that train. You won't get a bed in Marble. Colonel Meek don't permit it."

"That's where we're at? Marble?" I asked.

He examined me like he was settling on which cheek to bash in. But I had been nursing a nightmare through the dark morning ride and had no idea where we were. I knew from maps and memory that Marble was on the west side of the continental divide, south of Glenwood Springs and Carbondale. But that was about all, and I didn't even know why we were here. I guessed it was just the end of the line, and that suited me just fine. Good place to hide.

"Three kinds of men end up in a place like this: missionaries, mercenaries, and miscreants. Which one are you?"

I had to wonder. "Who's Meek?" I asked. "He run the town?"

"See the big finishing mill? That's his operation. He's the owner and manager. It's all part of the Colorado-Yule Marble Company, formed a few years back in Ought Four. Meek gave a strict writ for Creekers to clear out and stay out."

He tapped a shotgun hammer, evidently to clarify the word strict.

For me, 1904 was a vivid nightmare. Evidently, while Mr. Meek was musing over the formation of marble works here, I was embroiled in union strikes and violence, trying to stay afloat and trying to keep my men from getting killed. The year prior, my partner Sam Whitman had been brutally beaten to death by union thugs, and nothing went right after that. If Colonel Meek knew anything about that mess, I could understand the meaning of the sign, "NO CREEKERS."

The sheriff nodded at the two-hundred-foot wooden finishing mill. "It's the Marble Age. We're doing a new thing out here. Don't tolerate no professional agitators of no kind. Ain't no union here. No Western Federation of Nothin'. Now where'd you come in from?"

A team of four skinny horses and hay wagon drew up next to the sheriff, so I turned to have a look at his booming little quarry camp, a sight brighter than your typical timber camp or the many mining camps I'd been through.

In my experience, the types carving out communities like this were exactly the stoic and independent ones standing before me with shotguns at the ready. I got a look at what they had wrought.

A small hotel sat up the hill a stone's-throw and assorted stores stacked up around it, neat square-façade kit types from the catalogues. Faint explosions and an occasional whine of pneumatic tools drifted down from the eastern hills punctuating the constant drone from the big wooden building. The finishing mill was clearly the principle reason for the town's existence. But enough commerce had sprung up around it to actually be called a city, if one could see the potential.

The hay wagon pulled off and men began loading marble blocks onto flatcars behind the little Mogul 2-6-0 steamer while it took on water from a standpipe. That little train must have seen a passel of boomtown drifters, treasure seekers, and hard-luck cases in from Cripple Creek, where we had just come in from.

"I'll ask you just one more time, mister," the sheriff said, locking eyes and ignoring Levi who had pulled out a sketchpad and pencil.

4

"Where you from?"

"Well, I won't lie to you. We are from Cripple Creek, just like your sign says. But we're not union men, and we're not seditionists. I owned the Black Jack Mine in Cripple Creek. You've heard of it?"

The man shrugged.

"Well that is, until the Western Federation of Miners wrecked the whole shebang back in 1903 and Ought Four. Since you got this sign, I guess you heard about that."

"We heard… And it ain't happening here. So, you best move on."

"But we're not union men, remember? I owned the Black Jack Mine. We were the good guys." I smiled.

"So you say, but the mule don't kick flies for nothin'. Like the sign says, No Creekers. Understand? I got a writ." He cocked the shotgun right there before me, and stared me down, ready to discharge his duty at the slightest cause.

"Can we at least use your privy and get a sandwich?" Best not test the man beyond the necessities. I had learned enough from Sam Whitman, the old Texas Ranger to know when a man meant business. Cocked shotguns usually meant just that.

"You and your pard got one hour. Be back on this train or up that road to Crystal City. I can't allow you to linger."

"Fair enough, Sheriff. You got orders. We'll be back in an hour. Can we leave our kit here?"

"No one will touch it." I reckoned a cocked shotgun would see to that. "But you be back in an hour, or I swear I'll…"

Levi and I stepped off the platform to find a privy. One long road bisected the valley basin north from south, with old-growth evergreens virtually covering the narrow lane, the type you see in picture postcards from the high country. Collecting pine needles must be like baling hay. The big hotel stood high on the north side, with stores crowding for positions close by. A row of shotgun cottages lined the street for a quarter mile, all puffing little clouds of smoke into the clear blue sky. Unpainted outhouses and wood piles tucked in behind each one. Levi and I planned to meet outside a minute later.

"Okay, Park Street," I said, when we buttoned up. "We're on

Park Street."

"I like that one!" Levi said, pointing to a colorful shop down the lane. "It's a curiosity shop. I want to buy… umm… something for back home." He squirmed and consulted the treetops for words.

I knew what he meant. I had courted my own sweetheart back in Randalls Flats as a youth. But my prickly granddad was no man to consult on the art of sweet nothings. I hoped I was a better father to Levi, but probably not if the truth was known.

Levi double-timed up the street with me trailing behind with eyes on the towering ridgelines. A dense collection of marble statues, carvings, and raw blocks posed a maze to the shop entrance. A dozen barn swallows guarded the door, evidently out in the sunshine for a good feed before the hard snows came.

Levi cracked the door and peered in. It looked inviting. Neat as a pin.

A little brass bell over the doorway clanged next to a hand-painted sign reading, "For God so Loved the World." A little different than the one at the depot.

A thousand mingled scents of herbs and roots, flowers and flora, minerals and mud escaped the doorway in a little exhaling breeze. Purple glass jars with all manner of crushed plant and mineral lined the upper shelves. Exotic marble carvings below stood fixed in time, each begging the question of their curious poses. Grass and greenery contrasted snow-white marble. Everything to indulge the senses. An imposing brass cash register, two feet tall sat on a short wooden bar where purchases of the unusual crafts were presumably tendered. A rosy little sign tacked to the back read, "Your Credit is as Good as Your Word. Let's Be Friends!"

A little redhead in braids – maybe six or seven – marched out from the back room with windmill arms. She deftly navigated the potions and marble to greet us with an infectious smile.

"Hello, mister," she wagged, fiddling with her dress. A wildcat on wheels. "What do you want to buy? Do you like this one? My pa will deliver it for free. But I like that one with the angel wings." She sped over to a massive protective angel overlooking a pair of children at play. I had never seen such a stunning piece. It captured my emotions so deeply that I could not concentrate on the girl's words, but that didn't slow her well-practiced sales pitch.

"Which one do you want?" the whirling wonder repeated, tapping eagerly for a sale she felt forthcoming. "Can you make up your mind soon? Carey's Ice Cream Parlour has lemon phosphate now!"

A female voice came from the back room. "Please excuse little Harriet. She thinks she runs the—"

Just then, the dreamy marble creations darkened before a set of dazzling blue eyes. Diamonds in a sluice box was my first thought. Diamonds in a creek bed. The kind you mortgage the homestead for. Those diamonds reduced me to a speechless idiot, a wooden Indian without a word in me, even with the little redhead winding up for an answer.

Why would the eyes promise so much? With certain people you get everything you need just from the eyes. Not the face. Not the body. Not the hands. It's the eyes that do the work, and sometimes they do it very well. In those eyes before me, I saw everything I had needed for so long.

I saw healing. And tenderness. And strength.

Of course I also noticed a lively nature. Animated. Friendly and fun. Eager to please. An adult version of the dynamo in braids, waving me over for her next pitch. Most of that information came right out of those eyes. Sharp blue crystal that cut a passageway to the soul.

A moment of exploration commenced. Eyes locked, with generous information passing between. Nothing verbal, just unfiltered communication, soul to soul; understanding, compatibility, and desire. Enough to start my mind on a little journey, with or without my consent.

Had she begun her own journey too? What did my eyes reveal in return? Misery and dark depression? Or swelling curiosity and desire? Was she seeing the worst in me or some version of goodness my heart was able to dredge up for public display?

Levi had no idea.

"Afternoon, ma'am," he ventured, fracturing the invisible flow. The woman seemed to lose her balance as the connection broke. We both blinked and turned to the boy. What did he say? I guessed he just wanted to buy something and get back to the train station before that sheriff came looking. "Do you have any…" He paused and turned. "Father, go outside… go on."

"What? What did I–"

"Just go. I want to get–"

"Okay, okay, I understand," I said, reluctantly turning for the door. The curious marble works outside would entertain me while he did his lovey-dovey thing. But once outside, I caught myself stealing looks back through the rippled shop windows.

Minutes passed as the woman led Levi from item to item, lifting small carvings from wrought-iron stands and describing their unique qualities. I read their silent conversation; Levi choosing just the right object for his purpose, and the woman asking just the right questions to direct his search. Levi examined every item, even the ones I knew he couldn't afford. Their conversation seemed to expand beyond the purchase of marble craft. The woman wanted to know everything about this unique boy in her marble shop. She touched and admired him.

Banishment was too much.

"Levi!" I said, letting myself back into the shop. "Did you see that carving of King David with a lamb over his shoulder out there? It is absolutely–"

"Father!"

"Well, it is fabulous," I said with rising spirits. My reentrance was not exactly elegant, but at least I was back in. "And you should see the massive blocks out there. I'll bet they make some pretty interesting pieces. I just couldn't take my eyes off that statue of David. Is that cut from a single block?" I had no idea what I was chattering about. I just wanted to get back into the conversation.

"Is this your father, Levi?" The woman asked. "I'd like to meet the man who raised such a fine young gentleman." She turned to me with a smile, and then came the redheaded wildcat.

"That David statue is sixty-eight dollars," the girl informed. "Can you afford that? No? Then look over here." She grabbed my hand and dragged me to the other end of the store. I turned back, acknowledging the little zealot.

The woman's eyes said, "Sorry for you! Maybe next time."

Levi held up a blue marble rose mounted on a delicate green stem of stone.

"I'll take this one," he said. "I like the blue and gray veins." He twirled the specimen to admire its facets. Little sparklets danced across his eyes.

"Oh!" the woman shrieked. "Oh, Levi dear, your hands!"

Levi went dumbstruck. The alarm must have made no sense. But I glanced at my own hands and knew exactly what she meant. They were cracked and bleeding from mucking ore in the Black Jack Mine for the last nine months. Plus, we'd been pulling double shifts for three, just to save up to leave. Personal care had been a lesser concern, especially for me. I just wanted out of that place as soon as finances allowed. But we nearly worked ourselves to death blasting and mucking ore in the dark stopes and drifts a thousand feet under. We were tramming out thirty-two tons of ore a day, sending one-ton carts of high-grade up to sorting house chutes, which traveled to the stamp mills and processing in Colorado City.

Thirty-two tons a day will wear you plumb out.

And, darkness, choking dust, black powder, smoke, the black damp, dead canaries, and ten thousand jagged rocks will wear you out. The hands, the knees, and the elbows took an awful beating. Men died in places like that, but we had to make a living one way or another. And we needed traveling cash.

Now suddenly a pinch of guilt crossed my mind for subjecting little Levi to the harshness of labor in Cripple Creek. Maybe the lady was right, but I had worked like that my whole life, and the toll it took from Levi had never occurred to me. Neither had it to Grandpa Clark who had toiled in the black Missoura dirt behind a matched set of mules and a one-way plow. It was just a day's work, nothing more. That was how we lived. But Levi's hands were bad off. Maybe as bad off as his shredded overalls and blown-out shoes.

The lady storekeep returned with a bottle of pink ointment.

"Ouch!" He cried. "That hurts!"

"I know. I know. It's just the oil getting into the cracks," she

9

groaned with him. "You'll be better soon dear, just rub it in."

The fragrance was as intoxicating as the David statue.

But not as much as those crystal blue eyes I had affixed to my own. Little eddies of fantasy followed. Clean face with a little button nose. Slight muscular frame. Eighteen-inch waistline in a new cream dress with eight pillowed buttons leading to a crisp standing collar. Blonde hair flowed from under an ornamented silken hat.

And blue eyes as bright as the marble.

"Mister Clark," the woman began with no affection, now only three paces apart, and probably sensing the little eddies of fantasy in my eyes. "What type of man are you?" she asked.

"Ma'am?"

"This boy works the Cripple Creek mines with you?"

"Yes, ma'am, that's right," I said.

"And he's thirteen?"

"Uh-huh."

"Are you a hard man, Mister Clark? A sweat shop boss?"

I just stood there. Maybe I had missed the meaning.

"Levi, dear," she turned. "This will soften those callouses and stop the bleeding. I make it myself." She pointed to overhead shelves with a hundred medicine bottles. "It's mostly wild rose and bee's wax, which I gather from the marshy flats below Yule Creek. Here, take this bottle." She replaced the glass stopper, placed it into his breast pocket with a pat, and then continued working the fragrant substance into broken skin. Her expert strokes enveloped Levi's rough hands. A sweet fragrance filled the little shop, which mixed with a hundred other intoxicating scents and the eddies of fantasy.

I nearly felt it on my own broken hands. And nearly felt her in my arms.

"Now, let me explain this wonderful little rose you've chosen, Levi." He gripped the small stone with newly anointed fingers. It was delicately carved from spidery blue marble.

"Can you see the variations?" she asked, lifting the sparkling item before her face. "The tiny gray and blue lines are vegetable matter pressed into the limestone at its formation in the days of Noah. This is

10

Blue Marble, my favorite."

"Uh-huh," Levi said. "But how do you make it like a rose? Or does it come from the ground like that?"

"No, I carve them," she explained. "With special tools." She lifted a quarter-inch tooth chisel from her bench.

The little rose reflected light from each facet, casting colors onto the upper shop windows. The woman leaned in, touching and teasing each cut and surface of the stone – her artisan fingers gliding over the curves, presumably as they had a thousand times before in expectation of this very day. Her blue eyes widened, as if this single stone was the sole source of fire and passion within her.

I had to look away. And exhale.

"Um, how much is it?" Levi asked, eyeing the precious stone. "I don't have much–"

"These blue roses take a week to polish, Levi. I charge four dollars, but I like you, so I want you to have it for free." The woman glanced at me with no pleasant sentiment. Was it her answer to the hard labor in the mines of Cripple Creek? Maybe. But it hadn't been that way, and the woman must have known that, for there was more to the glance than spite. She had other things on her mind and that came out too.

Why? Because the eyes tell all.

The eyes do not lie, and you cannot hide all the meaning they intend to impart. They communicate the moods and meaning of the heart, and you cannot stop that, even if you try.

Her visual scolding was no match for the heart. Checkmate.

"Oh no, ma'am," Levi protested. "I can pay. I have sixty cents." But you wouldn't know it to look at him. We had barely made it out of Cripple Creek with a rice bag and some jerky, with Levi's duds as threadbare and ragged as mine. Worn to the drawers and raveled at the hems. Patricia never would have allowed us in public, but she had passed, and here we were. Levi, Micah, Caleb and I had made it the best way we knew, and that was the truth. If Patricia could see us now, she had to know that. We were four men untethered and set adrift, and making it any way we could. But I closed my eyes and apologized to her nonetheless.

The woman said, "I know you can, dear," caressing his hands with more salve from the bottle. "I know you have money. I just want your Adelaide back in Cripple Creek to have the best you can send her. And I'm putting a bottle of my rose lotion in the box too. She'll like that. A girl needs to know you care about the little things, like her hands, her skin, her hair, her eyes. You have to notice them all. Plus, you'll both be using the same lotion and that will give you something to write about, and to remember me."

I sensed a question rising in the woman's mind, but then she sucked air through closed teeth and turned away. "One more thing, Levi. I want her to have this little marble cross. It will remind Adelaide that you are a man of integrity. She needs to know that. Or at least her father does."

She packed the items in sawdust in a little cardboard box – hand-folded, hand-stenciled with little blue roses, not machine-made like everything else in this ugly world. Had those hands crafted everything around us, I wondered. My observations now fell on her lean muscular fingers closing the bright little box, creamy and small but intensely purposed, and somehow connected to the snow-white marble, the blue marble, the lotions, the smells, the dreamy crystal all around us. It was all one package.

The woman looked into Levi's eyes. "I have deliveries this evening. I will post this for you. Just write her father's name and street on top. I'll make sure it gets there. I like you, Levi, and want you to be happy with Adelaide. She sounds like the perfect girl. Homeschooled by her own mother, you said? Now that's not something you see anymore. She must be an exceptional woman. I hope you will come back to see me again, Levi."

"I will."

"Where does your name comes from, Levi?" she asked.

"Mother told me. It's not from Levi Strauss and his jean-cloth. I was named after Joseph's brother from olden-times Israel. They did something in the desert, but I don't remember exactly what. Mother read the scriptures to us kids."

The woman smiled. "This sounds silly, but I think Israel will be a nation again."

Levi's eye's lifted in mild interest. Even I had to admit, it was an interesting notion.

"They're scattered all over the world now, but I think God will bring them back into their own land, just like he said he would. Prophesies will become fact."

Levi half-smiled. I don't think he had any idea what she was saying. The notion sounded so foreign I couldn't even consider it. The ancient Israelites back in their own land? Wild speculation. Crazy talk. Never happen. But then, there was some mysterious stuff in the Bible I never fully understood.

"You mentioned brothers. Where are they now?" she asked.

"Micah and Caleb are stock brokers in New York City, ma'am. That's in the east."

"Good for them. They're making lives for themselves. You'll be doing that soon, Levi." She took his hands and smiled.

A man's face slid out from behind the curtain of the back room. "Harriet okay? I haven't heard her in a while. Where is she?" The little girl had grown tired of adult talk, and sat quietly in the corner with a marble slab and a draw knife.

"She's alright, Tom," the woman said, "she's right here with me."

I glanced over at the man who eyed me up. He sniffed lightly, but said nothing, and then returned to his work behind the curtain. He had been so quiet I didn't even know he was there.

The woman turned back to Levi. "My name is Lorena. Please let me know what Adelaide thinks of her blue marble rose."

"Yes, ma'am, I'll write you," he agreed.

Levi and I turned to leave. "Thank you for your generosity, Miss Lorena," I said, extending a calloused hand. She took it lightly, winced, but offered nothing. I bowed in embarrassment.

The woman excused herself and headed out the door in a sudden rush. "I just realized I must speak to someone!" Like a vision, she was gone.

The little brass bell clanged behind us, and once again the swallows buzzed the intruders below. The breezy mountain air, with scents of pine and mountain water struck my senses anew.

I blinked. What in blue blazes?

Had the prickly ash bitters opened my sinuses? Or what? I felt alive. Not dead inside. Not lost in grinding depression. And no menacing images of derailed passenger cars rolling to the bottom of a thousand-foot ravine to pacify my pain. Was it just the natural beauty of this wild place? The scents and smells? The remoteness from everything modern and industrial? Yes, the droning mill was here but it was nothing like the industrial wasteland of Cripple Creek with its massive tailings and cribbing tacked to every twisted mountain switchback. If Cripple Creek was a derelict drunk, this place was a freckle-faced schoolgirl. It was clean, and I felt clean just standing there.

"Guess we gotta git back, huh?" Levi said. "That sign said NO CREEKERS."

"Hmm…"

Levi brightened. "I like Miss Lorena. She gave me this bottle of hand liniment." He held up the rose-colored bottle and admired it in the rays of sunlight.

"I know you do, son. Let's talk to that sheriff, " I wished I'd had a pocket watch, but I was sure if the hour had passed, he would be out gunning for us.

A short walk down the hill revealed the self-same sheriff on his beat. He paced up and down the roadside with the 12-gauge in the crook of his arm. Evidently, nobody entered his town without a talk.

"Train leaves in five, mister," he informed.

I touched my hat. "We sure like it here."

"Mister, you are trying my patience. I gave you an hour. That was out of my own kind nature. But if you try me, I will see you and your partner incarcerated."

"Levi here is my son. But didn't you mention a town up the road a piece?"

"That'd be Crystal City," he said.

The sheriff turned and waved to someone; he cocked his head for a spell and then spun back with a new word. "Hey, there's gold up there." He pointed due east.

"The Lead King Mine?" I asked.

"Yessir, but it's a six-mile walk and you got two travel trunks. But it can be done, or you could hire that team you saw an hour ago. You'll see the Crystal City Mill just before town, just before the crick on your right. Once you cross over, thars yer town." He nodded up the dirt road into the eastern mountains. "But I'll warn you. They don't abide drifters up there neither. If yer gamblers or low-down trail bums, you best git back on that train. They are good folk up there, and I ain't afraid of traveling up that road after you."

"No sir," I said. "We're not gamblers. Remember? I ran the Black Jack Mine, but not anymore. We're muckers now. Or, we were. Until–"

"Well, whatever you say. I just don't want to hear no news of you two. Understand? They got a nice little community up there. There's a few rough miners and trappers, but most are good law-abiding folk. You best stay on their good side or I'll hear of it. And I'll come right up that road myself." He boosted the shotgun for effect.

"Yessir, I understand."

"So, this your son? And he's a mucker too?"

"That's right, Levi Clark. My name's Jeremiah Clark. We're not gamblers or union men, sir." Levi shook the sheriff's hand who finally let down his shotgun and offered the use of a goat cart for our kit. He was a good man, just doing a job. I wish we'd had a few more like him in Cripple Creek, or a little more temperance like Colorado Springs. Things might not have gone so badly up there.

"Awright, let's go, Levi," I said with a bearing on the eastern ridgeline.

We started up the dusty road with steamer trunks on the borrowed cart and a bag in each hand, past a little boarding lodge and a mountain lake where picnickers and rafters enjoyed the bright afternoon. Another five miles and we'd be in Crystal City, but I was in no special hurry.

15

"I like Miss Lorena," Levi said again, whistling the tune she had likely been named for.

"A… hundred months have passed, Lorena,
Since last I held that hand in mine,
And felt the pulse beat fast, Lorena,
Though mine beat faster far than thine."

Chapter Two

A Year Later, 1907

WOMEN WERE NOT ALLOWED at the quarry or in Quarry Town. But Colonel Meek permitted it as long as I dressed modestly and didn't present a safety hazard. Which I did... dressed modestly that is, with a black silk outfit and gray hat, trimmed in thin black piping and red roses, bought at Kobey's Clothier down on Center and Main. This was one of six new ensembles for the 1907 year.

But modesty and safety were not the issues. It was "luck."

"Bad luck" or "Le donne sono sfortuna," to be specific.

Everyone in the marble camp knew the harm females could invite upon mining and quarry works. Not from any supposed safety hazards or misplaced passions, but for simply being where they ought not. It aroused Tommyknockers and spirits of bad luck. Of course, it was a nineteenth-century notion, but still alive and well in 1907 among the Austrians and Italians who had come in from the old country to work marble in the newest and grandest marble works on earth.

"Sfortuna, signorina Lorena. Sfortuna! Izza bad-uh luck."

Colonel Meek stepped out of the Pea Vine carriage offering a strong hand. "Watch your step on this slick rock, Miss Lorena." He let his dog out to run the length of the quarry portal. "All the photographers are up at the pit mouth to Quarry #2. Are you excited?" He smiled broadly from a strong jaw, with robust and inviting features. Six feet tall, and physically able in such environs, eight-hundred feet above the town of Marble, on a ledge cut into the white cliff.

9,500 feet into the raw elements is a dizzying position for any female.

Everything is below you. You just want a man to hold on to.

Quarry Town was home to a hundred workers, mostly transients and summer help at the Colorado-Yule Marble Company, of which Colonel Channing F. Meek was principle owner and chairman. Homes consisted of dugouts, lean-to shebangs, and a few free-standing frame houses, suitable only for summer occupation, and only for the indigent and lowest men who ventured to occupy them. With eight feet of snow in February, nothing in Quarry Town was permanent.

Except the marble.

Build a shed; it's snow-covered and caved in by springtime. Dig a well; mud fills it in the next twelve months. Erect a picket fence; and cornices pull it down by March. Bring in workers; they flee when snow buries their cabin for the eighth time in a month, or slides off the edge of the cliff. Only the marble is permanent in Quarry Town. That… and the crisp and rarified air of the Elk Mountain range.

"This promotional shot will endear the marble works to our female buyers in Denver and Colorado Springs. They will love us! Miss Lorena, you are going to make us look so good! You know all the housewives down there want washroom accents, commode lids and linen shelves, faucet handles and backsplash tiles. And of course, washroom bowls and floors in the finest homes. It's the fashion rage for the newly affluent. Faux marble is out and solid rock is back in. Make us proud, Lorena. You are the apple of my eye!"

Colonel Meek wanted me on every photographic expedition in Marble and the quarry works. Nearly every photograph of women at the works were of me. Was it merely the avant garde curiosities it aroused in his investors? Or was it just my smart choice of dress? My friend Blanche never got invited, so maybe that was it. She was just too gaudy, but would she listen to me? Not on any point from fashion to fools. In any case, I loved the wild nature of this place and posed on any dangerous perch Colonel Meek put me up to, as long as there was a sturdy man nearby.

The hundred-foot opening to Quarry #2 was a hive of industry. It was alive with channeling machines, wire saws, steam-powered compressors, steel cables, the clickety-clack of the Pea Vine tramway, and dozens of the roughest men Colorado could produce. Only the most modern machinery could pick ten ton blocks off the quarry floor and swing them out over the cliff to waiting oxen carts – the job of the industry's newest Lincoln hoist, hanging off a fifty-foot boom-derrick.

A fair comparison might be the steamy new 1907 haute couture, full-breasted gown.

With broad-brimmed hat, complete with silk grass and stuffed hummingbirds.

Modern. And steamy.

Colonel Meek cut the first opening into the marble cliffs himself in a boson's chair, hanging over Yule Canyon back when his men all feared the 150 foot fall to the talus rock bottom. They slung him out over the edge where he hammered for a foothold to stand on. That was the original Number #1 from which this whole enterprise had arisen. Now you'd only fall to your death if you lost your footing too close to the edge, or was horsing around and forgot where you were.

The crystal formations on this ledge made gold mines look cheap.

Not three minutes into the photography session, where the finest Eastman Kodak dry film captured the most modern and interesting images set against milky white rock, I noticed two new men I wanted for a whole new idea.

"Ask those two over. I know them!" I smiled, pointing to the new men in Quarry Town. "Then lay that two-by-six slab on their shoulders. I'll sit on top and you take the image on your fancy Kodak's. Channing will love it!" I pointed to an eight-foot sliver left over from a sawed slab. "That one!"

The marble sliver would prove the hardness of Colorado-Yule marble and satisfy Meek's avant garde photographic interests all at once. Black silk on snow-white marble? Yeah, that would do it.

"Miss Lorena!" Levi shouted, running for me. "You're up here in Quarry Town. Are you allowed?"

"Hello Levi," I smiled, reaching for his hand. "Want to work for me?"

I nodded to his father. "Hello, Mister Clark. I'm glad to see you down here."

He tilted like a drunkard. "Down here? We're eight-hundred feet up! I could tumble into Yule Creek and never be seen again! But I know what you mean; down from Crystal City. We're just here for the summer. They reluctantly allowed it, but we had plenty of work up in the gold camp. The Lead King Mine shipped forty tons of concentrates last week alone."

"It is a prosperous decade," I allowed, unshuttering my blue eyes to Mister Clark, who seemed to animate at the mere sight of them. For what reason, I had yet to explore. He must have had some fixating fetish to blue eyes because I used them for the next two hours to command his strengths in inhuman ways, hoisting marble beams, lifting me atop marble ledges, and other such feats of strength and beauty the Colonel could exploit for his promotional materials. Two hours later Mister Clark and Levi fell out in a state of collapse. I had worked them like Roman slaves.

"I want these two again tomorrow!" I yelled to Colonel Meek. "I want to bring that cracked block up from Glenwood Springs. Can I have them?"

He smiled and waved a finger, then returned to his drawings and a new Sullivan Ingersoll pneumatic-powered channeling machine, just uncrated at the portal opening.

"I guess you're my slaves!" I twinkled at Mister Clark, an act that seemed to stun him on each occasion, which I decided to use to my advantage. "Can you be at the Larkin Hotel at 4 AM tomorrow? It's a four hour trip into Glenwood Springs. We've got a big block to haul back into Marble."

I had Colonel Meek's Stanley Steamer touring car with a good head of steam and puffing eagerly at the hotel at four. Acetylene headlamps gave at least fifteen feet of forward light in a nice yellow glow. We had all the horsepower needed to haul marble from Glenwood Springs – sixteen horsepower, Colonel Meek assured me. Of course, we could have it shipped, but I had other designs for the day. Young Levi and Blanche were soon asleep, as the rhythmic Steamer could rock anyone to sleep at such an hour. That left Mister Clark next to me, nervously fishing for words. The excursion must have been a little different than his normal tasks up in Quarry Town or out in the backcountry wilderness of Crystal City.

I turned to Mister Clark. "Don't worry; Colonel Meek says you're getting paid for this."

He just smiled. "Good. After yesterday, I may need medical care!"

"Do you remember me, Mister Clark? You and young Levi came into my shop last–"

"Oh yes. You made quite an impression. That is to say, you and your daughter. What a whizzbang. She wanted me to buy something real bad. Is she your... only..."

I think he realized he'd said too much, or stepped into a chuckhole and tried to extract himself as ably as one could.

"Umm, well, Levi was very impressed," he said, whirling back at the dozing boy. "You see, he was an orphan child, and had only recently come to live with Patricia and me when–" He puffed. "Well... when... Let's just say that is how we came to wander into your store back then. Levi hasn't stopped talking about you and your family. He was smitten."

"And you?"

Mister Clark blinked. "Smitten?"

"Mister Clark! I meant... umm... impressed. You know... with the marble shop?"

Now I'd stepped in my own chuckhole.

"Oh yes, but that sheriff didn't think much of us two bums. He sent us on."

Mister Clark shifted in the leather upholstery, which creaked with every jostle of the little steam buggy. "Sent us up to Crystal City, up in the mountains. Been at the Lead King Mine ever since. But then they called men down to Quarry Town for summer work so we decided that might be a little closer... you know... for convenience sake, better groceries and such." He paused and glanced. "You can get so much more down here in Marble." He smiled again, not entirely satisfied with his answer.

"Of course, we're glad to see you again, Miss Lorena." He added, and forgot to disconnect from my eyes. "And that little firefox, Harriet! Haha! And Thomas. I see him at the quarry from time to time. Your husband is a fine man; I admire him."

He peeked over to see where the words had landed.

I could have laughed at his boyish awkwardness.

So I allowed him to entrap himself for the next four hours, and mused at how transparent a man could be. He had evidently never acquired the guile so quickly perfected in social circles. Had he been in the wilderness with Jesus? Socially speaking, he could have been Levi's brother. Just a happy-go-lucky boy, swinging from trees at the swimming hole, but also with the cares of this world on his mind.

I determined to explore both.

The marble block at the Glenwood Springs depot was a sunrise surprise. It had been cracked by use of dynamite but undiscovered until it reached the train station. Colonel Meek was furious and took up the matter of dynamite with his foremen. "We must insist on saws alone. No more explosives," he had said. So that was when the channeling machines and wire saws came in. In any case, it meant the block could not be sent on to customers. Mr. Meek said I could carve a bust of his mother from the better half. It was mine if I wanted it.

Yes, I wanted it, and needed it if all honesty was bared. The shop needed it. That was always the case. I turned waste rock into darling delights, and into a workable livelihood in this unforgiving mountain enclave. I suppose I gleaned marble like Ruth in the field of Boaz, and the fact was I really needed it to keep the store open.

After loading the marble, we stopped at the Glenwood Hot Springs.

Mr. Clark looked around, waiting for his next assignment.

"Oh, didn't you know?" Blanche asserted. "We always swim at the hot springs when we come down here. Or the Penny Hot Springs, up the road. You can rent everything you need."

She winked and wiggled her hips. "See you in there, sweetheart!" Then went off like a little spring doe.

I rubbed rose oil into Levi's neck and arms. "This will help with the sun. See you in there!"

"I don't use swimming machines," Blanche informed me, which I already knew from our last fifty trips to the hot springs. "They are such a nineteenth century thing. I like to be modern. And I don't care if men see my bathing dress. I watch them. They like my ankles."

I nodded. "Someday you'll get what you're asking for."

"And what is that?" she said, lifting a shoulder and a snarled lip.

"You'll see." But the fact was, I secretly wanted what she was asking for too. A man. I wanted a man to tilt his head at my ankles and wilt when I lifted a shoulder. So what was I doing in a place like Marble? I had a plan for that. Problem was, it was a stupid plan and probably wouldn't work any better than Blanche's plan – which was to just show a little ankle and let men pine over your bathing costume.

So much for the stupid plan.

For now, I unhooked the massive swimming machine, preparing to roll it into the hot waters, and swim in my own little private room. That is how Christian women bathe at the hot springs.

Blanche grabbed me before the machine rolled an inch. "Did you see that? You're not going to believe it!" She pointed through the rising steam. Mister Clark stepped out of the bathhouse to the edge of the pool. "You never told me he was carved granite. Ooooh, sweet sister!"

Blanche nearly slipped under. "I want to touch it."

"Control yourself!"

But how could she? Mister Clark must have felt like a carnival freak. His rented swimsuit was evidently tailored for a less-endowed man. Under all that Italian stonecutting garb he'd evidently been hiding two tree trunks and a pair of anvils.

Blanche's tilting head sagged. "You're the seamstress between us... Just how much pressure can one cotton thread take?" She pointed. "Lookie there. That should be illegal."

I slapped her wrist. "Uh, you wicked girl!"

But I also strained at every stitch along the black suit – following two ample thighs up to the navel, over an expansive chest, and then out to each anvil. The thought of this garment giving way under such pressure was an alarming notion to consider. There were bulges and valleys I had never seen on a man, and we had been swimming here for two years. And to think, I had worked those anvils at the photography session without any thought of the actual tools at my disposal. Or what lay under that Dago garb.

"I bet he could knead dough," Blanche mused.

She tilted in every range of motion available, probably also tracing the stitching from bottom to top and back down again, scanning for signs of compromise in the woolen suit. "I would be like a kitten in those arms. Or a mouse. What would a creature like that do to a furry little ball like me?"

She looked up at me. "Can I have him?"

I giggled at the silly request. "He doesn't belong to me! Or anyone that I know of."

"Yeah, but he's your man-slave. Your Roman. You own him, right?"

I laughed. "I merely employed him to haul marble. He's hired labor."

Blanche cackled "I wasn't exactly sleeping the whole way into Glenwood."

She cocked her head. "You never told him, did you?"

"Told him what?"

She gasped. "He still thinks Thomas is your husband!"

"Tssss."

She grabbed my shoulders. "And Harriet your daughter? What is wrong with you, silly goose? Oh, for crying in the sink, didn't I teach you anything? I'm going right over there and telling him everything."

"Oh no, you're not! You're staying right here with me in the bathing machine. He doesn't need to know anything. He's just a Quarry Town transient, and that's all."

"Oh, you innocent little thing, Lorena. I swear. Have you ever been kissed?"

"What a stupid question! I have a brother, don't I?"

"Oh my gosh, you haven't! You poor child. I'll fix that!"

Her hawk-like eyes returned to Mister Clark, who had finally entered the water and stirred the steaming bubbles. Shoulders erupted beneath a neck of bronze, all tightened under a thin vail of black wool.

"You know I don't use them... bathing boxes..." Blanche slurred, with eyes still fixed on neck muscles inviting enough to fix any crying in the sink. "I don't use them..." She melted in. "I'm going over there if you won't."

"Not if you're a Christian."

"Yes, I am," she insisted, and strode right into the waters.

I puffed and retreated into the bathing box but still got a few glimpses out the little glass slits. It wasn't just neck muscles.

Levi, Mister Clark, and Blanche splashed and played in the hundred degree pool, so soothing and medicinal. But I was safe in my bathing box.

At least I was still a Christian.

Pitching woo. Pfft.

Blanche always knew how to draw men into her affections. A little shoulder-shake, some hips, and inviting talk. Plus the ankles. She was plying those arts right before me and probably didn't even realize what she was doing. She didn't know what I knew. And she didn't know what I felt. How my prayers had finally been answered after so long. But then Blanche moved right in, like she always did. I just wanted to go home and cry. Nope, Blanche had no idea. She was just being Blanche.

Mister Clark waved toward the little glass slits.

But he didn't wave for long. Three minutes later he had everyone heading for my end of the pool. Heading right for my little bathing machine.

Oh, no! What was he up to?

He wouldn't do that!

Mr. Clark tapped on the glass slit. "Did you think you could have this wonderful bathing machine all to yourself?" he asked, smiling and pushing all the laughing bodies inside. "Let's have a pool party!"

Chapter Three

I GUESS THEY DIDN'T hate us up in Quarry Town, because when they needed a pair of rousties to stack and polish baby headstones in the Marble finishing mill, we got a letter. Of course a job like that does nothing for your reputation in the community. Levi and I were already outsiders; shiftless transients, wastrels, heavy-footed lay-abouts and Cripple Creekers. You couldn't put much trust in men like that.

But still, there we were, released from Quarry Town and back in Marble.

Let's just say, you didn't put your best men on baby headstones. If you wanted a real bad job, that was one. It was for the lowest on your payroll, except maybe snow removal which went to the Irish. The low looks at the grocery and meat markets and liveries told me that much. But I liked the work. It was a service to the grieving and broken who had lost little ones to cholera, measles, polio, or other crippling and deadly maladies. I felt connected to those poor souls and put my whole self into the lowly occupation.

"Land Sakes! What in Heaven's Name are you doing, Clark?" Tolbert, my first boss asked. I wondered, did a shop this size really need three bosses? "What are you carving down there?"

I had taken to carving "J.H.C." for Jeremiah Hiram Clark into the lower-right corner of every baby headstone, down below the dirt line on the back side. It was my small message to the heartbroken and devastated, letting them know that somebody out there cared – someone other than a machine. Evidently, Tolbert did not appreciate the practice, and took the act as an invitation to upbraid me.

"I don't think babies can read yet, Clark. Haha! Especially not dead ones."

Of course, that invited the next boss in for a look. "Humph, you think that means something?"

"Maybe, Anson. Maybe." I said, tapping a cornered chisel into the stone.

Marley Brown, the top boss, could never resist a pile-on. "You'll have these ten stones done today or you'll stay here until they are. I don't care if you're here 'till morning."

And so the next hour consisted of me cutting, routing, and polishing under the watchful eye of not one, but three bosses intent on maximizing control over the workforce. An awful and oppressive experience. That is, until an envoy of businessmen followed Colonel Meek and Miss Lorena into the shop.

Hmm, something worth looking at.

"These are the finest examples of marble works west of the Atlantic. We are entering the Marble Age," Colonel Meek boasted before the eager businessmen. "We're not Italy yet, but you just watch. We have columns over there. Fluted Greek, and square columns. Capstones and Corinthian capitals. We have washbowls, tiles, accents, and inlays. Marble curbstones and walkways. And of course, there is a full line of headstones and monuments. Yes gentlemen, the Marble Age is here!"

Colonel Meek sought to engage the investors on as many levels as possible. "W.F. Frazier will demonstrate the fluting machines. Mortimer Mathews knows washroom accessories. And our ravishing Miss Lorena can demonstrate hand-tooling. She is an accomplished sculptor."

"Our investment interests are mostly with columns, facades, and those marble accents on capital buildings and municipalities." One of the businessmen stated. "Washrooms don't interest us. Does anybody buy that stuff?"

"Greek columns." Another put in. "And them fancy capstones. You know, the ones up top."

"That's what we want to invest in," the first clarified.

Colonel Meek smiled. "Excellent! We have an array of competitively priced bond offerings for your consideration."

I stood to make way for the entourage, including Miss Lorena, who tipped a half-smile as she passed. The men filed around my polishing bed, swiping stones and coming up with sparkling marble dust between their fingers. The route was a tight squeeze and the only one through to the next station. Sort of like little islands of industry floating in a sea of swirling marble dust, belts, pulleys, and hand carts. Ten feet of visibility was an exaggeration, if not a bald-faced lie.

"Excuse me!" I complained in faux surprise, bumping shoulders with the last investor through the line. "Are you even watching where you're going?"

The man spun around with flares in his eye. "Listen here, you—" He stopped short. "Jeremiah Clark!" he yelled, while the others moved on to the next station, presumably to the Greek columns and capitals they sought. "You old Cripple Creek robber baron! What are you doing here? Dang!"

The other men continued, but then waited at the monument bases for their partner to catch up. Graveyard monuments definitely didn't fall into their sphere of interest, but the router bits occupied them long enough for their partner to finish his conversation. After all, it was the same carvings used on capital stones and facades, Colonel Meek explained. They all clustered around the Colonel, who waxed eloquent over the Italian cutting and routing skills at his disposal. "It's a new thing out here!"

"I'm infiltrating the operation at the lowest ranks," I joked. "Give me five years, and I'll be the major investor." Of course it was all hyperbole, which my Cripple Creek friend could plainly see. But he obliged, not knowing how to respond to seeing me in loose overalls and an immigrant hat, under an inch of marble dust.

I could have been a filthy Irishman, if not for the Dago garb.

"Infiltrating the lowest ranks. I don't doubt it, after the circus act you pulled in Cripple Creek. You robber baron in disguise! You Andrew Carnegie impersonator!" Then he leaned in and whispered, although the racket of eighteen steam engines and sixty overhead pulleys did not require it. "You had the Western Federation of Miners groveling for mercy. On the run, is what I heard." He shook his head. "They are all gone now, you know."

"Ancient history."

"Will you ever go back?"

"Never. Had my fill. Plus, I like what I see here," grabbing a quickie at Miss Lorena in the hazy cluster around the routing tables. But did she even see me, I wondered? Or just another indigent mill worker?

The investor nudged. "Got any insider tips I can bank on?" He lit up.

"I have one or two, but I'll save those for another time. I've seen the Colonel on his grand tour. Don't cost me my job, Patterson." I nodded over to the group.

Colonel Meek pulled out a set of eight-inch calipers and leaned into one block, evidently likable to his line of persuasion. "Look at this precision, gentlemen." He applied the calipers to the carving and turned a smile. "Notice how the measurements do not deviate more than a tenth of an inch on every touch of this radius. I gave no specific instruction for this precision, yet here it is before us. And this is a random piece. That is the quality we produce here. Can you get that in the Greek Isles?"

"Oh, come on, Clark," the investor urged. "He's as busy as a basket weaver. Give me the inside rap. What's the next big thing from the Colorado-Yule Marble Company?"

Miss Lorena left the group and picked through the hodgepodge of routers and rubbing beds toward us, only mildly mindful of her loose clothing around leather belts and pulleys. She lifted an eye from time to time but tried to seem interested in the workings in the dark shop. Her movements around the belts and pulleys caught my notice. I had seen men lifted right off their feet and carried into the rafters by those self-same belts – practically snatched baldheaded and hanging there in no small discomfort. And it was not uncommon to see men with rags around bruised or severed fingers. This wasn't really the place for women.

But it wasn't just the belts and pulleys that triggered my emotions.

It was those eyes. Again.

I could be indentured to those eyes for a decade and never know the loss.

"Hey! Are you with me?" the investor laughed. He looked around at the whirling belts and tables, then at Miss Lorena who circled around the polishing bed where we talked. "Come on, Clark, give me something for our board meeting next month."

He seemed intent.

"Alright, Patterson. For one thing... look out over the shop floor. See anything odd?"

"No."

"There's no organization, that's what. You've got fourteen belt sanders, eight rubbing beds, six routers, and a dozen sanding tables, plus fifteen smaller machines. And it's not just marble; you've got wooden crate makers on the east end. A blacksmith's forge. A nail maker. Saw sharpeners. Everything is belt-driven from above, but it all looks like somebody threw a handful of candy corn into the air, and wherever it landed they slapped down a new machine. Did any planning go into this? You can't even walk a straight line through this shop. Every block is moved by hand. And it moves like a tangled spider web from one machine to another, from one end of the shop to the other and back again. Thrice. Blocks travel a tenth of a mile before completion. Does that seem right to you?"

Miss Lorena edged in. I noticed, but my blood was up for the passions rising in me, and that always made me a little heedless and neglectful. But still, I could see the investors clustering around Colonel Meek happily discussing dovetail joining. Of course, they looked over from time to time, and made signs of joining us, but I felt free to share the things that interested me most about the place.

Patterson looked around nodding, but not convinced.

"I would gut this finishing mill and install every machine in a straight line. See that entrance next to the oxen road?"

Patterson danced around the belts and dust clouds for a line of sight to the sunlit barn door at the far end of the mill. "Yeah, okay. I see it. Right there, right?" Staring about seventy feet off toward some vague and obscure source of sunlight.

"I would run a surveyor's line from that door to this other one. The full width of the shop."

The investor group began moving in our direction, probably just to collect their colleague and finish their tour.

"I would put rough-cut band saws right there at the entrance, right at that door. After rough cut, you move to planing. That gives you a rough product within twenty feet of the door. From there, it comes straight down the line to routing, sanding, polishing, sealing, final inspection, and then crating and shipping."

Patterson mused, "Yeah? What's your experience with industrial equipment like this?"

He wagged his head like an idiot. "Okay, okay, I just answered my own question. Continue!"

"Now look... right there's the Crystal River & San Juan rail line, right at the very end where finished product comes out. Every block rides on big wooden carts, pulled by a nice hemp rope. Maybe on a pulley, or maybe by hand; maybe on rails. Marble stays on that single line until it hits that door, where it's loaded onto railcars for shipment."

The big boss Marley swooped in. "Clark, you are stretching my nerves. You're not here to entertain guests. I need those baby headstones out that door. Do you understand?" He smiled apologetically to the investors, who had gotten tired of waiting and came back. "We can continue our tour now. Clark is just a baby headstone man. He's not really one of us."

Marley glowered. "Get those stones polished or–" he held back, seeing investors, all with raised eyes.

"I want to hear more," Miss Lorena interrupted. She stared Marley down.

Now, what woman can stare down a mill boss? I wanted to know the answer to that myself but didn't question the gift I'd been handed.

Marley leaned in. "After this shift, you're finished. Transients know their place. Got it, buster?"

Colonel Meek broke into the conversation. "Is there trouble?"

Marley tried to recover the happy mood and move the group onward. "Oh, just a little talk with the hired help. It's under control. Let's take a look at those drum saws and Greek columns. I do admire the designs Mr. Meek gets from the foreigners." He pointed onward. "Mortimer Mathews, let's get a look!"

"But Mr. Clark had some ideas," Miss Lorena reminded. "I thought Mr. Meek might like to hear them as long as we're here."

Patterson nodded. "Yeah, buddy. Do tell!"

Marley's glare turned to forced smiles and chuckles. "Not really. Just ramblings. We always get 'million-dollar' ideas from the transitory classes."

Tolbert put in, "And he's probably not even a millionaire."

The other bosses rolled their eyes.

"I can listen to any man with an idea," Colonel Meek said. "I'm pleased to meet you. My name is Channing Frank Meek."

I extended a nervous hand. "Jeremiah Clark. Jeremiah Hiram Clark."

Marley circled the finishing table. He mumbled something like "You just cost yourself–" and trailed into indiscernible mumbles.

"Well, Colonel," I said. "Have you ridden the Pea Vine tramway lately?" Of course I knew he had. Every morning up to Quarry Town and back. But I was making a point. "That little Pea Vine funicular is a dangerous piece of machinery. You're going to a have a wreck sooner or later. But don't get me wrong; I love the thrill of flying down through those canyon walls every morning. Have you considered an electrified tramway up to the quarry? You can move four times as much rock. We could build a motorized flatcar. A motor house on each end of an ordinary flatcar would do it."

Meek smiled. "Lay blocks between them for traction?" he added.

I raised an arm and looked up. "Hang a trolley wire overhead."

"Ah, for electrical power. Nice!"

"You'd need a new transfer crane. And upgrade that Lincoln hoist to fifty tons."

"Good ideas! Send me your plans. Ah, Mr.–"

"Jeremiah Clark, sir. Glad to work for you." I gloved a hand to hide the nerves.

I probably should have stopped there. "Also, you're bringing slabs in on oxen carts. Or mules. For the cost of forage and vet care, you can get yourself a new eighteen horsepower steam tractor. BEST Manufacturing has them. And it will never contract blackleg or hoof 'n mouth. I'll bet you could haul a thousand cubic feet of sound marble down that hill every day except the Sabbath."

I guessed he didn't hate that idea.

Meek nodded and lifted a hand, then smiled widely. "I like the way you think, Clark! Go on."

I pointed to the long mill wall. "Put a twelve ton traveling gantry along the back side of this entire mill and pull blocks right through those doors." We all turned to the same wide barn doors I had drawn Patterson's attention to earlier. "Do you understand? Envision a two-hundred-foot-long traveling crane along the back side, rail lines on the front side, and the mill right between them like meat on a rye bread sandwich. Blocks come in from the gantry and out to the railcars. We do the work in the middle. It's a straight line from one end to the other."

The men cogitated the wild idea.

"A set of gang saws can divide five-ton blocks onto every shape and size you need. After that, every block travels down the 'line' where workers like me finish them off. Look across this finishing mill and envision twenty straight lines from the back side of the mill to the front. Seventy-five feet long, each. Straight as a schoolmarm's rule." I turned and pointed to the door nearest us. "Monuments on one line. Columns on a line next to it. Capstones and capitals on about four or five others. Headstones on ten more. And then all the scraps go into washroom accents, wainscoting, and wash bowls. You can make fruit stands, ornamental vases, sun dials, garden seats, flower stands, even those little card receiver bowls. Don't waste a scrap. Every marble chip has a commercial purpose. Heck, you can grind this stuff up for chicken feed and fertilizer. It's just calcium carbonate." I turned and faced the far wall again. "Every 'line' produces only one item."

Marley and Tolbert jumped in and laughed. "Lines. Haha… Clark will have us so exhausted they'll bring in the Ladies Aid Society to scoop up our weary bones."

"Actually, it's a lot less work than you're doing today." I asserted, but suddenly realized my livelihood hung on those few imprudent words. But still, I stepped out again after noticing Miss Lorena's widening blue eyes. They gave me power beyond what good caution allowed. "The shortest distance between two points is a straight line."

"Where did you hear that?" Tolbert jumped in. "It doesn't have to be a straight line. The shortest distance could be—"

"Shut up, Tolbert," Anson demanded. "He's right. But still, it just sounds like twice the work because everything is moving twice as fast. I don't think we could keep up. We'd be exhausted in a week."

The Colonel frowned, "What about that? Could workers keep up with straight lines of blocks moving from one end of the mill to the other? It does seem too fast for human capacity."

"On a line like that, I could produce baby headstones for a dollar each. Right now, it costs you four."

Tolbert whispered to Anson. "How does he know? Has he stolen the books?"

"I think he's just guessing," Anson replied, just a little too loud.

"You're right, I am guessing. But how far off am I?" I turned to Colonel Meek.

"Not far," he grimaced. "It's about four bucks each."

"I can move baby headstones down a single line where each worker applies his small improvements to the slab. When it comes out the other end, it's smoother and more appealing than what you've got today. Plus, it saved you three bucks a slab."

"Do you want more babies to die, Clark?" Tolbert asked.

Marley piled on. "You're going to produce so many baby headstones, we won't be able to sell them all. They'll call us the Death Shop! Headstones will be stacked all the way to Carbondale."

"Haha," Tolbert laughed. "They'll pave the Redstone Road."

"And line the Redstone coke ovens," Marley added.

Anson jumped in. "Hahaha, and cover the Redstone Cliffs!"

The three bosses all laughed, gauging their exuberance against Mr. Meeks reaction.

Problem is, he didn't react at all. It was all mental cogitation with him.

But the investors did. Patterson grabbed Meek by the lapel. "This is exactly what you promised, Channing." He shook the Colonel's hand. "I want in." The other investors did likewise, and never did get to the fancy fluted columns that had sparked their interest back in Cripple Creek.

"I'll send over the bond contracts!" Meek exclaimed.

Miss Lorena's bosom swelled as the whole mood changed, and how Mr. Meek didn't hate the idea, and how the investors tripped over the machinery to shake his hand. I think her brain also swelled with excitement. I know mine did. This was a whole new idea that seemed to flutter around the finishing floor, sparkling off the marble clouds, and bouncing right back into our brains. I didn't have to say another word. The idea just gained lift on its own wind, silently glancing from one investor to another, and finally into Colonel Meek's understanding.

Lines. What a novel idea!

But our dreamy love connection had no such reaction in the public square.

"That Quarry Town tramp will get us all killed," I heard at the bread store.

"Marley explained it all. Clark is like a know-it-all."

"If he's so smart why is he polishing baby headstones?"

"Colonel Meek says it will ruin the operation."

"What a shame. It was good while it lasted."

Fortunately, Miss Lorena caught me at the crossroads leading down to the little Sears and Roebuck house we rented on Roebuck Row. West Park Street to be exact, but I called it Roebuck Row for obvious reasons – cabins so small you could fire a shotgun through the front door and have it come flying out the back without striking an interior wall. Four dollars was reasonable rent for such a place, especially with the convenience of an outdoor water spigot and electric light bulbs. A broom and a washtub hung on every porch wall. You could wash up right there on the street before going into work, or down at the Crystal River. I'd never had it so nice. Or, for eleven dollars you could have an indoor enamel bathing tub. Another eleven got you the recirculating kerosene heater for your tub; then you only needed to haul in a little water to bathe in private. I planned to order one from Detroit when finances allowed.

Miss Lorena rubbed a little rose oil into Levi's hands, and turned to me. She had tried to broom the long black dress free of all the marble dust from the mill but that was an impossibility. Men came out of the finishing mill after every shift like walking flour sacks, but with a sparkling ambiance. I called them glow sticks because you could see them in the dark. Me included. And now, Miss Lorena, like a little sparkling angel from Heaven dancing around me, lifting her arms and letting off little sparklets that caught the moonlight.

"You put on a little show back there!" She shimmered and skipped, and I could not tell if she was real or an apparition from over Jordan. Of course I could tell, but I didn't want to. I just wanted to let my head go, and touch her glittering skin, and see if it was as smooth as–

But Levi shouted. "Do you want to cook supper for us?" His eyes popped in anticipation. "Do you know how to pluck a chicken? Cuz–"

"I would, Levi dear, but I do not hold company with men after dusk. It is not a Christian virtue. I'm sure you understand." She smiled and braced his shoulders. "You understand, right?"

But I know she wanted to, the way her bodice lifted as she spoke; the way her eyes opened and how breath escaped her swelling breasts. She wanted to sit and pluck chickens with us and gaze up at the rising moon. I could tell.

"I would meet with you any time," Levi smiled. "I like you. And I bet you could fix a fine chicken and dumplings stew."

She laughed. "And I like you too, Levi."

She rubbed his rough hands again and touched them to her sparkling cheek.

Little marble sprites lifted off her skin and disappeared into the evening breeze.

Her shoulders swayed to some silent hymn, lifting her bodice up to the mountain silhouettes around us. The black silk dress left its own silhouettes in the moonlight, and its own effects on my halting breath.

I stood there thinking, I would pluck chickens with this woman any night.

Chapter Four

"I DID NOT TAKE you for an Episcopalian, Mr. Clark." I set my Bible and purse down on the red velvet pew next to Levi. He looked every bit as haggard and wrung out as a fifteen-year-old could, working ten-hour shifts, six days a week, in a marble town where he competed for shifts with men twice his age. I laid an arm over him and kissed him on the cheek. He brightened up, so I rubbed some rose oil into his hands and cheeks.

"Do you think I need Doan's kidney pills?" Levi asked. "You know, for my back? It says if your back aches, it could be your kidneys, and Doan's pills are the curative for sick kidneys."

I flinched at the idea. "Where did you hear that?"

"The Marble City Times. It says Doan's cures even the serious cases. Maybe I–"

"You can't trust a word in that paper. Sylvia Smith brings that stuff in. No, you don't need kidney pills." I grumbled. "You probably just need a little rest. Or a cigarette."

He nodded. "Okay. I'll draw a likeness of you after church, Miss Lorena!"

"I would like that, Levi. Down by the Crystal River?"

"I'm not really an Episcopalian," Mr. Clark answered. "My kin were more like fire-breathing Baptists, if the truth was told."

I smiled and teased. "Then remind me never to sin in your holy presence, Mr. Clark." I lifted my eyes with a silent snicker, which Mr. Clark seemed to enjoy. When service let out I headed to the entrance where my friends waited. Blanche and Millicent walked out looking radiant and beautiful, both with contrasting black skirts and white blouses with four-inch celluloid collars. Each with cloisonné pendants around their necks. They could have been twins. If only I could match their style. But I never really tried. That was their game, and they played it well.

Black hats with wide silky ribbon towered another twelve inches over their heads, and nearly touched the foyer ceiling as they lingered. The grand entrance drew all eyes. Of course that was half the point.

Blanche and Millicent always had a crowd. And it made me wonder how many men throughout history actually married the fashion rather than the women under them. The engaging 1908 fashions held that very spell over men like never before in history, and maybe never again. It seemed women in these new times need only ply fashion to get their man.

Or in Blanche's case, fashion… and a little ankle skin.

Mr. Clark noticed Blanche. And I noticed that he noticed.

But then I wondered, aren't fashions just a reflection of the woman herself? So maybe men are getting the woman, and not just the fashion.

Blanche swayed enough to reveal her cheekbone under the voluminous hat. And like a magnet, Mr. Clark followed. Drop a little honey and bears will follow.

Yep, it was the woman, I concluded; not the fashion that men get. A modest woman doesn't add the lifting laces option to her corset order. And the woman with men on her mind doesn't stop at the eighteen-inch daffodil hat; she adds the six-inch silken ties and the gold and pearl hat pin. A quick scan of Millicent's ensemble confirmed that very theory. So yes, men get what they pay for. Fashion is the woman.

As it turned out, St. Paul's twenty pews hosted three denominations every Sabbath. An eager saint could worship all day long if the mood struck and nickel offerings allowed. Blanche was

Episcopalian, and she was evidently dragging Millicent in for a taste of the good life.

I wasn't really Episcopalian either. More like a fire-breathing Baptist also, if my friends were put to the question. Especially Blanche who claimed I scorched paint when the mood came over me. That wasn't true in any sense, but she liked to say it whenever she needed to bend the scriptures a little.

After church, I grabbed Blanche by the four-inch collar. "I need a chaperone. Want to go to the river? Thomas can't go because Harriet is down with whooping cough again."

"Maybe."

"Do you know who's going to be there? We're leaving now."

She didn't even ask to powder up. Her efforts with Mr. Clark had not gotten past the cordiality level, and she said if she could only get him down to the Penny Hot Springs or even the banks of the Crystal River, her new bodice frills and insert pads might interest him. She didn't exactly use those terms, but I learned to interpret. I had never tried the lifting remedies, and the fact was I didn't need to. Blanche did, so I couldn't blame her. We kissed the Pastor and took off for that very spot.

The Crystal River meandered only twenty yards from the railroad tracks and finishing mill, but if you crossed a little footbridge near the west end of the mill, you could find a secluded spot under the elm trees at the base of the mountain. It was so covered you could barely see the industrial works. Mill Mountain rose up sharply on that side of the river.

You got tipsy just looking up.

Snow sometimes flew down Mill Mountain and slid right across the frozen waters to the edge of the mill. That was fun to watch, and the whole town waited for the spectacular events like a new picture show. Stands of quaking Aspen usually limited such slides to about fourteen chutes until they were mowed down. In the spring, it all melted into crystal eddies of fascination. That made the river a romantic and special place for me, especially this very spot where I sometimes took breakfast and devoted mornings to scripture. Whenever I walked along the rushing and roiling waters, I dreamed of the man God had picked for me. I pictured and caressed his features in my mind. He was a perfect

40

gentleman and protector. And he wanted me more than all the fashion of this world.

He wanted me. Maybe that summed it up. He wanted me. And I wanted him.

Truth was, I knew exactly which man that was. It was my own secret, one I never dared mentioned to Blanche or Millicent. They wouldn't understand. And why would they? No normal female had put this much time into one man. This much passion and obsession.

Mr. Clark stood next to me at the water's edge. "Does it whisper to you, Miss Lorena?"

I smiled at his eyes. Sure, those same eyes had lingered at Blanche and Millicent's loops and laces like any eyes would, but he sincerely tried to marshal them. What he really seemed to like was my eyes. And that excited me more than fashion and form.

He stood next to me trying to take in the whole of Mill Mountain. His hands fell limp at the slope and enormity, hundreds of feet above us.

"I do love the mountains," he added.

And then he touched me. Or maybe only one hair on his finger brushed one hair of mine. Maybe only that. But it gave me a start. The kind of start that goes straight to the organs like strong medicine. And stops the words in your mouth. And makes you wonder if anybody is watching you stand there and wilt like a star struck adolescent.

That kind of start.

The water did whisper, as Mr. Clark observed. It said that I should tell him–

Levi spun me around in his impatient way, begging my attention. Where was the lad's sense of timing? "Sit right there on that rotten log," He pointed to a decaying stump and fallen tree. "I'll sketch you."

"How about that flat rock?" I suggested instead.

"Oh yeah, that's better. Hey, I forgot my pencils so I'll make your likeness in charcoal." He pulled a chunk of blackened wood from an old fire pit on the river bank and commenced sketching on the back side of a wrinkled railroad schedule.

Mr. Clark asked me, "Where's Thomas?"

I frowned. "Little Harriet is sick. You should look in on them. I know he could use a friend."

Levi never looked up. "Did you like Father's mill ideas? The Three Blind Mice don't never know good ideas when they're spoken right at them. I call them the Three Blind Mice: Marley, Anson, and Tolbert." He scribbled and backhanded the paper. "Plus, Father is brave as a badger."

He rubbed the charcoal with his finger. "Did you know he killed a bear with a sword?"

Mr. Clark jumped up. "That's an old rumor. It's not even—"

"No, it is true." Particles of black dust fell from the paper. "Mother told me the story before she—"

Levi looked over at Mr. Clark and nearly lost his implements. "Sorry, Father."

Of course, I knew the story was probably true even before the telling of it. The boy had not the slightest guile he could be shed of. He might not have even been capable of lies. So now I wanted the full particulars. But I wanted it told by the bear killer himself, standing there before me.

"Oh, do tell!" Blanche fawned. She visually traced his shoulders and arms.

An image of the wool swimsuit two sizes too small came to mind, and what virility must lay beneath it. I traced the same lines and stitches in my vivid memory. If any man ever slayed a bear with a sword, it must be this man.

"I'm sorry, but this is no dime novel account," Mr. Clark began reluctantly. "There's just not much to tell. It happened so fast I cannot recount anything of notability, so don't be disappointed."

Nothing about this man disappointed. I even looked around and hoped a bruin might come roaring out of the mountains so Mr. Clark could demonstrate the act just for me. Blanche had equivalent ideas in her own head; her body rhythms told that much.

"You never disappoint me," Blanche added. She exhaled but forgot to breathe.

"Don't fidget," Levi scolded. His hand had slowed, and final touches were in process.

Mr. Clark began, "It was 1895. The month of May, I reckon. We were on the Colorado City skid road just west of Colorado Springs, heading into the Ute Pass, just out of Kansas and into the wild and western frontiers. This was back before trains ran into Cripple Creek. I'd never even seen a mountain like Pikes Peak. It had been a month-long trek out of Kansas, and we were finally within a week of the gold fields."

"Were you there, Levi?" I asked.

Mr. Clark lifted a hand. "No, Levi was an orphan. He came to us on an orphan train three years ago. I guess that was Nineteen-and-ought-five."

"Yes, I remember now," I said, reaching for Levi's cheek. He allowed it, because I think his work was nearing completion, and I think he wanted to hear the story again too. But he also needed his inspiration back, and my movements probably annoyed him. I tried to keep still.

"That old she-bear came out the Ponderosa pines like Elisha's child-mauler in the Book of Kings. When I spun around, I noticed her two cubs just yonder, and we betwixt them. A seven-hundred-foot drop into Seven Falls on our left, and a granite wall to our right. That's a tight spot!"

"Did you slay the beast right there?" Millicent laid her hand on her heart.

"No, I had a family and two mules to attend to. And I'll tell you, mules do not cotton to the presence of bears in any imaginable way. Especially Rosebud, who was as twitchy as an aspen leaf."

I envisioned Elisha calling down the true and righteous judgements of God, like Joshua when the walls of Jericho fell. "Where did you get a sword at a time like that?"

Blanche angled in. "Or did you fight him barehanded?" She swayed and touched her lip.

"It wasn't really a sword. It was my Uncle Olin's old Arkansas Toothpick. A Bowie knife. The children called it a sword. Heck, I even called it a sword. This was one fine example of Southern weaponry. Still is to this day."

Mr. Clark began slashing and plunging with the imaginary implement. His hips hinged and bucked in the telling. Feet shifted, and back bowed. Dust lifted beneath him. Muscles tightened to the point of rippage. The wild acts flexed shoulders and legs, a visual focal point I had difficulty ignoring. After all, you didn't see maneuvers like that in the pews of the Episcopal Church. Or even amongst the fire-breathing Baptist.

He suddenly stopped.

"Before I knew it, I stood over the slain beast," he said, breathing heavily from the exertion. "The old she-bear was dead on the skid road before us, and I cannot tell you exactly how. Of course that didn't calm the skittish mules, but they settled down when I threw an oilcloth over the carcass. We had rations for the rest of the trip."

Blanche and Millicent finally exhaled and tilted.

"What about the babies?" Millicent asked with great concern.

"Oh, we ate them too!" he answered. "That was a true gift because I was down to a grubstake of $128, and had to make that last six months. Cripple Creek wasn't cheap in those days."

Levi handed over the charcoal image.

He must have thought I was Eve's firstborn, the way he made me out. I never was handsome like that, but he evidently saw some kind of forbidden vision. And then laid it out before us. The image struck your soul when looked upon. It induced you to eloquence but hamstrung your vocabulary in the very same stroke. We all handled the image on the old railroad schedule like a holy scroll, standing silent at the marvel.

"Let's play Hang Man!" Levi finally burst forth. More youthful timing.

"Oh, no!" Mr. Clark protested. "That's not a good game for today."

"Come on, Father!"

Blanche giggled and raced around us. "Roll up your sleeves, Mr. Clark!"

Levi waved me over. He positioned Mr. Clark between us, with his hands raised to shoulder height. Mr. Clark reluctantly obliged, with his sleeves rolled to the shoulders. "Miss Lorena, grab onto his hand and hang on!"

Mr. Clark grunted and lifted Levi in his left hand and me in his right.

We both hung from an arm.

"I don't know how to play," I shrieked, hanging a foot off the ground.

Levi yelled over, "If he lets go, you win! All you have to do is hang on. That's why it's called Hang Man. Do you get it?"

Levi began barking, shaking, and blowing into Mr. Clark's eyes and ears. Anything to effect an early release. "Do like me, Miss Lorena. Do like me! Make him drop you. But don't let go!"

I tried, but soon realized my breast had pressed deeply into Mr. Clark's swelling forearm and I had little chance of extracting it unless I let go. A dilemma. The jostling only set off new sensations, throwing off my concentration. I'd never been in a position quite like this, and wasn't entirely sure what the feelings were. Should I slap the man and bolt over the footbridge to safety? Or act as though it was of no account? Of course, the man had no idea. He was just playing his part. And I realized I'd lose the game if I let go, and that would disappoint Levi. My only hope was to employ Levi's tactics to win. After all, how long could a man hoist two bodies at ninety pounds each?

That logic alone did nothing to assuage the physical changes my body soon melted into. His four-inch forearm stiffened against my silky blouse from navel to chin, with me clinging to a hand that had only yesterday handled five-hundred-pound marble blocks. Name one hardboiled female who would not melt in proximity to heat like that. Add one growing bicep and a heaving chest twelve inches from my eyes, and logic melted like chocolate.

I got physical changes that defied explanation.

Changes in new places.

But still, I was determined to win. And I figured I had only about two minutes to make good. My own strength would give way soon. Actually, I had handled my own marble blocks, lifted and hoisted them, polished stone for eighteen hours straight until my fingers ached, but my resources were still limited. After all, I was only a girl. So I gave Mr. Clark all the playful torture Levi advised me of.

I blew into his ear. I bit his fingers. I chewed his hair.

Nothing worked. He just smiled and whistled a little tune.

"Bite his ear!" Levi instructed, and began growling and lunging for an ear of his own.

It couldn't hurt. Blowing and chewing hair wasn't working. So maybe an ear, if I could only lean in and get one. That of course meant grinding both bosoms into the reddening muscles before me. Only the thinnest of 1908 fashion fabrics separated skin from skin.

I peered into an engorged bicep. And pressed deeply into it.

Knots and valleys appeared before me, and new veins — reddening and enlarging against my breasts. And with them, new physical responses invited themselves into my own loins.

"Hello!" they said to my whirling mind. "We're new. Glad to meet you, Miss Lorena. Can we stay a while?"

My answer was, yes. Stay a while because I like you, you warm new feelings.

Millicent circled around. "Bite him Lorena. Bite him!" But she didn't know I just wanted to hang there and play with my new friends. I didn't want to win. Losing was so much nicer.

Blanche yelled, "Bite him!" And she was right, because I guess some feelings make you lose strength and make you want to lay in the grass and whimper. I had to act, even if I didn't want to.

I lunged for his ear. And ended up with a lip.

My teeth sunk into flesh as soft as cream pie. And deep into that cream pie. Like a week-old calf on a nipple. I could not let loose. My mind would not let loose. My body would not let loose. I could have fallen into a dream and not known the end of it. A hot wind blew through me, from foot to forehead. It swept me clean of every crumb of logic and right-mindedness.

All I could do was stiffen up and close my eyes.

A warming rivulet trickled down my neck and into my corset. Was it the after-effects of the hot wind? A new physical sensation hitherto unknown to women, except those hanging from anvils of iron and biting into cream pies? But did I really care what physical sensations visited such women? It felt so good.

So warm and so smooth. It inched past my navel.

Ohhh. Let the dishes go dirty; I could hang here 'til Tuesday. Mmm. Ooh.

Of course I could still hear. Levi had long since dropped, and circled around to my side with admonitions to also drop. Blanche too had begun pleading, but I could ignore their voices a little longer, like covering an alarm clock on a sleepy morning under two new quilts and a fire in the hearth. My new friends were here, and I didn't want to leave them.

Mr. Clark gently let me to the ground.

My toes touched, and soon came to rest on solid rock.

I opened my eyes to Mr. Clark's swollen lip, and a generous flow of blood down his chin. His chest swelled and contracted a handbreadth, which I measured against by breasts. Sweat flowed from his brow and neck, mingling with the red stream from his lip.

When I finally blinked, I stretched out my own collar and touched my finger to his lip.

Chapter Five

I LEARNED THAT FAIRIES used the glittery sparkles from the finest statuary golden vein marble as monetary currency when buying and selling in the settlement of Marble. And not just any glittery sparkles, as Marble had no shortage of polishing dust and the delicate crystal emitted from it, but only those fallen from Miss Lorena's eye lashes after a day of polishing stone in her little shop on Park Street.

Or so last night's erotic dream informed me.

It was one of those dreams that went on for hours and you're floating in a sea of warm maple syrup and you wake up with a stiff neck. This one lasted three hours, even after a quick trip to the privy and back. When the alarm finally sounded at 5 A.M. I was sure I had gained new insight into the magical nature of Marble. Of course, I forgot half the dream by the time I washed up, but the basics stayed with me throughout the day. It wasn't until noon that it occurred to me that I had either been love-smitten, or had too much cabbage and onion the night before.

By noon I stood covered in marble dust at the rubbing beds, laying twenty-five-pound weights onto baby headstones, loading them onto abrasive wheels, and deciding which parts of the dream were real. Was it the fairies? Or the glittery sparkles fallen from Miss Lorena's eye lashes? Or both?

"Come with me, Clark," a voice sounded over my shoulder. I

turned to see Anson, Marley, and Tolbert with hands on their hips. "We're going to the office."

Had I been negligent in my daydream? Dropped a block onto somebody's foot? Allowed one to shoot off the whirling bed through a window while I daydreamed of fairies and crystals? I tried to think back. Any of those were possible.

The three marched me out of the finishing mill and up to the east end, where the austere company office building sat, attached to Shop #1. The office of Colonel Channing F. Meek. His late-model 1909 Ford sat out front leaking oil, so I pretty-much knew where I was headed. No words were exchanged. At least it was a break from the mill where conversing with fellow laborers ten feet away was a challenge. The rushing Crystal River next to the mill was always a treat. I loved coming and going every day.

And I loved the moment Miss Lorena and I shared beside it, where she bit through my lip and didn't even know it, and I didn't know it either, and I didn't want to put her down, and she didn't want to let go. Was that also true? Both the glittering sparkles, and the equally magical Miss Lorena? Both were true? Had I really met the most thrilling woman these hills had ever produced? A single minute passing the Crystal River reminded me that it was.

Glittery sparkles and all.

"Take a seat, Clark," Colonel Meek said, barely appearing over a letter he was pecking out on an LC Smith typewriter. "Do you know the contents of this letter?" he asked. The three bosses stood over me, pursing their lips and shaking heads. One hissed through clenched teeth.

I assumed it was my letter of discharge.

Colonel Meek battled the contraption, one finger at a time. "Confounded new machines and fat fingers." He shoved the typewriter aside, licked a pencil tip and commenced editing the reliable way. He looked over his glasses. "It says your machinery is to arrive Monday and Shop #1 is yours to manage. All shop personnel will be restructured under your command." He looked up at the Marley, Anson and Tolbert. "That includes you three. See Mortimer Mathews or W.F Frazier for details."

Just then Thomas came through the door, smiling, as his good nature always allowed. "You called?" He shook hands with the mill managers and me, as I stood to thank Colonel Meek.

I don't believe Thomas ever earned an enemy in this world. I believe he liked everyone and everyone liked him. Me included. We spent more than one Sunday pulling trout out of Beaver Lake and a passel more down at the river. One time we hiked Whitehouse Mountain. He was one of those fellows you could confess anything to, and would do anything asked of him. That didn't mean Thomas didn't have a mind of his own, or didn't see the wrong in things, or didn't point out the rough bits. He was just able to pitch those ideas in ways everyone liked.

I guessed that included my plans for the mill.

The meeting ended as soon as it started. Thomas and I stood outside the office blinking and shaking our heads. We were suddenly in charge!

Bottom rail on top, as Uncle Olin used to say.

In the months following, Thomas and I set to gutting the shop and installing new equipment. Narrow-gauge rail ran straight across the shop floor. Diamond and gang saws at the entrance, and polish and packaging at the end. Before this, no one in Marble had even seen a gang saw, and its means of operation became a topic of exploration and conversation.

"Looks dangerous," Miss Lorena commented, on her way to see Thomas, and staring up at the eight-foot frame with thirty blades suspended horizontally from it. "What if one breaks?"

"Sister... Jeremiah Clark is the new expert on these mechanical matters and I trust him. He's spoken with the Ajax Saw Blade Agency and they assure us of complete safety. Have you seen their advertisement in the Rocky Mountain News? It says, 'Warranted for Absolute Safety.'"

I nodded. "Plus, we can now cut blocks thirty times faster than with the single diamond saw. See how thin the blades are? One sixteenth of an inch, and twelve feet long. Thinner blades mean less scrap. That's how we can fit thirty into one gang truck. Pretty modern, don't you say?"

"They seem high strung. Tight," she said, not convinced of the claims of safety and modern materials. "Do they bind?"

"Of course not, sister!" Thomas remarked. "We put dogs on the top of the cuts, and that widens the cutting line. Nothing binds."

I nodded, but then shook my head. "But if you forgot one of the wooden wedges, or if one worked loose, then you could have–"

Thomas interrupted, "The blades don't even have teeth, Lorena. See? It's abrasive material that does the cutting, not teeth... not the blade... so they are completely safe. They can't cut you." He rubbed his hand across a blade and produced it forthwith and unharmed.

Thirty baby headstones in the time it took to do one could change everything. And not just headstones. Wainscoting, flooring, washroom mosaics, anything thin and flat. We could now do it more economically than anyone in the world. Gang saws were the newest and brightest idea in the modern industrial world. Only good could come of them.

Band saws followed the gang saws. Planers followed the band saws. Routers followed the planers. And then rubbing beds and hand polishing. Every step along the line improved blocks in one small way. Until they reached the end and were crated for the Crystal River & San Juan Railway. You could not get any more efficient by any means known to man.

Four weeks of smooth production proved it.

We finished a month of orders in the first week. All the gravestone orders stacked in Meek's inbox were cut, polished and shipped. That meant he could focus on bigger things like selling more investor bonds. Or winning the Cleveland courthouse deal. Or the Denver Post Office. Deals like that would prove that Marble stone was the best in the world, and the Colorado-Yule Marble Company could deliver it. Of course, Meek needed the investors to make it happen, which is where the bonds came in.

Anson collared Colonel Meek in the shop one day. "If you remember, this is exactly what we talked about, even before Clark came to Marble. I think we can take it from here."

"And don't think he's here to stay," Marley added. "He's still just a transient in a black twill suitcoat. Watch him pack up and move on to the next boomtown. If silver comes back, he'll be up in Leadville romancing the Tabor Mine bosses, teaching them how to process ore buckets. Or back in Cripple Creek, if gold stocks ever get the curative for their ills."

Tolbert had his own take on the changes. "I don't have nothing to do no more, boss." He threw up his hands and walked around dazed and dumbfounded. "Nobody needs me no more. And that's his dern fault."

And so the three bosses sought to poison Colonel Meek. But I don't think he took the pill. Things were running too smoothly. Meek had bigger plans and the new shop proved those plans could work. What if we did get that Cleveland deal? What kind of mill would that take to deliver? How about that marble post office with Greek columns over the mountains in Denver? You needed big production for jobs like that.

"Big jobs, big investments. More bonds, more bonds, more bonds," Colonel Meek repeated. "We'll sell more bonds."

The BEST MFG steam tractor was pulling down eighty tons of sound marble on a load, and those came in twice a day. No more four-horse teams. The quarry was at full capacity and the block yard was filling up.

"Let's get one more block cut today," I said, pulling Thomas back to the gangs. "That little twenty-tonner wants done up. Don't you think?"

Thomas didn't look willing.

"Oh, come on. We can have that sliced up like sourdough before the whistle blows. Then we can say we finished a hundred tons this week. That's never been done before. Come on, Thomas. We'll make history!"

"The planers are already backed up." He pointed to a stack of headstones waiting to pass over the planing bed, where they skimmed layers off each side of the headstones, making them perfectly smooth and true. Planers were slower than saws, which only meant we needed more of them, or needed newer cutting beds for the job. Or stronger motors. Or more electrical power.

More bonds, more bonds, more bonds.

Thomas waved it off. "They can't take another thirty blocks anyway." He looked wrung out.

"I'll set up the gang trucks and walking beams," I said, ignoring his tired eyes. "We can have this finished by the end of the day. A hundred tons in one week. Think of that! I'll get 'em set up!"

"No, I'll do it," Thomas reluctantly conceded. It was his job anyway. I just egged him to the point of action. Maybe that was a mistake. Limits were never in my vocabulary. Human limitations… human frailty… an end to human endurance… never even considered. When I saw an achievable goal, I just put my forehead of flint down and set off running.

Ten minutes into the cut, Thomas set the wooden wedges at the top of the block. We called them dogs because they kept the slabs from shifting, plus they opened the cutting slot so the blades didn't bind. Think of little terrier dogs biting the tops of those marble slabs and stopping them from jumping around, kind of like a dog on a calf's lip on branding day. That's where we got the word. Thomas and I came up with silly stuff like that to make the work light and easy.

Dogs.

All the little dogs were in place. All thirty – one for each blade – holding marble slabs apart.

Or so I thought.

That is, until a sudden crack rocked the dusty air and a thousand marble chips blasted me in the face. The last blade on the block buckled and shattered the end slab. Marble bullets shot across the wooden shop floor and chopped down six able men, including me. All the windows shattered. All the lights went out. Boards on the external mill wall busted loose.

A marble explosion!

But the gang truck just kept pushing. Twenty nine of the blades never knew there was a problem But that last one glowed red hot at the point of buckling. Thomas rushed to disconnect the electrical power, because machines don't know how to do that themselves. Machines don't think. They just go. Like me. And sometimes when they go bad, they really go bad. Especially ones with ten tons of force behind them.

The red-hot blade snapped and exploded.

Twelve feet of red-hot steel whipped back at Thomas and

cleaved his shoulder from his body.

His arms swayed as an aspen in a stiff wind, and then he fell limp where he stood, not six inches from the electrical switch. A gallon of blood formed before I could even fall on his wound. Before I knew it I was covered and coughing in Thomas' own lifeblood. I don't think he even saw it coming.

An hour must have passed. Or maybe five minutes. I could not tell, for I was now floating outside the realm of time and space. I laid over my best friend's chest soaking in his own blood and searching for that one sure reason this block had to be cut today. For why it could not have waited until next week, like Thomas said. Was 'a hundred tons' a number they would speak of for generations? Was it some grand achievement we had to reach?

And was the slaying of Thomas Thayer worth its magnanimous achievement?

Oh Lord, couldn't we just back up a few minutes to recheck those dogs? Just one minute, Lord. One minute, and I'll look them over myself. And then Thomas could come back, and we could shut the saw off and go fishing in Beaver Lake with quarts of buttermilk and ham sandwiches. We could wait a few days. Just one minute, Lord. I just want—

Somehow I became aware of the cloud of witnesses about us. The bloody pool had expanded ten feet across the wooden floor. And floating in the pool was the very shimmer of crystal I had seen in my strange dream. To be exact, it was the sparkling crystals falling from the eyelashes of Miss Lorena, for she was the first person my eyes set upon. She stood at the edge of the witnesses with manifest horror in her eyes, without the very air to speak, and those glittering and sparkling eyes slowly burned out at the scene before her.

I must have laid there for hours.

But I woke up at Thomas' graveside. Or maybe I had walked or had been carried. I was not sure. But there I was, next to a black lacquered casket I knew the contents of without looking.

I obviously knew how I got there. The last four days had been spent equally getting my face patched up, and sitting on the quiet shop floor next to Thomas' blood with shattered saw blades in my hands. But I could not tell how I went from place to place with any certainty, even here beside him this last time.

The four hundred mourners behind me seemed to be split into two even groups. Half that wanted me dead, and the other half that just wanted me hung. Each one filed past the lowering casket to Miss Lorena, who sobbed deeply under a black vale.

"I would not trade a hundred Quarry Town transients for your brother," came the frothing words of one woman, as she touched Miss Lorena.

"I wanted to marry that man," another said. "But I'd probably be slain in my bed."

"My uncle is a county commissioner," a young man said. "Do you need help with this?"

"Miss Lorena," I whispered. We had not spoken since before the accident.

No answer.

"He's ruined a whole town in one day," a man added.

"Miss Lorena, can I explain?"

"What is he doing here?" another asked. "Isn't he the one?"

"Yes, he's the one," Anson answered. He and Marley came to Miss Lorena's aid when they spotted me. "None of this would have happened in the old shop. It was safe and orderly. None of those gang saws. None of those–"

"Shut up, Anson," I said, and then turned to Miss Lorena.

"Lorena–"

Anson protested. "Listen, Mister. You will address her properly, or not at all. Were you raised in a barn?"

"Transients…" someone said, shaking his head.

"Miss Lorena, I know why this happened. I know the reason–"

"I don't want reasons," Miss Lorena snapped. "I know the reasons, Mr. Clark. I thought you came to apologize and see if there was some way you could stay here in Marble. But it looks like you're only here to justify your actions. Thomas is dead, and all you can say is that you know why." She sobbed and turned away.

"I just thought that might—"

"Why don't you leave, please?"

"It was the Ajax blades, Miss Lorena. The blades were—"

Miss Lorena boiled. "I want you to leave, Mr. Clark!"

A few sturdy men stepped in and slid off their hats. One handed his to another. He rolled up his sleeves and spit on his hands. A pair of fisticuffs? I'd seen that aplenty in Randalls Flats and Cripple Creek, and I never did scare worth a cent. But I felt Miss Lorena should know what found.

I edged around the men. "The blades were hardened too long and that made them brittle. That's why the blade broke when buckled. It was the Ajax Saw Blade Agency's fault."

That must have invited a fist to my gut. "Back off, Mister," the man warned.

I sucked air but rose and ventured another word. "I looked at them myself, Miss Lorena," I said, holding my aching gut.

And just as the man stepped in for another gut punch, Miss Lorena pushed forward. I figured she was ready to finish me off herself.

"I asked you to leave. You've killed my brother, and now you blame saw blades?"

"I thought you should know. Thomas was my—"

She hauled back and slapped me. "I don't care what you think."

I must have been a lunatic. Or maybe I had never been slapped like that before, because I repaid the slap with one of my own.

Her eyes turned sideways but never lost their steel.

And then I said, "You're enjoying this. Wallowing in your misery."

Miss Lorena never flinched. She just hauled back for another. This time twice as hard. The smack echoed half way up Sheep Mountain. "I asked you to leave."

By this time, twenty men backed her up. "Better get the sheriff," somebody said. "Before I get a rope."

"He's on his way," another said. "You best git, mister. Or we're pressing charges for the murder of Thomas D. Thayer."

"We're going to undo every stupid thing you did to the mill," Anson said.

Cheers went up and Miss Lorena nodded.

I raised my hands, "Alright, Miss Lorena, you can keep this howling wilderness. I only wanted to help this town and the mill. I loved Thomas like a brother. And I loved you. Yes, I loved you. I guess that was a mistake."

I tramped down to the railway, pulled a hand-car onto the rails, and pumped the handles north to Carbondale.

To heck with them.

Chapter Six

UNCLE OLIN BUSTED OUT laughing when he saw my cut-up face. "Sorry you got shot up and run out on a rail, Jay. Did they tar and feather you too?" He then proceeded to lift his shirt and display four bullet holes in his back, and repeat a story I had heard twenty times back in Missoura. "Pa and me got shot up and run out of—"

"I didn't exactly get shot up. I got blasted in the face with a thousand marble chips."

"They loaded a danged canon and shot you up?" He looked scandalized. "Dern… Jay!"

"No, it's a long story. But I did have to git out of Marble before they really did shoot me up. Or hang me. Glad you wired money." I looked around the train station. "So this is New York City! Is J.T. here? I was hoping to see him again."

Uncle Olin shook his head. "You picked the wrong day, Cornpone. J.T. is in Paris with yer cousin Buford. I'm all alone with a hundred thousand Yankees. Got to do all the killin' myself!"

I just smiled. After all this time, Uncle Olin still stood the very image of the rebel bushwhacker — mangy hair and mustache, with a hand-stitched drop-shoulder Missoura border shirt and Bowie knife under his belt — but I doubted he actually harmed any Yankees here in New York City. Maybe in the back hills of Randalls Flats, but not up here. But still I glanced back for signs he might be serious. You never knew with Uncle Olin.

He smiled. "Can ya hep yer old uncle? A murder a day is all I ask."

He shoved me in the shoulder and headed for the exit. "So why'd the Northern hordes run you off? I told you not to go to Colorado, didn't I?"

Did I really want to recount the whole story? "Guess I messed up," I finally said, but didn't really want to get into it. "Where do you live? Here in the city?" It was still hard to believe that Uncle Olin and Cousin Buford joined J.T. Martin's garment company in New York City. Did Confederate rebels do that? And a Missoura border ruffian, to boot. But here he was, ready for Yankee killing and in the right place for it.

"Me and yer cousin live out at the east end of Long Island. That's not a real city. It's out near the ocean. J.T. lives in his pa's old place. But we work in the city, cutting cloth mostly. You know, Buford is the genius behind the operation. J.T. is the money. And I'm just the unreconstructed rebel they trot out to whip up customers." He laughed and whistled an automobile taxicab. "We're ridin' in style, Jay. Lookey here! The dumb-heads come a runnin' whenever I whistle."

On the long ride across Long Island, I admitted most of the story with Thomas and the gang saw. But I still couldn't find the fault in it. Sure, it was an accident, but industrial accidents happened all the time, didn't they? Men lost fingers. Arms and legs. Or the occasional eye. The shop floor was stained with the blood of a hundred little mishaps. Couldn't they see that? And couldn't they see that Thomas was a beloved friend I would protect with my own life? Why did it have to be him anyway? And the brother of Miss Lorena too. What an awful mess, and one I could not erase from my thoughts.

I guess I just messed up. That's all I could think.

Uncle Olin lasted about six minutes into my saga before tapping the hilt of his Bowie knife and preparing oaths of vengeance. "I'd slaughter every dern one of 'em. Remember that little affair down in Centralia? That was me and Jesse! We drunk Tennessee whiskey out of stolen boots, and then slaughtered about twenty of them blue bummers.

Yer grandpa was thar too. That thar's what I'd do to them Colorado bummers if they ever run me off."

"I don't really need revenge," I said, but wasn't sure if that was really true. Maybe I did, but I wasn't about to admit that to Uncle Olin or he'd turn the taxicab around and head for Colorado with about four .32's in his belt shouting the rebel yell.

Uncle Olin sniffed. "Alright then… what about you buy them white-livered Yankees out?"

"I'm broke. You know that. You had to send train fare."

Uncle Olin's house came into view at the end of the island. I could tell on account of the huge sour mash cooker smoking in the dooryard, tall weeds surrounding it, and shingles falling off the roof – just like back in Randalls Flats, Missoura. And the fact that we'd go into the water if we went any further.

"Revenuers all about these parts," he whispered. He stepped out of the automobile and checked around for the aforementioned revenuers. "Cantrell's ain't paid no whiskey tax since 1792. Taxation is theft."

"Is that the ocean?" I asked. I'd never seen the ocean and wondered what it looked like. Did it really roar and swallow up whalers? To me, it just looked like a really big lake, calm and peaceful. Uncle Olin's place sat right on the edge and appeared to be in no obvious harm.

Uncle Olin nodded. "Yeah, that's the danged ol' ocean." He raised a Missoura bushwhacker finger. "I'll tell you who ain't broke! Yer bully pal, Roosevelt. I'd git him to put up a million dollars and buy them whole lily-livered abolitionists out. How many are there up there in Marble City? A thousand?"

"Eight hundred," I said. "But the Marble Booster says—"

"That's what I'd do, Cornpone. Buy 'm out. Either that or burn their homes and scalp their evil children." He danced a little jig with a wagging finger.

"Old Dan Tucker were a hardened sinner, he nebber said his prayers at dinner. De ole sow squeel, de pigs did squal. He et de 'hole hog, tail an all!"

Sometimes I wondered where Uncle Olin got his ideas. Not the scalping. I knew where he got that. But the Roosevelt thing. That was pure genius. And they called Buford the brains of the outfit.

Uncle Olin paid the taxicab driver and promised him another hundred if he brought some customers in next week. We went into his house. This was no salt-box cottage; it was enormous. But without a stick of furniture. When we stepped into the front room, there sat two dirty cots and a galvanized wash tub. A quick look around revealed nothing else. The house must have had fifteen rooms, each with marble floors and high gilded ceilings. But virtually devoid of civilized trappings.

One room seemed to be devoted solely to some sort of tribute to William T. Anderson, the man Uncle Olin and all Missoura referred to as Bloody Bill. A hero to all who knew him — the leader of the Centralia massacre Uncle Olin claimed to enjoy so much. I was too young to know the details.

Uncle Olin had somehow procured four huge oil paintings of the man, each framed in what I judged to be pure gold. Not the gilded stuff; this was real. They hung on each of the four walls. Numerous wet-plate glass photographs filled the gaps, all of the same man: Bloody Bill. Some were of him riding into battle and others of his death with his bullet holes on display. In the center of the room stood a life-sized stallion rearing into the sky. It too had five bullet holes with blood leaking from them, recirculating in a pool at its base by some means of electrified pumping. Drip, drip, drip, the blood poured out without end, and the bloody stallion rearing into battle.

Nice touch.

Hanging under the Bloody Bill death daguerreotype, was the same bullet-ridden shirt shown above it. Uncle Olin had somehow gotten the blood-stained shirt off some enterprising trader. I could not imagine how, because I knew no less than a dozen men who wanted it for their own cabins and shacks back home. This was no rag. The hand-stitching approached fifteen stitches to the inch. Some mother had obviously spent a whale of loving hours by hearth light, and now the man was shot up and kilt in it. She must have cried herself to death.

"You kin bunk in Buford's cot," Uncle Olin offered. "He's got the better blanket." Which looked to be a woolen horse blanket from the 1880's. "We got electric lights! And lookey here; water comes trickling right into this little water closet." He pointed into a little indoor privy, with a shellacked wooden seat. Snow white marble lined the contraption and the baseboards of the little room, just like all the big rooms in the rest of the house. I thought of Marble, and wondered if the ornaments had come from there or the Vermont Marble Company we fought so vigorously for contracts. "Buford won't use it," Uncle Olin observed. "He still does his dirty work in the outside privy, like back home."

Uncle Olin smiled. "Remember that glorious two-holer? I brought that up from Missoura just for Buford."

"Tell me more about that Roosevelt idea," I begged. Uncle Olin's house was fascinating, but this new idea had me by the fingernails. I wanted to hear everything in Uncle Olin's genius little mind. Because if it was anything more than a stupid joke on me, then I wanted to soak up every drop. They said the Pinkertons claimed there was no trap Olin Cantrell could not sniff out, and I felt trapped right about now.

Uncle Olin just stumbled around the empty house with little more to say. He stepped into one goodly sized room with steamer trunks lining the walls. I opened a few and found them filled with hundred-dollar treasury notes.

"That's from garment making. But my side business," he glanced out at the smoking still in the dooryard, "hardly brings in enough to feed the livestock. Your Cousin Buford won't take paper money," Uncle Olin informed me. "He only takes gold dollars, and he counts them about ever third day." He opened a few trunks to reveal the shimmering contents. "Too heavy for me," he said shaking his head. "Got no use fer it."

"Now what did you mean by Roosevelt?" I asked impatiently.

"I got too lazy totin' gold. So I started in with them federal dollars," he complained.

"I can understand that." I nodded. "So... ah... Roosevelt? What about that idea?"

Uncle Olin finally growled. "T.R. was yer mess pal from Cripple Creek, weren't he?"

"I guess. Not really a mess pal, he just took the Black Jack Mine under his wing and gave me advice from time to time. He brought in some investors. Helped sort things out. That kind of thing."

Uncle Olin rolled his eyes and huffed. "Alright, you call it whatever. We called 'm mess pals. If Roosevelt ain't got a million dollars, I'll guarantee he's got mess buddies what do. Remember all them Rough Rider generals? Sherman Bell, an' them Cuban invaders? They're all rich now. And they all live in that rotten Washington D.C. swamp, not ten days ride from here."

Uncle Olin still referred to distances by the number of days on horseback. I guess that explained the dozen horses in the riding stables behind his house, but I knew he also traveled in trains like the rest of the civilized world. And I thought I saw a few motorcars in the horse barn too.

Uncle Olin continued. "Or, Roosevelt could scare up a million dollars' worth of marble contracts in that Washington pesthole alone. I'd like a nice big Anderson monument, wouldn't you? With Bloody Bill sitting inside a big marble chamber with fancy Greek columns about him. And Yankee invaders dying under his boot. And the rebel flag carved in marble over his head. Git me a monument like that, and I'll put in a trunkful of my own money. Buford's too. Get a contract like that and you're on the wire road to a million dollars. Then you kin buy out them what run ya out of town."

But then he wrinkled up his face. "Why do ya want to go back anyways? Why not bring them sons of yourn out here with me and Buford? I'll get 'em all stock trader jobs on Wall Street. Or they can tend my corn-liquor still. I need brave boys from the hills to hold off revenuers."

That was a good question. Levi refused to leave when I did, and for good reason. He had his girl, Adelaide back in Cripple Creek, and he wanted to stay close. The older boys, Micah and Caleb had found their way to New York, but I didn't know where just yet. They had lives of their own somewhere. But Uncle Olin's point was valid. Why go back to Marble?

It didn't take long to cypher that out.

And it wasn't just for Levi.

So I stayed with Uncle Olin for a time, bunking on Buford's cot under the dirty horse blanket, tending the sugarhead still and sitting by the ocean. That's when I figured I had some business to attend to. I got up one sunny morning with a new idea.

"Uncle Olin, could you grubstake me for a trip into Washington?"

Chapter Seven

LITTLE LEVI SHOWED UP at the door a week after the funeral. "Miss Lorena, are Christian women excited by good belches?" he asked, and then let out a long forced one. "I've been practicing now that Father's not here to whollop me. Are you still mad at Father?"

He bounced into the house like a month-old puppy and went straight for the ice box. What if I had had a gentleman caller? What would that man think right about then? He'd take me for an unscrupulous woman, letting young men tramp in uninvited. But then, I never had gentlemen callers, except for Levi and Mister Clark, back when he was here in Marble. I guessed Levi had gotten into some routine of familiarity he thought was okay with me.

But it wasn't. Not now.

He didn't know I had rehearsed my meanness all week, and it was about to come crawling out with slow malignant tentacles. Problem was, with Levi's sweet and innocent spirit I forgot the words. I forgot to explain how his father had taken everything from me. I forgot to describe how my life was over and there was nothing more to live for, or that he should join his negligent father wherever that might be, or that Marble would not tolerate their kind another hour so Mister Clark had better not return. Those were the very words I had recited all week. But they failed to emerge.

Instead I just said, "Do you want chicken and potato cakes?"

Dang. That was not what I rehearsed.

The large wood stove had been going hot since breakfast while I lay around in bed clothes. I just kept throwing in logs with no regard to cost or austerity. Plus, I went through the entire 1907, 1908, and 1909 Montgomery Ward's catalogs and Kobey's advertisements in the last four hours, and swore off all the latest fashions contained therein. Page by page, I fed the fire on fashion, and cried for Thomas, and cried for Harriet who went back to Denver to live with my sister. Why place an order? Why even consider the new black leather shoes with only half the eyelets as last year's? Or silk hats with seventeen "like real" roses? What good would the new Sears and Roebuck slimming corsets do me? Could I really achieve the fifteen-inch waistline they guaranteed?

I might just as well throw on a barn coat and men's trousers.

No man would ever look at me again.

And if I thought hard on the matter, that was the real problem. I wanted a gentleman caller, but no man even knew I was alive. I just wanted to lean up against a sturdy man and let him surround me and carry me about the house. And chop fresh pine and bring in logs and feed the stove so I could lay on the couch and cry. And what if he did try to kiss me? Would I stop him? Maybe not. I might just let him have his liberties if he said Thomas was a good brother and everything was going to be okay and I could sit by the fire as long as I liked. I would throw whole catalogues in if I had a gentleman caller.

I poured a cup of hot cocoa for Levi. He had his own troubles, and leaned in with weepy eyes.

"Miss Lorena?"

I took a chicken breast out of the ice box, and rubbed salt and onion and garlic into it. It would roast up nicely in the hot oven. That and fried potato cakes would make a nice little Sunday meal for the boy. Most of the single men in Quarry Town or Marble lived on salt beef and hardtack because you could get a paper box of that for a nickel at The City Market and Grocery. Of course The City Market also had fresh beef most of the time, but that went for twenty cents a pound and most men didn't have the time or inclination to cook it up. I figured that was the case with Levi, now that Mister Clark was gone.

"Miss Lorena, I want to marry Adelaide. You know... back in Cripple Creek. But I'm a baby and I don't think she will marry me."

"Why do you say that? You're not a baby."

The garlic chicken began filling the kitchen with promise. Real women can cook by smell alone.

"I only saw her once this year, on account of it being two-hundred miles away. And we just played around and didn't do any grown-up stuff. She just wanted to play with my fingers and hair, and push her nose into my ear and stuff like that. I don't know if she even wants to marry me."

If I had a gentleman caller right now, I would push my nose into his ear. But I didn't tell Levi that. He had picked up a pencil and The Marble Trading Company circular and began sketching me in front of the big smoking stove. "What did you expect, Levi? She wants to be next to you."

"I thought we should build a house next to the Black Jack Mine. Or at least dig the privy."

I smiled. "Sometimes women like different things. And sometimes digging a privy isn't what women want to do when a man is in their hands. Do you understand?"

He didn't even look up from the sketching. "They don't want a nice house and a privy? Like you got?"

"Yes, but other things too." And I knew exactly what those things were. I could feel them in my tenderloins. And I could feel them on my white skin and breasts. Breasts that heaved with certain feelings I never really understood. My own body told me what it wanted, so much that I hardly had to think about it. That's probably why God did not see fit to send me a gentleman caller when I had prayed so hard for one. He knows better than to give you everything you ask for.

"Tell me, then!" he begged. "What do women want?" He finished the sketch and handed it to me. I should have framed it because it turned me from ordinary into elegant. There next to the nickel-plated oven doors stood a slender barefoot female with all the sensual qualities a gentleman caller might desire. And I hadn't even changed out of my silky night clothes. "Sorry, it's just a quick drawing, Miss Lorena."

I held up the pencil-sketch and laughed. "That's not me. Probably something you saw in a book somewhere." The stunning figure had all the right lines, the kind of lines gentlemen find inviting for whatever ideas they have in their little minds. But it wasn't me, not by a country mile. This woman made the nickel-plated stove look old and busted. This wasn't me.

"No, it's pretty-much what you look like right now. See how the silk curls up into–"

I went straight in and changed.

When I came out Levi asked, "Were you beautiful back in the olden times?"

I smiled and stoked the nickel appliance. The answer was yes, I was. But I was older now, and still had never had a man. There was a reason for that, and only I knew what that was. Blanche didn't know. Millicent didn't know. And I wasn't going to tell them. They would laugh at me for wasting the best years of my life. But it was my life and they didn't have to know.

"Tell me how to make Addie like me. You said women like other things. Tell me what they are. Root cellars and vacuum cleaners?"

I patted him on the head and checked the chicken and potato cakes. A nice aroma now filled the kitchen and front room. Sage and garlic. Paprika and onion. And a little hickory smoke from the bottom of the flue pipe where the damper rod runs through. "They don't care much for good belches, so you can safely leave off practicing that. I can only tell you what I would want, if I were being courted by a handsome young man like you. Not every woman is like me, but maybe it will help you."

It took me some time to compile his list, but this was the core of it.

First off, I wanted a man with integrity who held his convictions even when opposed. I'd seen too many man-pleasers with compromising morals and words. The business world was full of them. Even the church. I wanted a man that knew what he wanted and could not be bought. A man that could take bruising and come back for more. Conviction and patient persistence.

Money meant nothing.

Prospects meant nothing.

Fashion and tailoring meant nothing.

I wanted a man that wasn't hard to look at. Because I would look at him every night, and he would look at me. A sturdy man. And one I liked the feel of when I my fingers slipped over strapping steel, but I didn't tell Levi that one.

Levi didn't think much of those qualities, but he nodded in partial agreement. Plus, I probably didn't go into enough detail, as discretion and modesty forebode the mention of certain topics. But still, I think he got the general idea.

Levi prayed over the meal, and he did well. At least his father had taught him that. He was a sweet boy and I didn't feel he had any trouble with Adelaide. She would take him just as he was. But he didn't know that, and I didn't know how to convince him of it.

"Don't you think I need a professional job? I can't have babies by sanding headstones at a dollar a day. I only bring in six dollars a week, and rent is four. I don't even think Adelaide's father will let me marry her until I have prospects."

"You have an artistic talent. Why don't you design marble buildings? The Colorado-Yule has a drafting room. I've seen it. It's fifty-feet square, and they lay out full-sized patterns right on the office floor. You know the Cleveland courthouse job? It's being drawn up right now. Right up in that office, this week. All the columns and flutings. The arches, cornerstones, and capstones. All drawn up, right there."

"I could never do that. I was thinking of moving up to band saws. Those fellows make eight dollars on account of the danger. But you can lose a finger—"

"Levi, stop. Draw me a building. Right now. Draw it on this chicken wrapper." I wiped the blood off it and thrust it into his hands.

Levi laughed and took up the wrapping paper. Two minutes later he handed back his creation. I had never seen anything like it. And I didn't know if the Colorado-Yule Marble Company could even produce such a structure. It would certainly require all the Italian artisan talent the firm possessed. Fortunately, they had the finest in the world. But still, this thing was something new.

"How can these arches even be constructed?" I asked.

"It takes eight cuts, but it can be done. I'll draw it out if you want." In sixty seconds, he sketched a detailed miniature of the spectacular arch, with the aforementioned eight cuts, along with angles and dimensions. I sat staring at the chicken paper wondering how God could share this much of His own creative capacities with mere men. Wasn't He a jealous God? Evidently not. Or not in that way.

"Do you mind if I take this to Colonel Meek?"

"No! If the Three Blind Mice hear about it they will fire me. Anybody that tries anything new gets fired and ran out of town. Everybody knows that now."

"Levi, that's not true. Your father got somebody killed. That's why–"

Levi stood up. "No he didn't! He just wanted to help the company. And now I get yelled at if I even lift my head at work, or show my face at Carey's Ice Cream Shop. Them three want me fired real bad. The whole town does. I don't even talk to them three anymore. If they see that drawing they will fire me the next day. Adelaide already thinks I'm a baby, and what do you think she'll say if I come back to Cripple Creek without nothin' but my hat in hand. Her father will–"

He began shaking and rubbing his forehead.

"I miss Father." He began to sob. "And I miss my real mother and father back in Kansas. I want to go back and be with them and…" He hung his head.

"Levi–"

"Maybe I should just give up and leave Marble. But then Adelaide will never like me."

"Let me take care of this, Levi. I'll show your design to Colonel Meek. The Three Blind Mice will never see it. I promise."

Levi laid his head on my breast and sniffled.

I was probably the only one he could cry in front of.

Chapter Eight

Nah, I didn't need men. My little marble shop was enough. It was bright and cheery next to the Crystal River at the base of Mill Mountain, where Ponderosa Pines bend to the ground in winter and let off their fragrance in the sunny summer. Heck, I probably wouldn't know what to do with a gentleman caller if God ever figured out how to send one.

I could stand in the center of my shop, spin on one foot and see snow-white marble across every inch of the walls and nooks. I lived in a little corner of Heaven. Why would I ever need a man with so much beauty before me? I probably wouldn't even have time for gentleman callers.

No, my little shop was all I needed. No men for me.

"What's the good word, Miss Lorena!" a voice came through the door. Mortimer Mathews stepped through with that very thought on my mind. For a man with deep lungs, and an officer in a million-dollar marble concern, he could be a little goofy and awkward. Especially around me. He reminded me of little Levi, and he was sometimes fun to watch. Men always are.

I sometimes gave Mister Mathews impossible tasks, just to watch him twist.

"Oh, Mister Mathews! How nice to see you. Can you grab that

bottle of rose oil? My hands are so dry. Can you just rub a little in, right here?" He fumbled with the bottle, trying to figure how to apply it without breaching that invisible barrier of intimacy men are taught to observe. Mothers teach their sons so well. A gentleman never touches a woman in certain ways. Never touches a woman's hair. Never her hands. And he must make certain to never brush against her when walking on the avenues. Even the Beadle's Dime Book of Practical Etiquette for Ladies and Gentlemen says as much. I figured I could use such instruction to my social advantage in torturing the poor brutes.

Mr. Mathews touched his finger to the oil, tested several approaches, each with its own set of impossible challenges. I just kept working the statue of marble before him. A chisel in one hand and a one-pound hammer in the other – chipping and stepping back to choose the next gentle tap.

I was roughing out the outline of Jesus on the Via Dolorosa, the Way of Suffering, with a crown of thorns on his head and wounds on his face. When finished, Simon of Cyrene would reach down to the stricken Messiah and offer to carry His cross. Mary and the disciples would be faintly visible behind. I wanted something like a painting, but in marble, cut from a 1x4x5 foot block. The block had deep cracks and a line of blue flint marring it. Blue marble had no commercial value to the mill, which made it perfect for me. I could gently carve around the cracks and use the dark flint line to my advantage.

It would be a year-long project, for which I would have to charge a full hundred dollars.

I never charged by the hour. Instead, my prices reflected the measure of love that poured from my soul. The little shop was lined with love, what little was still left. God had not filled it with what I needed – at least not yet. Crosses, statues, figurines, swans, cemetery monuments, pillars, columns, anything to sooth the eye and lead viewers to the love of Christ. Size and price had no relevant connection. Prices came from the measure of fleshly extractions from my own heart. This piece depicting the scourged and suffering Christ was already shaping up to be the last of my reserves. It would have to be a hundred dollars. I would not take a dime less.

Mr. Mathews had tallied eight failures with the rose oil when I laughed to myself and handed him a hammer and chisel. Men can do hammers. They grow up with them in their hands – either hammers or guns. But, can they touch a woman with a drop of rose oil? Not likely. Mr. Mathews was no dunce with a hammer, but he was actually a wizard with numbers. Colonel Meek had tapped Mathews to set up and sell bonds. He could do bonds. The Colorado-Yule was mostly financed is such ways, and Mortimer Mathews was the manifest wizard behind it all.

"How do they work?" I asked, just touching the angle chisel to the crown of thorns.

"Beg pardon?" Mortimer inclined his ear. "How does what work?"

"Bonds," I asked. "How do bonds work? How does the company make money off them?"

"Oh!" He looked at the hammer and set it down. "Bonds are just loans. We borrow money and use it for expansion. Shop #3 is all bond money."

"Don't you have to pay it back?"

"Hey, let's all go down to the Penny Hot Springs!" Millicent yelled, breaking through the door behind Blanche. Blanche and Millicent were already dressed in striking new black and white wool swimwear, with their hair tied up and towels over their shoulders. White leather belts cinched the girls tightly at the waistline. Exploring eyes landed directly on the bosoms and hips, just where the ladies wished them to land. Fortunately, the swimsuit designers included ample layers of black cloth, obscuring any true womanly forms. Blanche and Millicent were free in their movements and you could practically see their ankles as they leaped through the door. I think they liked it that way. Plus, the new French fashion allowed a touch of collarbone. And you would soon conclude that Blanche's most alluring feature was the collarbone by watching her tug at the neckline to let it out.

Mister Matthews's stolen glances were proof.

"Don't you have to pay it back?" I reminded him. Plus, I liked to watch a man's head spin at the various attractions he simply could not pass up. "It's a loan, so you have to pay the bonds back, right?"

Mister Mathews spun awkwardly back. "Oh yes, Miss Lorena," he said, raising a finger. "With interest." He oscillated between me and Millicent in her tight striped swim apparel, and Blanche with just a hint of collarbone and a promise of so much more, and then back to me again.

"And Miss Lorena, how could I forget? That was actually the true reason for my visit. I wondered if you might accompany me to the Penny Hot Springs this afternoon."

Oops, a little late on the draw, gunfighter.

I stood wondering if I had just been asked to the Penny Hot Springs by Mister Mathews, or if Blanche and Millicent had actually asked Mister Mathews, and he decided to include me as an afterthought. It didn't really matter. God had answered my prayers. I had a gentleman caller.

Now if I could just keep Blanche from stealing him.

But, I also needed Blanche as a chaperone, hence the dilemma.

Penny Hot Springs was little more than a bricked off pool about four feet deep, situated between the railroad grade and the Crystal River. One-hundred-degree water bubbled right out of the hillside and produced a steaming white cloud over the little brick-lined pool. Nobody had thought to charge money for it like Glenwood Hot Springs, but the citizens of Marble, Placita, and Redstone used it every Saturday and Sunday. Today, it was ours. You could not reserve it; you had to just show up early and fend off attackers.

"He's no Jeremiah Clark," Blanche observed with slanted jaw. Mr. Mathews slid beneath the steaming vapors, sucking and blowing for protection from the shockingly hot pool.

"Good. Then he's no murderer."

Blanche wagged her head. "From what I heard, you had no problem with Mr. Clark before he was a murderer." She cackled and wagged. "I know everything about everyone in Marble."

I slapped her. But not hard enough, which only invited a little dance with swooning gestures and certain erotic words I could not repeat with a clear conscience. Mister Mathews didn't notice. He was still contending with temperature challenges, and probably computing the face value of a new stack of bonds sold on the New York market and maturity dates.

"It's gotta be a hundred and four," he shouted from under the mist.

Was that the face value of bonds or the water temperature, I wondered.

"I guess this is no place for delicate females," he teased. That gave Blanche and Millicent ample information to plan their own entry and catch glimpses of the manly figure Mr. Mathews displayed between blankets of vapor.

"Remember Glenwood Springs?" Blanche tormented. "Remember that little black swimming uniform the murderer wore? I do." She danced around, poking and imitating what had shocked even her sensitivities at the Glenwood pool. She covered her eyes, then peeked out behind at some imaginary scene of Mister Clark in the black woolen suit, and swooned and picked herself up again.

"Murder me, Mister Clark. Murder me tonight." She danced and teased.

"Now… I forgot…" she added. "Did that swimsuit keep absolutely everything inside? Or did anything accidently slip out?" She skipped around me. "And later… didn't you accidently bite your lip?"

She laid a finger on her chin in faux contemplation. "Or was that his?"

"That was an accident."

"Little liar." She stuck out her tongue and twisted her head. "You liked it."

I just ignored her.

"Yeah, you suuuuuure admired the murderer back then!"

I pulled her hair. And slapped her again. Soundly this time.

I had not the least admiration for Mister Clark. He was out of Marble, likely murdering other brothers wherever he had landed. He wasn't hard to forget. Except for the wreckage he had left behind. I would be the first person to have words with Mister Clark if he ever returned, and I knew exactly what I'd say. But he wasn't coming back, so it didn't matter. I could sneak peeks at Mister Mathew's swimming outfit, even if it wasn't as shocking as Mister Clark's.

A little Italian girl no older than twenty had joined us uninvited. I think she was Millicent's friend, because she seemed to sneak in behind Millicent like a little puppy. She spoke no English, but I think she understood the topic of conversation. She emulated the older girls, and stole looks at Mister Mathews when prompted by Blanche and Millicent. I guessed Millicent was her guardian for the day, for a father intent on safekeeping his daughter's innocence. And yet here she was getting the very education the man must have feared.

Twenty-year-old Italian girls don't know such things. They need instruction.

Mister Mathews peeked out of the mist. "Is anyone coming in?" He tried to wave a window through the drifting vapors, with little success. "I'm sweating under water!"

"We're coming," Millicent shrieked, laughing and urging the Italian girl to be the first into the boiling waters. Her delicate figure and expanded breasts seem to interest Mister Mathews as much as any collarbone; maybe more. Blanche had a competitor she never counted on. But really? What man wants a jiggly little twenty-year-old that speaks no English? So Blanche was probably safe.

Plus, Blanche and Millicent had prepared their best defenses for times like this – fashion! New York does not produce a feathered bathing costume exotic enough for that pair. But I had to laugh, because the little Italian matched their style with nothing but raw beauty. Jet-black hair and striking facial lines, combined with the perfect Greek mathematician's proportions actually made external fashion a detractor. She was a golden Greek goddess in threadbare white cotton, who probably never had to work for her fifteen-inch waistline.

And then there was me. With neither fifteen-inch waistline, nor fashion.

I wondered if Mister Mathews even noticed my second-rate costume. It was last year's slimming bodice, intended to look old fashioned yet modern at the same time. I think the idea was to harken back to olden times with modern treatments added. No feathers. No black lace. Just a simple hook-and-eye arrangement for viewers to muse over and consider how advanced we had become in the last fifty years. I wondered, could that much planning really go into a swimsuit?

But does a slimming bodice compare with Greek proportions? I glanced at the little creature, dipping her toe into the hot water, and turning shyly from Mister Mathews, who just wriggled at the awkward moves.

But he also noticed the red bodice, so it wasn't just Greek proportions and collarbones on his mind.

"I'm all alone here!" Mister Mathews howled again. He splashed a little water out of the mist.

"Lorena won't go in without a bathing box," Blanche taunted. "But I will!"

Mister Mathews made his best effort to gain views of the three girls entering the little pool, which only proved Blanche's point about the bathing box. In such a device, I could wade and enjoy the steaming vapors the same as her, but without the eyes.

I knew exactly how to combat Blanche's little schemes. I knew the one topic Mr. Mathews enjoyed almost as much as bathing fashions or bouncy little Greeks. Business.

"Mister Mathews, did the Colorado-Yule meet its financial objectives last year?" I asked, immediately recognizing the obvious danger. It was a huge risk to try business at the Penny Hot Springs with so many attractions at hand. I could easily be ignored in favor of silly girl-talk and flouncing lace, dripping with hot water. And then I'd be all alone.

"Does the Wichita Public Library really need twenty-ton blocks?" I asked, doubling down on the risky strategy without a thought to how deep I was drilling in. I had no idea of the validity of such statements, but it seemed to work. Mister Mathews fell dumbstruck when he finally got full view of my faux-fashioned silk bodice with red laces. It must have shocked his system as much as the hot waters, and temporarily left him without the function of speech.

"I think.. Umm…" He puffed, as if the heat had gotten to him. "That Wichita contract… Ooo…" He finally caught up with his wits. "We're going to make a killing on that deal. It'll be at least two thousand dollars in the end, if we can get the right artistic talent to bring it forth."

He nodded to the little foreign girl. "Your father is the finest artisan from the Old World. He is the man for this job. Giuseppe Zanotti."

The girl understood nothing but perked up at her father's name.

"Zanotti," She repeated, and wiggled like jelly, which seemed to please Mr. Mathews and turn his whole attention to her. Oh great... my whole strategy had just been nullified by a little wiggle and a smile. But at least Blanche was sidetracked for the moment. And I had no real fear that Mr. Mathews would be attracted to a little foreign girl who didn't know anything about business.

Men just don't think that way.

"Is Wichita getting a full façade or just facing blocks?"

Mr. Mathews turned back, albeit distracted to the edge of exhaustion. "Ahh... just the facings. The library itself is built of brick and mortar, like most public buildings. But they want a modern and elegant frontal elevation. We'll carve Greek images of higher learning on twelve-inch facing blocks, and then bolt them on with brass escutcheons. The whole presentation will be awe-inspiring when viewed from the ground level. I'm going to visit and inspect the final creation myself. I travel a fair bit, I'm sure you know."

Blanche deduced my strategy and formed a counteroffensive. "The Colorado-Yule should quarry granite too, Mister Mathews. Everybody uses it. It's more popular than marble."

I laughed my mind off. She really stepped in it. Granite. Hah!

"Question to you, Blanche," Mr. Mathews asked. "If the Greeks had used granite, would the Parthenon exist today? Or the Temple of Zeus? I speak rhetorically." He smiled. "The Greek structures exist today because of their natural beauty, not structural integrity." He glanced under a cloud at the little Italian girl. "The most attractive building material on earth is marble. The finest and hardest is right up there on Yule Creek. Vermont doesn't match it. Georgia is a distant third. Even Carrara is back in the squalling pack somewhere. And I don't think granite will ever come close to the beauty of crystal-white marble with good polish. In a hundred years, the world will all be using Colorado-Yule marble."

Defense foiled. Hah!

Blanche would have to resort to dripping-wet swimwear and collarbones for attention.

And we all knew that never worked.

"I hope you and Mister Meek remember my little shop in the forest," I reminded him. "You know… for cast-off blocks with seams and cracks that you can't use. I can work around that. Tourists like everything in my shop. If you could get me another–"

A railway pop-car pulled up next to the pool.

"Oh yes, Miss Lorena. We won't forget you. I won't forget you." He smiled and tilted his head thoughtfully. But he never should have lingered in that position. I had to lay an arm over the red bodice laces and look away.

He continued with some interest, "I've actually been thinking a lot about you and–"

Three men leaped off the railcar and skidded down the embankment, nearly landing in the boiling water themselves. "Emergency, Mister Mathews. We've had an accident. The BEST Steam Tractor went over the shoulder at Smelter's Curve. You know… about a half mile from the mill yards? It rolled a hundred feet into the canyon. The tractor and all the marble is crushed up against the canyon wall."

"Any loss of life?"

"You should come now, Mister Mathews."

Chapter Nine

BA-BOOM; THE HAND-CRAFTED double-barrel went off beside me, both barrels nearly at once. Eight quail escaped into the forest but one dropped into the deep grass. "Bully for you, T.R." I said.

"Thanks, Jeremiah. Next one is yours." Teddy Roosevelt walked up to retrieve the bird and placed it in his bag. There were already two in there, and none in mine. He turned to me. "I'm sorry, Jeremiah, there is no way on God's good earth the federal government will erect a monument to Southern traitors. I have a lot of influence in affairs of public works but not that much!"

"But what about—"

"Especially with the dubious moniker of Bloody Bill." He laughed and stomped his foot. "But you got sand coming out here asking for it. I can just see William Taft's face when they unveiled the thing! He'd probably come out, guns up. His father was Secretary of War, for bully sake! And President Grant? He'd come out of retirement to fight the thing with all his war generals. I'm sorry, it would never pass."

I tried to argue, and at the same time pick a line toward what I hoped would be a nice cache of quail on the other side of a wet bog we found ourselves in. If I could find a nice covey up next to the trees, I could bag two or three, and maybe catch up to T.R. by the end of the hunt. Of course, there was no way I was going to up-stage the president of the United States, but I also wasn't going home emptyhanded neither. He had a point about the Yankee powers in Washington. But Uncle Olin's idea wouldn't let go of me – a monument to William T. Anderson, the hero of all Missoura.

"It's just that my uncle–"

"Olin Cantrell?" T.R. shook his head and laughed. "Isn't Olin Cantrell still a notorious felon and fugitive from the federal justice–"

"He's an upstanding citizen. And he's willing to invest in a national monument, and I'd like to bring a contract back with me." I paused. "Actually, I need this. Plus, Olin claims his son Buford and his business partner J.T. Martin will throw in too. You know the J.T. Martin Garment Company, right?"

"Of course."

Circumnavigating the swamp meant no quail for a few nervous minutes. Quail feed on ants, and ants don't like water. Ants, beetles and grasshoppers: that's where we'd find the quarry. Not in this swamp. So I tramped hard for the tree line and tried to explain.

"Uncle Olin is now partners in the J.T. Martin outfit in New York. He claims to be the biggest supplier of men's coats and trousers. They're premier clothiers. Olin is bonafide."

T.R. chuckled.

"He is! I swear."

But then my mind filled with my last image of Uncle Olin feeding sticks into a rye whiskey still in torn overalls and hillbilly hat, with a sawed-off shotgun slung over his back just in case of revenuers. That image was just three weeks old. But I presented him to T.R. as bright as I could.

"Olin is the J.T. Martin company image and marketing vice president."

I looked over to see where that landed. Nope. Nothing.

Only a hundred yards of high grass and occasional mud sumps separated me from a bag of fresh birds, and renewing my manliness with T.R. The President had seen me bust rocks up in Cripple Creek back when McKinley was running, and he'd seen me bust heads to keep up gold production at the Black Jack Mine, and bust axe handles to keep the miner's union in line, but this was my first quail hunt with the man. I had to prove myself or he might not accept the marble monument idea. T.R. was notoriously competitive in the gaming sports, and I worried that his opinion of me and my idea hinged on my performance here. I would not go home without a half dozen quail. And I would not fail to display my own virile constitution. I would bag my share. But I also had this crazy new idea consuming half my mental capacities and distracting me from the success I felt I needed.

I stopped and faced Roosevelt. "Yes, Olin Cantrell is a polished New Yorker now and—"

"Don't lacquer it up, Jeremiah." T.R. laughed. Plus he had just stepped into a mud hole up to his shinbone, and the slurping suction amused him. With boot laces up to the knee there was no fear of losing footwear. "I've read the security reports on the Cantrell family. But I understand what you're saying. And I know he's kin." He stooped to pick mud from the laces and said. "I'm also sorry about your grandfather, Hiram Cantrell."

That was a hundred year old memory from another life.

I turned to Roosevelt who now squatted to retrieve a lost sporting button from his hunting coat, the nice brass Tally Ho types you didn't want to lose, because replacement meant writing London for new ones.

"If we can't build a William T. Anderson memorial, are there any other ideas you think might interest Olin? He is the principle investor so far. I've got to bring something back he can swallow. Ulysses S. Grant is a definite no for Olin. What about Jefferson Davis?"

Roosevelt snickered. "Jefferson Davis? You're missing the point altogether, son. Congress will never appropriate funds for rebel monuments. And every man of power up here will have his say."

"But weren't those Confederate heroes also patriots, fighting for their countrymen? Hearth and home? State's rights and limited government? Brave and sacrificial until the bitter end? I could see a monument for them. Half the country would applaud the nod to the Southern patriots who gave invaders a sound whipping before the end." I stopped and raised the bird gun. A covey rustled the underbrush just fifteen feet off. Twenty birds, maybe. Me and T.R. spotted them at once. He nodded and turned to the rustling, pointing silently.

Both barrels went off the half-cock. Click... click.

Another slow step forward. And then one more.

Suddenly the birds exploded into flight. Thirty miles per the hour. Maybe forty. Twenty birds took flight, then another twenty. I had the bird gun up, and it let off. The first load decimated the covey. I had just a half second to swing the shotgun into line and let off the second load, which scattered the next covey. What a lucky providence of God. Birds dropped on each flight. How many, I could not tell. But Roosevelt's dog retrieved six, plus a live chick which I returned to the nesting grounds.

T.R. four, me six. Uh-oh... not good.

"It's not a question of patriotism. And nice shooting, Clark. I believe you are up two birds to my four. I'll need to get this gun resighted and rebored if I'm to keep up with you." He stooped to pat his dog and feed a little dried meat. "Yes, the rebels were all patriots to their cause, but they called them rebels for a reason. And there's just no way I could sell a monument to disunion to the American people. How about a monument to 'The Unknown Soldier?'"

"Which soldier?"

"Any soldier. It doesn't matter. And it doesn't matter which conflict. The War Between the States. The Cuban Conflict. Or even some future war. It doesn't matter. What matters is that they are not forgotten. What about a marble block dedicated to an unknown?" T.R. spotted the next covey in a distant thicket and headed for it. "But why are you so fixed on marble? And marble contracts?" he asked. "Aren't you still up in Cripple Creek? You're a gold digger aren't you? Is this a financial scheme to get the Black Jack Mine back?"

"It's a long story."

"We've got nothing but time, and I may know a little of it already. I have my sources. You're not the only individual I talk to. I'm the President of the United States, for bully sake!" He stopped short of the next covey and raised his double-barrel. "But just a minute; I'm going to bag one right now. Maybe two." Two minutes later, his birddog returned three.

T.R. seven, me six. Much better...

"I'm no longer in Cripple Creek." I sighed and looked into the overcast skies.

"I'm sorry to hear that, Jeremiah. I know the story of the Black Jack Mine. That was hard luck." Roosevelt laid a hand on my shoulder. "But you're planning to recapitalize and recover the mine, right? Isn't that what this marble monument business is all about? You've got a new scheme in play?"

"I'm up in Marble, Colorado now. I left Cripple Creek. I've still got a small house in Cripple Creek, but we're no longer there. Caleb and Micah are stock brokers in New York. And I now have an orphan son by the name of Levi. He's also up in Marble now."

T.R. sniffed. "I heard about Patricia. I'm sorry about that. You've had it rough, friend. But I did not hear about the orphan boy. I hope he's a good boy and a comfort, and I hope he's in good hands while you're out here. Someone watching over him?"

"Yes, thank you. We're getting along. I'm just a little lost right now. I feel like I've got something to do. There are unresolved things back in Marble I need to–"

I paused to rethink.

"How about a really big monument?" I asked. "Bigger than a house. Uncle Olin talked about Greek columns and a plaza. That big. And all built of snow-white Colorado marble. Not granite."

"That's a million dollars' worth of stone!" T.R. said. "Wheeu!"

"Like I said, my uncle–"

"That's another thing." T.R. said. "There's no way the government, or any other investors I could imagine would be involved in a project with your uncle. His background is a little too questionable. I don't think the American people would stand for that."

"They might. If they knew how bravely he–"

"I can get the investors, Jeremiah. Or Congress could appropriate the full amount. A million dollars is a big deal, but we're a big country now. It might go. I could float the notion on Capitol Hill. See what it flushes out. Get it?" he said, holding up the bag of birds with a wide smile. "But not with Olin on the ticket. But hey, let's get some big banker money!"

I smiled. "I'll be ready to shoot!"

We walked a ways and another idea arose. "Could you help me get a contract for the Denver Post Office? She would like that."

"Patricia?"

"Oh, nothing." I shook briskly. "Never mind. I'm just fixating."

"She, who?"

"Never mind."

We started back to the automobile. T.R. liked the White Steamer for its power and lines; I had to agree because it just looked like it would go fifty miles an hour. The birddog raced across the field, ready for more, urging us back into the thickets. But both of us were jaded and dragging. It had been a ten-mile hunt through tall grass, thickets and bogs, and I was ready for some rest. T.R. was too. I had proven my gamesmanship with the President, and felt sure he liked the marble monument idea too.

T.R. asked, "You said you're in Marble, Colorado. What are you doing there?"

"Well, I'm not running anything." I paused and looked into the dark and swirling skies again. "Just polishing marble in a finishing mill." I didn't tell him about the accident or getting banned for life. Or that they all hated me for carelessness with Thomas' life. And how I'd probably never polish baby headstones again, as if that were some life goal, but I still secretly longed to stand next to that whirling six-foot rubbing bed, and lay stone on it, and live in the same town as the one who had pulled me back from depression and despair, and inspired me to new life.

I would do that again.

"Are these marble ideas a way to get back into the game? Are you planning to take over the place?"

"Oh, no. I'm happy right where I am."

"Sure you are! I know you better than that, Jeremiah."

I hung my head. "No, really. I like the baby headstone job."

He laughed and threw his kit into the automobile. "Then what are you doing in Washington D.C. inquiring about million-dollar marble contracts?"

That was a fair question. I wondered about that myself.

"And what about this 'she' thing? I heard that, you know."

"Nothing. Never mind."

Nothing was clear in my mind. There was no grand plan. But I felt nudged by the Spirit of God to follow this marble contract idea. Somehow, God had worked His plan through Uncle Olin, and it had taken hold of me in a way I could not resist. In reality, I felt no compunction to resist. The idea fascinated me beyond understanding.

Roosevelt clucked and shook his head. "The thing about men like you is that they never stop. It's a mental deficiency. I'm the same way. And I know you. You are planning something. There's a scheme rattling around your head somewhere. You've got a plan." He stopped and faced me. "But the thing is, I can't get Congress involved or bring in private investors if you're not completely open with me. I can sense you're not telling me everything. Like I said, I've got my sources and I might know a few things you don't."

"No… yeah… I'm happy polishing–"

"No, you're not! And even if you were… which you are not… there's a reason you're out here. Who sent you? Who are your partners? What company are you representing? Is there a woman?" He laid a hand on my shoulder and released his breath. "There's just something you're not saying, and I want you to come clean. You're holding back something, Clark."

That was an understatement.

"This isn't about your Uncle Olin, is it?"

"Not entirely. But he gave me the–"

He smiled and laughed so hard he dropped the gun. "You're in love aren't you, Clark?"

Chapter Ten

I LOVED MY LITTLE electrified iron, the Hotpoint, with the hottest point at the front tip. It just took too much time for those Sad irons to heat up. I preferred my little Hotpoint. But there seemed no point in buying a whole new stove, just to be considered modern. After all, what could electricity do in a stove that wood could not?

I had just left an argument, where Blanche claimed all new brides were getting electric stoves and electric lamps when their daddies built new homes for them. And that nobody wanted wood cook stoves anymore, not even the nickel-plated ones like mine. Her further claim that in a hundred years, nobody would use wood in the kitchen made no sense. Millicent and I both told her so. At least she was on my side. After all, burning wood had been part of human existence for thousands of years. Why would that suddenly change now? But Blanche had to have her way and make sure everyone knew it. I guess some people just can't accept good logic.

And it was not just the effectiveness of one cook method over another that Millicent and I argued for. It was also the smell. What housewife would give up the smell, and even the sound of burning wood for a sterile kitchen with neither? It would be like living in a bread box. No wonderful scent of wood smoke in the early mornings. No soothing aroma in the evenings to go to sleep by.

Just a sterile breadbox. Sorry Blanche, that was just stupid.

But I guess it wasn't really the dispute over Sad irons and electric stoves that set me off. Or that she had to be right all the time. Or even that Blanche no longer considered my kitchen modern. Heck, I could go straight down to Kobey's with seventeen dollars and rectify that. None of those things really mattered.

It was that phrase she used: new brides.

Fortunately, there was no time to dwell on that stupid subject either. Mr. Mathews was heading up the walk to my front door, and I had a good idea what he had in mind. So maybe I'd rectify that too.

But really, would I? That's not what my heart said. It had a mind of its own, completely separate from my own mind, and it seemed to get what it wanted most of the time.

"Lorena, dear, I have a question for you. I'm only in from Cincinnati for the week. Would you accompany me up to the quarry, where I might pose it properly?"

The answer was yes!

Yes, I would take just about any blocks of marble the company set aside. No matter how many twisted seams of green and blue and black they might have. I actually liked the spidery lines of minerals and vegetable matter pressed into the rock by the hot finger of God. To me, it had character, even if not commercially viable by the Colorado-Yule Marble Company. Sure, I still had the big block for Jesus on the road to Golgotha, but I needed a whole lot more for the many new projects handed down by that self-same Jesus, given in meditations of prayer. New projects He assured me would interest my customers, in my little marble shop on Park Street. So the answer was, yes, I'd take them all.

But my quick answer seemed to put Mr. Mathews back on his heels. Until I spoke, he seemed uncertain how to pose his question. He sure brightened up at that answer.

"Would you accompany me up to the quarry then? I want this to be just right. Overlooking Marble and the whole valley is perfect. We'll have an enjoyable outing." He smiled and loosened up. This clearly wasn't easy for him. But how hard could picking out some cracked and discarded blocks be?

I smiled too. "I don't have a chaperone. I couldn't possibly–"

"We could call Blanche."

"Nope. I'll be fine!" I grabbed my coat and smiled.

Plans had been drawn for a new electric tramway up to the quarry, plans largely suggested and put under way by the absent Mr. Clark. Even the plans of a transient man-killer could be useful. Or was that too harsh? Mental images of the man fully occupied me, just as Mr. Mathews took my hand and escorted me to Colonel Meek's Stanley Steamer – about the only auto transport capable of climbing the mountain or hauling blocks I could use.

Until the electric tramway was in place we'd have to take the oxen road up to the start of the funicular cable tramway curiously named, Pea Vine. It wasn't so bad, as long as I closed my eyes. But Mr. Mathews left little opportunity for that.

"That's Forest Lawn," he pointed to a flat spot on the hillside leading out of Marble. "That will be the first station on the new tramway. And then... do you see the old smelter's mill up there? We can take the railway right around that curve if we cut the mountainside back about ten feet. And then it's on to Windy Point." He lifted his arm to about a forty-five degree angle and squinted into the distant trees clinging to granite cliffs. "Those are the first three stops. They'll have to pick their way up the rest of the mountain from there. This will be the steepest regular-adhesion railway in the world. They don't build railways up mountains, you know... I mean, except the cog type in Manitou Springs."

The narrow leather seat of the 1906 Stanley left no wiggle room for shoulders and hips. F. O. Stanley must have been a slight man, and had evidently not anticipated women without chaperones riding abreast with men in his new invention. Our bodies pressed together and rubbed rhythmically all the way up the steep road cut. At least it kept me warm. And it was sort-of nervy, so I almost liked it.

"I've heard the 1909 model is an inch wider," Mr. Mathews said, sensing the privations and terrifying proximity to hundred-foot mountainside cliffs. "Would it help if I lifted my arm over your shoulder? It might give you an extra few inches. My shoulders are–"

"Oh no, Mr. Mathews. I'll be okay." I smiled and wondered

about returning for Blanche after all.

"Call me Mortimer. I would like that."

I nodded and shied off with a blush. "Mortimer."

"I now feel quite at home in these mountains," he ventured. "You know, I spend a fair bit of time in railcars. I visit the New York office regularly. And building projects in all the states." He stopped to think. "And traveling abroad. Did you know I have been to France on business? But I have a sweet tenderness for the blue mountains over Marble." We looked out over the mile-wide valley, nearly eight-hundred feet above town. Yule Creek emptied into the splashing Crystal River, and the town of Marble lay under a dense canopy of Ponderosa pines along the riverside. The river was no longer audible, but still wild and free. Puffs of smoke rose up from fifty little chimneys in the valley.

"I have a tender heart, Miss Lorena." He stopped in nervous introspection. When he sensed my uncertainty at the statement, he added, "It is not all bonds and business with me."

"Um, do you have blocks to show me? I'm glad you brought the steamer." That is what Christian women say when they know what's in a man's mind, and they're pretty sure they like it, but don't have a chaperone to throw a loop over the man to draw him back. I might have liked just about everything in this man's mind. I looked over at his nervous eyes. Um-huh, just about everything.

"Blocks?" Mortimer asked. "Oh yes, blocks of marble. I do. The workers ran into a whole seam of blue marble, which we naturally had to discard. There's a hundred foot of it below the quarry floor that no man has ever seen. But only the snow-white crystal clean marble will do for us. The company reputation is built on it. It is the cleanest in the world. You know that, right? Not a speck of discoloration."

"Why don't customers like blue marble?"

"It's not a question of liking. It is a question of strength. You see, all those beautiful blue veins are potential stress cracks. They are mixtures of non-crystals and not as strong as the pure white rock alone. Only snow-white marble can bear weight without cracking, and only ten percent of that is suitable for building material. I suppose we could use blue marble in household settings, but still, most people prefer the crystal white rock. But I don't really know for sure; we're serving the monument and architectural markets mostly, so I don't really know about home use. We normally just pitch that spidery blue stuff over the Crystal River bank. That's what you see all along the river bank. It has no value."

I smiled awkwardly. "I like blue marble." What I didn't say was that blue marble was the very picture of my lonely heart. It was the discarded... the cast off... the undesired... the unwanted and valueless. My own heart had been blue marble for too long. Maybe all those spidery blue lines had hardened and cracked, and left my heart useless for the applications of love. Maybe it could not bear the weight. Or maybe it had become altogether undesirable. God had looked down and seen my broken and useless heart and set it aside. It has no value, He probably said.

But I still had a plot to redeem this blue heart of mine.

It was a risky plan, an underground plan. A long-shot, I believed they called it. Gambling halls would put million-to-one odds on its success. Especially now that God had danced all over it, smashed it into a million pieces, left me crumbled and broken, and then set me aside. Who bets against The Almighty anyway? But I wanted it to come true nonetheless. And it had been my secret obsession for more years that I could remember. Maybe a million-to-one was generous.

And here sat a man that could nullify the whole plan.

"Did you know you're beautiful? Far more beautiful than your friend Blanche," Mr. Mathews said, but soon backed off the risky statement. "I am so sorry, Miss Lorena. I have forgotten my protocols. Sometimes I get nervous fright and I forget—"

I smiled. "You're forgiven. And thank you." That small statement brightened my eyes. He said I was beautiful. He said it out loud. I almost cried.

Mortimer squirmed. "The question I wanted to ask is... oh heck... let us at least get up to the quarry. It's so wonderful up there at the top of the world." Mr. Mathews tried to bounce in the leather seat to shake off his ungainliness. "It is a bouncy road, but the oxen don't mind. They just plod along. But you know the BEST traction engine goes right up this. It's eighteen horsepower and enough foot pounds of—"

He remembered himself again. "Oh, you're probably not interested in foot-pound of torque and man-talk. We do have some blue marble. It is beautiful and interesting, just like–" He smiled. "I mean, you will love it."

I smiled. "So the question you want to ask is… is which blocks do I want?"

"Here we are! Are you ready for the Pea Vine to the top? It's a thrill!"

I looked up. "Can I close my eyes?"

"You can do anything you like. Just have a seat on one of these wooden planks and brace yourself against the next one. You know, you've done this many times. How often have you come up here for photographic outings? A dozen? Two dozen? Henry Johnson does fantastic work, doesn't he? Did you know he documented our entire works for the investors back east? They like progress. And they love the mountain shots. You know, looking down on the mill as it progresses from fledgling to world-class marble producer. Just look down there! That's the money shot, and we're not even at the top yet."

Mortimer looked up the last hundred feet of cliffs and waved it off.

I closed my eyes.

"You're missing some of the best views in the world. You see how Yule Creek rushes down the mountain and empties into the river? You could roll a boulder down this canyon and smash every tree in its path." At that point, Mortimer's enthusiasm gained momentum. "Nothing could stop a good ten-tonner. That would be a sight for the tourists. They would pay for a sight like that! Smashing everything in its–"

He noticed my horrified eyes. "Well, I just mean–"

He touched my hand. "We're almost at the top… and… I should probably confess… I ahh… I don't know where they stashed your blocks. But the quarrymen did run into that vein of blue marble in opening number three… and… you and I could spend the afternoon looking. I know we could locate some nice pieces. I'll ask to have them brought down to the load-out area. Have you ever been inside the works?"

"No, but I have a few questions. How do they get the marble out? I never hear dynamite up here. Colonel Meek said the company doesn't use it anymore."

"Oh, gracious no! Dynamite would crack the blocks. Colonel Meek is firm on that. Everything nowadays is done with saws. Channeling machines and wire saws. Want to see them? Come on!"

"What about the quarrymen?"

"Nobody is here today. We're all alone."

We stepped off the Pea Vine funicular railway transport and crossed the flat marble ledge to the yawning portal in the cliff side – the opening to quarry number three. I had been on this portico many times, but never inside the belly of the beast. Women weren't allowed. They weren't allowed on the portico either, unless the photographer Mr. Howard insisted, but definitely not inside. Bad luck is bad luck, and you don't tempt bad luck with a female on the premises, not under any circumstances. I guess I could understand that.

I stood musing and remembering the photographic sessions, and Mr. Clark trying so hard to please me. I guess my stupid plan had worked after all, but then broke into a million pieces. No sense lighting that torch again. I would not give it another thought, not with a man so tender beside me.

I supposed it would be dark inside, but the still-rising sun poured through the Eastern facing portal onto the marble beds.

Mr. Mathews pointed to a modern new machine. "That's a channeling machine. It extracts the marble blocks."

"How does it work? I don't understand how you can pick twenty-five-ton blocks right out of the ground." Of course, my little shop could not handle anything over a ton. And I needed help with anything over fifty pounds. I stood there looking at ledges of giant marble, stepping from the floor to the ceiling in big stages, each one inset from the last. The cavern extended two hundred feet into the mountain. Ten ledges of marble were exposed, like steps a giant could walk up. Ladders stood against each one, evidently used by quarrymen working the various levels.

My head shook instinctively. "You can't get under the blocks to cut them out. And you can't get behind them either. Do you know what I mean? So, don't you have to use dynamite to get them out?"

"That's what a channeling machine does. Do you want me to turn it on?"

I reached for my ears. "Oh, Heavens no!"

Mortimer walked over to the nearest machine on the ledge we stood on and pointed down to the floor. "There are six sides to a block, right? For this block, two sides are already cut. The top has already been cut, which is this floor we're walking on, and the front side was cut. So we have four more to deal with: these three sides, and the bottom." He walked around the perimeter of an imaginary block, drawing three lines with his boot heel. "The channeling machine will cut vertical channels down these three sides. See that bar with cutting chains? It will–"

"I understand." It had become obvious how the vertical bars cut deep channels into the rock, and that accounted for the four sides of each block. But it didn't explain the bottom. I peered into the deep channels and wondered how the bottom got cut. You couldn't get down under the rock.

I stepped up to a machine and touched it. "How do you pay for all this?"

"Bonds. Investors. One man can't own the biggest marble works in the world. It's a big operation. I guess you could say I'm just another investor too. But bonds are great because investors get no equity. They just get paid back with interest at a later date when the bonds mature. We don't give away the company." He looked into my eyes. "I could use another investor." And then he spun around and stepped over to another machine and started mumbling about the qualities and means of operation.

Of course, he didn't mean me. Mr. Mathews had investors up here every month. He probably wondered if I knew someone. But then my heart figured it out.

I went back to safety. "You've accounted for five sides. What about the bottom?"

"That is feathered out with steel wedges, or cut with a Corsi pulley and wire saw."

"Huhhh?"

"They just drop a wire cable into those three vertical sides that were cut by the channeling machine, then push it to the bottom."

I peeked in for a look.

Mortimer edged in closer and touched me. "See? Around the entire block, right at its base."

What if I touched him back? Nope! No chaperone! "So, you have a steel cable at the bottom of the block, and it goes into these channels all the way to the bottom?"

"That's right. They just circulate the cable. With a little sand and steel shavings in the kerf, it will eventually cut the stone out – about six inches of progress a day. Once free you can lift it out with a mast-and-boom derrick. That's what those big arms are for." He pointed to an iron contraption with steel cables and pulleys. "The Lincoln hoist will lift a hundred tons. We upgraded it."

"More bonds?"

He smiled and slid around to my other side. "Aren't they a marvel?"

"Where's the blue marble?"

Mr. Mathews pointed to the bottom ledge. "I don't know where the workmen stashed your blocks, but under that white marble ledge lies a hundred years of flinty blue marble yet to be exploited, yet to ever be seen by any man and in a completely unknown state we can only wonder at its qualities. It has been hidden even from the sight of God since the foundations of the earth. No man has ever set eyes on your blue marble."

True statement.

He touched my wrist again. "But let's go out to the portico. I still have my question for you."

Mr. Mathews took my hand and guided me out into the sunlight. He breathed deeply and lifted his face to the sun. We stood admiring the expansive valley for several silent minutes. Mortimer had not loosed my hand. He seemed content with my hand in his, the sun on his face, and the thin air through the Ponderosa Pines. But worry soon overtook him.

"Did you know the mill workers are talking strike?"

"Uhh... no!"

"Oh, never mind. It'll be okay." He scanned the sea of trees and took in their calming effect.

He finally turned to me. And I understood that his question did not concern marble blocks, or spidery blue veins, or channeling machines, or investors, or even the uncalculatable beauty before us. My heart had figured this out eight-hundred feet below, but only now let me in on the secret.

He took my other hand. Our eyes connected. I was ready.

"Miss Lorena, have you ever considered joining the Yule Marble Company?"

I blinked. "As an employee? Was that your question?"

Mr. Mathews wrinkled his nose and shook his head. "No, not exactly." He tried to relax a tortured face. "I'm not good with some things, especially when I'm–"

"I could work for the company from time to time. But I have the shop, you know."

"No, let me try again." He breathed deeply.

"My question is this, Miss Lorena, would you consider joining me in holy matrimony?"

Chapter Eleven

"MISS LORENA, I'M SORRY; but you can't just wear an article of clothing and then bring it back for refund. If you leave the store with something, you can't just bring it back. That's the store policy, and it's against all laws of decency. You should know your size before purchasing."

"Kind sir, it is not a matter of size. I simply do not like the style."

"But didn't you look at it before you—"

"Miss Lorena?" A courier dashed into the store. "Miss Lorena, I have an important message for you!" The storekeep threw his head back and growled. He knew he'd been superseded and could say nothing until the urgent matter was resolved. No one trumps a messenger boy. Or a telephone.

I turned up a lip at the storekeep.

The boy was dressed in crisp blue wool, a blue cap with black leather bill and new patent leather shoes. He had come skidding in on a new black bicycle – the type with friction brakes and headlamp you see in the Sears and Roebuck catalogues. Black piping on both cap and coat set him off as a true professional. He was efficient and courteous and looked the part for his employer.

Take that, mean little store man.

I had not realized Marble started a courier service. A shoeshine service, yes – the traveling cart showed up downtown a month back, but a courier service was special. At first, I assumed the boy from Denver or Glenwood Springs. But why send a boy? Why not a wire or telephone if it was that important? It seemed an inefficient use of manpower in such modern times. But here he was before me, bouncing and pulling off his cap for manners sake. Out fell a tuft of sandy blonde hair, which he pushed back out of continual practice.

He thrust out an envelope. "The message is from Mortimer Mathews of the Colorado-Yule Marble Company."

"Yes?" I stuck out my chin at the Kobey's manager.

But he took that as an invitation. "Miss Lorena, you cannot return items just because–"

I raised a finger.

"You can tell Mr. Mathews I already know the content of his message. Inform him that it has only been a week and I will answer him in good time." But the first thing to mind was, I could not marry Mortimer Mathews for I had no man to receive a blessing from. Father and Mother were long passed. Thomas was killed by that transient I would not even name. And no uncles worth seeking the blessing from still lived. I could not ask little Levi. Perhaps the circuit pastor of Saint Paul's Episcopal Church might do. But it made me wonder; did I really want a blessing? Was Mortimer the man for me? Of course he had all the qualifications: A Christian man with a gentle spirit, a creative and inventive mind, handsome and easy in soft conversation, and a man of means – an executive of the Colorado-Yule Marble Company. I could not name a woman in Marble who would not drop a dishpan in answering him.

"Mister Mathews says you don't know the content of his message."

The manager opened his mouth.

But I didn't yield. "Young man, I do. I do know the contents of–"

The manager persisted. "Miss Lorena, I must return to my duties. In the future, you should look more closely at items before you purchase. I am sorry."

I turned to the storekeep. "Don't go. I really must–"

The boy tugged my shirtsleeve. "Mr. Mathews says that if you say you know the message, that I should say you don't. He says you must come at once. He's in Colonel Meek's office now, at the mill. Both of them are waiting. And it took me a long time to track you down. Please, Miss Lorena?"

I tipped the boy a nickel and left for the office. But only after failing to convince the store manager to refund my sixty-eight cents. The dreadful hat would stay with me.

First off, the hat only had half the flowers of last year's models. And the silk ties were half as wide. What was happening to styles these days? Smaller, with fewer adornments? That made no sense. But I could not go out without one. Or could I? Maybe the boy would carry it for me in its box, or I could pitch it under a bush and forget it. In the end I decided to wear it, as hideous and unpleasant as it was: green roses and green silk. Who came up with colors like that? Roses aren't green!

With a hat like that I decided to drop down to State Street, under the cottonwoods and out of sight, and then skip over to First. That would keep me off Main Street where Blanche and Millicent might spot me and mock the green calamity. Then I could jog streets down to Fourth where the mill office was, next to the train tracks. Then only the mill workers would see me. What do men know of style? And Italians at that?

I entered Colonel Meek's office and pulled the wretched thing from my head and laid it behind me. Mortimer Mathews stood by his side.

"Mortimer, can you get on this labor thing?" Meek lamented. "We don't need a strike. Find out what they need, and make it work. I don't care what."

"On it."

"Have a seat," Mr. Meek said, authorizing payroll. His office was small and efficient. Not like the ornate trappings of Denver or Kansas City, which I had seen on my travels. And I think he used the office only about two hours a day. He was out in the operations the other twelve. He looked up by and by, with a smile. "Nice hat, Miss Lorena."

Mortimer Mathews emulated his boss. "Nice choice of headwear,

Ma'am. Very festive."

Mortimer's smile faded. He said, "I won't dally. I have a shock for you, and I want you to be ready for it."

I laughed. "I thought you already shocked me last week. There's more?" I wagged my head and smiled. "If there's more, I absolutely must hear it. The whole town is stopping me on the street saying, oh Miss Lorena, we've heard the good news, and–"

"Miss Lorena."

He wasn't smiling, but that's probably because a full week had passed without word of my decision, and successful men don't like delay. Another week would likely pass, and he knew that. I might just as well have slapped him across the face as delay a week. The two were likely synonymous. Of course, my mind understood the excitement of the proposal but my heart had not gotten the go-ahead. Perhaps it needed a crisp little messenger boy to send it.

"Miss Lorena, you have a suitor," the bicycle-boy would say, handing me a yellow slip, typewritten by a new Royal typewriter. And then maybe my heart would leap and dance until midnight. What was wrong with my darned old heart anyway? Broken and put away ruined? Had my heart been–

"Miss Lorena, are you listening?" Mortimer said. He waved a hand before my eyes.

"Oh yes, I'm sorry. Proceed."

"Please brace yourself, Miss Lorena. I have news from the saw blade manufacturers in Cincinnati. That is why I have come in to Marble. I've done some research and just got the answer by wire. The manufacturers say the blades were defective."

There was silence in Heaven for the space of a half hour.

But that only lasted sixty seconds in Colonel Meek's office, here on earth.

"I don't want to hear this. My brother was killed out of negligence! Everybody knows it!"

"Miss Lorena, that may not be the case. Acme Sawblades is saying the–"

"I said, I don't want–"

"This is information you must hear. I'm sorry for Thomas. He was a friend of every good and decent man in Marble. And if you will receive it, he was a friend of Jeremiah Clark."

I threw the hat at him.

"I am so sorry," Mortimer said, setting the hat aside. "Acme says there were defective welds on the saw blades."

Colonel Meek explained, "The blades never should have shattered like that. The blades on those gang saws are under no load. They rest lightly on the stone and act by use of recirculating abrasives. I don't know if you knew that, or cared. We pump the abrasives up to the top of the stone where they do their work. Water and abrasives. The blades just grind it in. They barely touch the marble, and there are no actual teeth on them."

"So, what?"

"Well, I'm telling you that the blades were not used incorrectly. They were used exactly as designed. And they were not under excessive load. Mr. Clark–"

"Then how could they shatter like that? There were metal shards all across the finishing floor. And one went straight through Thomas' breastbone like a–"

"They were pinched. Simple as that," Mr. Meek clarified.

"Pinched?"

"Yes, pinched," Mortimer confirmed.

Mr. Meek leaned forward in his chair, "The little wooden dogs we use at the top of the blocks keep the slabs separated. Oh… I'm sorry; we call them dogs, but they are actually little wooden wedges. Mr. Clark invented them, and we use them still. We believe one of those dogs was either missing or slipped out. The blades became pinched inside the big marble block and bound up. But there were no safety limitations on those electric motors. They just kept pushing. And when they did, the blades doubled up. But the thing is… they're not supposed to break, even when pinched."

"But they did."

Mortimer stepped up. "Like I said… Acme is saying the blades were defective. The welds–"

"The welds broke and killed my brother."

"We believe so. Jeremiah Clark had nothing to do with it," Mortimer explained.

"I don't accept that."

Mortimer added, "Remember what Mr. Clark said at the funeral?"

I rotated my head and raised a hand, but he persisted.

"That the blades were not properly tempered. Heat-treated, that is. We believe he was right."

I left Colonel Meek's office in a mad fog, where you expect to see red but you don't because that's just a stupid expression people use, and people like to repeat things they hear. But still, I didn't care which route I took or who saw my stupid hat. Or even if I had a stupid hat on. I walked right down Main Street past that stupid storekeep at Kobey's, past the stupid City Hall, past the Yule Hotel, the steam laundry, and the moving picture house. I could have been half-naked and wouldn't have cared. That whole stupid sawblade story fried my butter.

Plus, I found out I wasn't the first to get the news.

When you walk down Main Street of Marble, Colorado, the townsfolk are not the first thing you notice. Especially when a meteor like shattered sawblades has fallen on you. You walk around with your head in the clouds, and all you see are the Ponderosa pines and booming mountains above you. The citizens at street level don't even register. That is just what you see in Marble, and that is that. Your only sense is how small you are in this world, and how meteors can fall on you without warning.

But I did finally notice the people. And everyone was talking. And looking. What a time to be wearing a stupid and repulsive hat. Green roses? I mean, really?

Mr. Kobey ran up. "We heard the news, Miss Lorena. And everyone is praying for you. Oh, and you can bring the hat back if you want. But I like it. I think it makes you look modern and smart, not like last year's old stock. But you can bring it back." He touched my hand but stepped back; I guessed ready for a punch in the nose.

"You look so pleasant," the druggist said, and then slumped. "I'm sorry to hear the news. Do you expect Mr. Clark to come back? He was such a nice boy." The druggist was eighty-eight years old, and I had to stand close to him to catch his soft words. He always held my hand between his own for entire conversations that lasted longer than any woman ever felt comfortable with. I think he liked it. "Ida and me saw you down at the river with that Clark boy and his son. Levi, right? Is that Clark boy coming back? Ida likes that Clark boy."

"I really don't know, Mr. Lundegaard." And I probably didn't care.

"Ida liked that Clark boy. He fixed our roof and wouldn't take a nickel." Mr. Lundegaard kept on. "When do you expect him back?"

Twelve people gathered around Mr. Lundegaard. Half the gawkers narrowed a malicious eye at the mention of "that Clark boy" and the other half wagged their heads and smiled. I sided with the mean-faced ones.

My mean face stayed for two full weeks. I guess I liked it that way.

"Miss Lorena," the eager little courier hailed a goodly number of days thence. "Mr. Mathews requests your presence again. And Colonel Meek. They both request your presence." He tried to act like he didn't need a tip, but I think he had gotten used to them and could not resist the emotional rush of receiving nickels for nothing but delivering slips of paper. A boy of his age could live high on money like that.

Fortunately, the hat was long gone.

"I'll see my way. Thank you." And handed him two nickels from my change purse.

I did not really want to go, but the shock had worn off. Maybe this would be okay.

"Mr. Lanceworth," Colonel Meek said. "I would like you to meet Miss Lorena Thayer. She has the most interest in your findings – even above my own. Can you explain the situation? I'm sure she is very interested."

Not really.

The Acme Saw Blade man spoke in lofty mechanical terms only a physical science scholar could enjoy. He expounded upon stress coefficients and mechanical bonds and the effects of heat on materials of all types. Heat treating. Tempered steel, doused in oil. Wild flailing arms helped immensely. And then the breaking points of various alloys threw his eyes into an ethereal world of his own design. Mr. Meek had to stop him on three occasions and pull him down below the treetops, only to see him fly into the wild blue yonder in the next utterance. The Colonel forced the Acme man to speak in terms even a woman could understand.

"So the blades were junk?" I finally said.

"Yes, ma'am." He laughed freely. "That is the final analysis our engineers have settled upon. Junk. The accident would have happened even without this Clark fellow. The blades were installed and used correctly. All speeds and loads were within specifications. They were just bad. Bad from the factory. Junk, as you accurately stated. You're really smart for a woman!"

Mortimer turned on the Acme man. "Is this something you knew about?"

"Oh sure. We've seen them fail all over the country. Same as yours. We sent a letter to the Colorado-Yule Marble Company. But I guess it arrived too late. A wire might have been better."

I rolled my eyes. Thank you, Professor Obvious.

He turned to Mr. Mathews. "Of course, we will replace the blades at no cost. You have my solemn assurance. All Acme products are warranted for–"

My eyebrows went up. "And the death of my brother?"

He sank and lifted a hand. "You have our deepest condolences, Ma'am."

"Do you assume responsibility?"

He blushed. "We are replacing the blades. And that is at great expense, believe me." And then he excused himself on the evidence of his train schedule. A yellow ticket in his hat band, which he made obvious enough to force the issue, permitted a hasty escape.

Mortimer turned to me. "Now that that issue is over…"

It wasn't. Not to my satisfaction.

"Colonel, could you give us a moment's use of your office," Mortimer pled, with hands folded. The Colonel's eyebrow flicked twice, but he stepped out in compliance. Of course, he knew what came next. You didn't just pull a flour sack over Colonel Meek's eyes.

Mortimer whispered. "Now that that issue is over, I was thinking we might return to our previous discussion." He laid a hand on mine "You remember… from up at the quarry."

I know he wanted an answer. His eyes wanted it. His breath wanted it. And his body wanted it. He could not disguise a desire so deep it filled his daily routine. He had changed. He was not himself. And that fact became evident in his actions. I followed his eyes down my neck, where they lingered somewhat lower, but then returned to my own eyes after catching himself.

I wondered, did men always do that? Allow their wanton minds to linger in places they ought not? Don't mothers warn their sons? Or the church? It was a pardonable sin for sure. A sin I didn't altogether hate. After all, he was warm-blooded and full of every passion and desire any human ever possessed. Sometimes I forgot that. One could easily make that mistake with Mortimer Mathews. He was so compelled by ambition and vision that you forgot he was also a man with carnal needs.

And in this case, a man who wanted nothing more, and needed nothing else…

But me.

Chapter Twelve

JEREMIAH CLARK IS COMING back! Mad as a jackal, declared the Marble City Times. But could the words of Sylvia Smith ever be trusted in Marble, Colorado? Maybe down in Gunnison, but up here? Was she even a journalist? Evidently, some thought so. The Marble Times never lost its readership, even when its columns were considered sensational and opportunistic at best. Who could resist words like this?

A Day of Reckoning
The Awful and Terrible Day of the Lord
Visited upon Marble, Colorado

Marble Colorado is finally getting its comeuppance. After years of worker mistreatment and preference to Yule company policies, set forth by the sole dictator on Fourth Street, the struggling mountain hamlet will at last get its doomsday. And why? You may ask, Dear Reader? Jeremiah Clark is coming back. And he is mad as a jackal. The ousted designer of the new mill operations has designs on his enemies. This won't be a child's scolding.

Our sources have uncovered the awful truth.

Mr. Clark, who has lived in our nation's wholesome capital for the past year has learned of the Acme saw blade debacle. He has learned of his innocence. He has learned the depths of treachery in Marble, Colorado, two thousand miles from his eastern refuge. His furious responses cannot even be printed in ethical and honest publications such as this, the Marble City Times. Dear Reader, expect the worst.

Ongoing coverage will include every detail we learn, as we learn them. We are all certain to face a showdown this summer. Let us pray we are on the right side of this conflict. Most right-minded citizens know this is not the side of corporations, their progeny of dictators, and disingenuous stock swindles like the C. Y. M. Co.

Dear Reader, would you consider supporting the Marble City Times? We are the sole voice of truth in this dark corner of Colorado. For only five cents a copy, or two dollars per Anum, you will receive truth in your post office box. Subscribe next week!

"I don't traffic in speculation, hearsay, second-hand news, and manufactured controversy," Frank Frost, the editor of the Marble Booster stated. He handed the Times back. "This story is as thin as the pulp it's printed on. I could not find a shaving of fact in it. It's designed to keep the paper in black ink, and that's about all. You will not see a single story about Jeremiah Clark in the Marble Booster. He simply is not that interesting. So what if he comes back?"

A citizen stepped up. "It's not even a real publication. Sylvia Smith publishes the whole thing from a hotel room down at the Marble City Hotel. She takes her meals on premise, and never leaves the place."

"But isn't that proof of her dedication to the cause?" Another asked. "Somebody has to expose the rottenness in Marble."

"Rottenness? Not hardly," Mr. Frost said. "It only means her readership is too low to afford her a printing floor and journalist offices.

What's she got? Two hundred copies a week? I'd guess only forty of those are local. This drivel is for eastern ears."

"But what about her eight years in Crested Butte? To me, that spells dedication and vision."

Mr. Frost smirked. "Or lunatic tendencies. In any case, The Marble Booster is just not interested in how mad Jeremiah Clark is, or if he is coming back, or if he wants revenge, or even if Miss Sylvia howls at the moon four times a month and pitches the tortured wailing as news. I'm the Marble Booster editor, and that's what I say."

"Then you're not coming to the town meeting?" I asked.

Mr. Frost sniffed. "Didn't know there was one."

I held out the paper. "It seems this article has set off a debate."

"About Jeremiah Clark?" Mr. Frost said. "Miss Lorena, there is nothing to this. It is pure sensationalism. Muckraking scandalism, not news."

I said, "W.F. Frazier at the Colorado Yule called a meeting for next week. He's not happy about this article. Are you going? It's at the Masonic hall."

Frank Frost did go. And so did a hundred other concerned citizens. I guess those forty local copies got around. And if Mr. Clark was as mad as a jackal, those hundred attendees were wolves.

W.F. opened the meeting according to Robert's Rules for Meetings. A chairman, secretary and officers were appointed, as W.F. directed from the Robert's manual. No meeting in Marble would be misconstrued as a lynch mob, he said. He wore that book out, and allowed no deviation.

"I believe the first order of business," W.F. spoke, "is to determine if there is any truth to the assertion that Mister Jeremiah Clark is actually on his way back to Marble, Colorado. And secondly, what that might mean for the Yule Company and for the town of Marble. And lastly, what our official response should be to his eventual return. Can anyone second the motion to adopt those three planks for our discussion tonight?"

"I second the motion," a voice rang out. The secretary's inkwell began draining.

"So moved, and seconded."

And so ended the tidy Robert's Rules for Meetings, and began a free-for-all that W.F. Frazier had little control over.

A loud voice came from the back. "I say Colonel Channing Meek and the rest of them Yule bosses line this town with Pinkertons. Bring in some muscle. Soon's that bum steps in, arrest 'm and put 'm on a rail for the Kansas outposts. That's how they done it in Crip-Creek."

The gavel came down. "Sir, that topic is not on our agenda—"

Another voice rang out. "Meek better keep up the ban. Remember that NO CREEKERS sign? Bring that out again. And a good double-barrel. That's all I got to say."

The first voice responded, "You know he's fixin' to take over the mill."

Three more gavel hits. W.F. raised his hand. "Order, order. This discussion is afield. Now if anyone has an opinion that is not on the agreed-upon agenda, or extra information to share, it ought to be Miss Lorena. If she wishes to alter the agenda, she may step forward with a motion to adopt new discussion. We all know she has given the most, and must have her say in any actions this assembly takes."

Frazier raised a hand. "Miss Lorena, this assembly will now hear your voice on the matter of Jeremiah Clark."

A small voice slipped in. "On account of her being sweet on him."

Laughter erupted from that area of the hall, and heads turned.

Another hidden voice squeaked, "I'd take a slapping like that. Ooh, yeah!"

More howling from hidden sources.

"Preach it, brother!"

The gavel went down again. "Sir, you will exit the hall. You will not speak to a lady that way, especially one who has given so much for this town. Please find your way out." The man slid on his hat, ducked his head, and stepped out. But he snickered and peeked up at his friends on his way to the door.

"Miss Lorena?" W.F. motioned.

All eyes fell to me.

I just stood there in a disconnected stupor. Did I have any

opinion on the man? Had I even spoken his name in the last year? Or allowed a single memory into my thoughts? Probably not. Well okay, a few, but not with any regularity.

I didn't love him; that was for sure. In fact, why did I even think that?

All I could do was look into the tin-stamped ceiling tiles and wonder.

In my detached thoughts, Thomas stood before me in kind of a hazy daydream. His left arm was wholly cleaved off and blood drained from the fresh wound. But he didn't seem killed or even agitated. He just walked through the assembly in the Masonic hall with sad eyes. Mr. Clark was there too. Blood fell down over Mr. Clark's forehead as he dropped to his knees and scrambled to gather up the cleaved arm from the shop floor, with marble dust swirling around, and clattering machines, and workers bumping into him, and Robert's Rules for Meetings getting blood-soaked on the finishing floor. Mr. Clark lifted his arms and cried out with a loud wail, and threw himself at Thomas' feet.

Thomas only had two words in the distracted vision, "Forgive, sister," and then faded out.

As hard as I tried, he would not come back. Thomas did not condemn, as hard as I summoned him to do so. He would not reappear. Would not speak. And would not denounce. He just said, "Forgive" and that was that.

This had been my only clear vision of Thomas in the last year. And he had to go and say a stupid thing like that. I wasn't forgiving anybody, and I didn't care what Mr. Clark did, as long he didn't come back here.

I said, "I don't care what Mister Clark does. He can come back … or not… that is his business." What I meant to say was that if he ever came back, he would get a dose of my business. But I guess it didn't come out that way.

W.F. nodded. "You are a gracious Christian, Miss Lorena."

The hall went silent at those words. Right up until it erupted again.

A voice sounded. "You all know Clark is in Washington D.C. for a reason, right? He's got crony friends from his days in Cripple Creek. President Roosevelt for one. Taft is another. They ride around in motor-coaches together. And eat steaks for breakfast."

"So?" a voice demanded.

"So… he's getting marble contracts with his uncle. That's what I heard."

W.F. asked, "And…"

"Golly geez, are you all in the dark? He's getting marble contracts. And he's bringing them back here with a war chest. I hope Colonel Meek has a bigger one. Or some Pinkertons. Clark will take over this whole operation. You want to lose your jobs? We banned him, remember?"

"That's what I was saying!" the first voice let out. "Revenge!"

The golly geez man said, "Don't you think the Yule Company should get those contracts reassigned to the mill? They got agents in New York. Send them over to Washington and get those contracts under Yule control."

The first man added. "He's a millionaire, you know. From Cripple Creek. Jeremiah Clark is a gold baron from Cripple Creek. Remember the Black Jack Mine? I heard he sold it for all the money in the Denver Mint. And, he's got millionaire friends in Washington and New York. Men like that don't mess around. They will clean you out in a blink."

The assembly groaned. Every face looked to his neighbor. Little discussions cropped up like bean sprouts. Murmuring and arguments threw Robert's Rules for Meetings by the wayside.

W.F. called out, "Miss Lorena. Miss Lorena, do you have any–" But his voice was overwhelmed by the rabble. He just laid the gavel down and shook his head.

When I exited the Masonic hall, I expected men with pitchforks ready to defend. Ready to throw up earthworks. Ready to arrest and detain the evil Mr. Clark if he should come up that road from Carbondale and Redstone. I expected Pinkertons.

But what I actually saw was this: A throng of naughty girls with designs on Mr. Clark.

"I hope he does come back. I want to marry him." One said

smiling and bouncing.

Another added. "I'd give him five children, if you know what I mean."

The first naughty girl upped her, "I'd give him a dozen if he had the fortitude! Do you know what I mean? Teehee!"

All the girls snickered and each put forth hot-blooded fantasies for the man they called tender and juicy. Fantasies arose, like throwing out their teddy bears and using Mr. Clark instead. Or being stranded in the mountain wilderness with nobody but Mr. Clark to defend them with a sword. Or having him over to paint their houses on a hot day so he'd have to work with no shirt.

All the girls skipped and laughed.

"Wait! Wait! I know…" one of the naughty girls said. "What if there was a terrible rainstorm and Mr. Clark came to your front door soaking wet and freezing from hypothermia. Which would you do first? Put wood on the stove for coffee? Or, offer to get those wet clothes off before he caught his death?"

Another round of giggling and fantasies followed.

I thought about the rainstorm fantasy, and all I could think was doilies.

Table doilies. Those little white ones on coffee tables.

A newspaper advertisement came to my wandering mind and the girls soon faded. The ad stated, Doilies as thin as gossamer are now being used with crystal glasses and dainty china. The latest importations of these are as fine as cobwebs. Each disk is embroidered with the finest linen floss.

A fanciful vision of the new doilies on my dining room table included the image of a bloody and rain-soaked Mr. Clark in the chair across from me. He sat for tea and cakes while the rainstorm ravaged outside.

We chatted cheerfully until Thomas' blood began running off Mr. Clark's forehead. It ran down his arm and into the teacup, and then onto the doilies. I scolded him for ruining the new importations as thin as gossamer, but he didn't care anything for the doilies as thin as the finest floss.

He just leaned over and kissed me deeply. I slapped him, as I had done so forcefully at Thomas' funeral.

Mr. Clark just smiled and kissed me deeper.

So I only slapped him half as hard that time.

Chapter Thirteen

November 2, 1909

I RETURNED TO MARBLE to find West Fourth Street lined with armed men, even spilling into Park and State Streets. To say it didn't alarm me would be the height of folly. My first thought was to turn right around and go back to Long Island and fend off revenuers with Uncle Olin. What was I walking into? It looked exactly like Cripple Creek only five years earlier, minus the union busters with Gatling guns, but still bristling with arms. Nineteen and Ought Four was the worst experience in my life, and I did not want a repeat.

I saw no signs of the Colorado militia, as had occupied Cripple Creek for almost two years, and I knew what to look for. No uniforms. No Pinkertons. No gun pits.

So what was this?

Every armed man on Fourth Street was local. I recognized them all. Not a good sign.

I figured I could either step forward, or jump right back on the passenger car of the Crystal River & San Juan Railway. Just duck my head and be in Carbondale in two hours, Glenwood Springs in four, and catch the midnight express for Denver. The Brown Palace Hotel started to sound more and more interesting.

The more I thought about it, that probably was the best option. This did not look like the typical labor dispute. There was either a bank robber in town or a manhunt.

But I'd never been one to run.

Plus, I had a reason to stay.

I marched right up to the armed men. "What's going on here? Somebody rob the bank? Jesse James is dead." I chuckled.

"Ahh, Mr. Jeremiah," a man answered, an Italian stone carver on the column capital line. "You-a go right back now, Mr. Jeremiah. This-uh no good place for you. You-uh uomo pazzo." He touched his forefinger to his thumb and lifted it to his mouth. "Crazy man. Pazzo, you know? Pazzo! "

"Might be pazzo," I said. "It's good to see you too, Giorgio. What's going on?"

Giorgio had come in from the old country three years back without a lick of English, except the words, "Ellis Island" and "America." He even carried a little glass figurine of the Statue of Liberty in his coat pocket. Of course, all the foreign men were required to learn English, abstain from liquor, maintain a civil household, and obtain citizenship if they wanted long-term employment with the Yule Marble Company. What option did they have?

Turn down three dollars a day and return to poverty?

The thing was, Giorgio wanted to be an American; he was proud of his home in the New World and the money he sent back to his mother, so he happily complied.

Another armed man rallied the men from horseback. "Gather around, fellas! Right down there next to the gantry crane. Come on now, men. Move! You got lead boots?" The man trotted back and forth along the line of tired and haggard men like a Mexican general, brave and heroic, and high in the saddle. "Let's get organized, gents!" He waved a red flag, and herded the men from the corner of Fourth and State all the way to the traveling crane near Shop #1, right where Giorgio and I were talking. They didn't look pleased. But hey… maybe he was bringing them all to me and they'd all brighten up when they arrived to see me. It was either that, or I was already the subject of their manhunt, and in the perfect position for capture.

"Gather 'round, men," the rider hailed. "We got new business right here!"

"What's going on, Giorgio?" I asked.

"We're all-uh on struck. Iss-uh struck." He said in his labored Italian accent. "This is our new task-uh maker."

"No, Taskmaster, Giorgio. Task… Master… And it looks like you're on strike."

"You-uh such-a good with American, Mr. Boss. It's-uh strike, and this is the new task-uh-master."

The rider circled the men like on a cutting horse until they formed a half circle at the edge of the twenty-foot traveling crane, where he could dismount and climb to the top. He could have been a revolutionary, waving his red flag and drawing all eyes to him.

"Half of you do not deserve the bounty you are about to receive." The Revolutionary stood shaking his head, miserable and disgusted at the undisciplined men below, the men around me who seemed too limp to stand picket another night or heft strike signs or even lift their heads. "Three quarters of you do not deserve it." He paused and shook his head again.

"Do not deserve the victory!" He repeated with a fist in the air.

"Listen fellows," He entreated, "We are about to claim victory here in Marble, and only a handful of you have been true to the cause and put forth the effort asked of you. Yet you will all share in the spoils. When the battle is won here, it will be won again in Kansas City, and again in Dallas, and again in Detroit. All over this country, men are looking to you for victory. You've got to toughen up for them. For the nation. For the fight we are all engaged in. Collectively."

He raised his arms and shouted, "Every man oppressed by the capitalist devil is looking to you men right here in Marble for that win, for your strength, for your triumph over the red-faced devil! The exploiter of working men. The capitalist. The cost-cutting, wage-slashing, shift-cutter himself. The great slaveholder of labor and industry!"

The Revolutionary stamped across the iron crane beam with hands high.

"Men, I implore you. I beseech you. One last push. One last good one, and the Man will be toppled. The capitalist devil will fall, and you will own Him. He will be your slave and you the master. You will be the heirs of those riches he now withholds from you. One more push is all I ask. I implore you to hold fast another day, another week, a month, a year, whatever it takes. Whatever it takes to put the red devil in your place and you into his!"

The Revolutionary thrust his scarlet flag skyward. "Rally around the flag, boys! Rally once again!" With that, he slid down the iron ladder to his waiting followers, where he waved the banner violently with full strength.

And like a cat, I was up on the gantry to replace him.

I raised a both arms and shouted.

"Every word the man has spoken is true," I hollered from the ironworks. The men probably didn't expect another orator on the traveling crane that day and slowly turned back around to focus on my words. The Revolutionary had been so eagerly heaving the red flag from side to side and leading men up Fourth Street that he did not notice me.

But he heard the next words.

"You are within a gnat's hair of getting everything this man has promised." I pointed straight at the Revolutionary, who cheerfully received the accolade. "I believe you will win this battle; you will defeat your enemies. You men will take down everything you see around you." I threw out an arm and drew a wide circumference around the whole valley, and then up over Quarry Town, eight-hundred feet above us.

The man smiled widely and whirled around, hoping everyone was finally seeing his vision, now that some stranger was articulating it so boldly from the same heights he had just descended from. This was perfect.

"If you men continue, you will defeat Colonel Channing Frank Meek."

I nearly cried as the next words came out. "And lose the only true friend you ever had. The only man who loved you and gave himself for you, besides the Lord Jesus Christ himself. How many of you were drifters and transients? Came on your last dime? Had little left to live for? And did Colonel Meek lift his capitalist fist against you? Did he crush the bruised reed? Or, did he instead offer you skilled work at three dollars a day? Six times what they're making in the beehive coke ovens in Redstone."

The men shifted and peered at their boot laces.

"And what is the red devil's evil plan when he looks in on you and your families? Pays your doctor bills when you're short? Brings in groceries and clothiers? And builds a town with nine-hundred-thousand watts of power and piped water? Is it to become the 'slaveholder of labor and industry?'"

I too paced the ironworks, like the Revolutionary before me. "How many of you know my history?" One or two hands went up. "How many know that I ran the Black Jack Mine in Cripple Creek? A two-million-dollar operation in its day? And that the Western Federation of Miners, an organization so-called to the well-being of the workingman destroyed every opportunity the workingman ever had up there? When they were finished, hundreds were deported or destitute. Women bereaved of their menfolk. Businesses shuttered. Jobs gone. Opportunity, up in vapor. All because they too, just like this man who leads you now, were so blindly bent on bringing down the capitalists that they took the whole shebang with them – jobs, trade, security and all."

The Revolutionary waved his flag and raged, but every eye remained fixed on me.

"Do you remember the sign posted right here at the depot three years ago?" I pointed behind me at the railroad tracks. "Remember what it said? It said, NO CREEKERS. Do you remember why?" A few eyebrows went up. "And now you have become them. You are the Creekers. You are the–"

"Alright, alright, we take your meaning, Clark," a voice sounded from the rabble. "But what can we do? We've got to make a living. We've got to organize."

"What are your demands," I asked.

Another voice came forth. "We can't work twelve-hour days anymore."

"And not get paid for them," another voice boomed.

The first man added, "We can't work seven days a week."

"I will," one man said eagerly. "I'll work seven days a week. But

118

I just want a few extra dollars. On account of my wife and babies don't see me 'cept after the sun goes down."

Levi and Miss Lorena walked out of the trees and appeared before me.

I sat down on the craneway, mostly because I thought I'd fall off. I started worrying about what I'd say, and if the sheriff was not far behind with a rope, and if I should make a run for the depot.

"I'll bring a deal to Meek," I offered, after pulling my eyes off Miss Lorena and back onto the distressed men. "Time-and-a-half after eight hours, and on Sundays."

"Hey, Father!" Levi said. He had just spotted me. "Father!"

"Come on up, son."

Levi joined me on the iron works, which rebuilt my confidence. It was good to hug his neck and have him by my side. It probably meant he didn't hate me. And I was glad for that. Plus, I was glad he stayed and became a voice for me. I guessed he had a lonely time of it without me.

"Double-time," the man said. "Double-time on Sundays. Six dollars a day."

"Now don't get greedy. But okay, I'll try for double-time on Sundays. Anything else?"

The men looked around. "When can we go back to work?"

"I can't promise Colonel Meek, or even Frazier or Mathews will take a deal. They might just arrest me and haul me down to the Gunnison magistrate for disturbing the peace. I have not spoke to Colonel Meek, or Frazier. I just stepped off the train an hour ago and found you all here, following this man I don't know. Meek doesn't even know I'm here. If he did, he'd probably have the sheriff on me."

The men chuckled. But Miss Lorena just stiffened her lips and gazed into the trees. I wanted to jump from the iron beam and fall at her feet. I would weep and wipe my tears with her dress. Every word from my mouth would be: forgive me, forgive me, I am a worm. And then I would grovel without an ounce of pride in front of the men, because I had no pride left in me, and what I did have I'd gladly spend on her. I'd be happier at her feet than in Glory with Moses and the angels.

And maybe she felt the same, and maybe when I fell at her feet she would say, No! Forgive me, forgive me, I am addlebrained and silly. I never should have slapped you, and she would rub my face and ask if she hurt me and if I could ever forgive her, and would state her love for me.

None of those things materialized, and I probably lingered a little too long in the daydream.

Then I said, "There may be some that no longer want me here on account of Thomas. I will respect that, and I will leave if that's how it works out. I'm here to make amends if I can."

Our eyes met for less than a second, but then she looked away.

I almost fell off.

But I had learned early I could go a good spell on a stolen peek at Miss Lorena's eyes. Heck, I had just lived a full year off a few slaps and the look of her fiery blue irises. I could live in this town without another kind word from her and be satisfied with nothing but stolen looks.

Levi laid a hand on my shoulder and beamed at me like I was Atlas holding up the world. I needed that. Having my son by my side, up on this gantry in front of every one of his crew was big medicine. Salve, and Balm of Gilead.

"I'll tell you one thing," I said with confidence. "This is going to cost every one of you. It isn't going to be free. How long have you been at this walkout?"

"Three months," came the answer. "Started in August."

"August, huh?" I grimaced. "My best guess..." I drew ragged breath. "Is that you probably cost the operation a hundred thousand dollars in lost business. They may survive; I cannot say."

The Revolutionary waved his flag with a loud huzzah, but got no takers. The men just grimaced as ugly as I had.

"There are two types of men in this world," I responded. "Makers and Takers. The Takers of this world have never built anything. Never risked. Never ventured. Never struggled to support workers or make payroll. But they are whirling dervishes at tearing down the works of other men."

The Revolutionary just spat and thrust his flag into the air.

"Fact is, boys, this loss has to be made up somehow. Either short shifts, less pay, or more efficient operations. If Colonel Meek doesn't have me arrested, I'm going suggest even more efficient ways to process marble. Like–"

"Like you did with Thomas?" one man said.

The breath went out of me. I looked at Miss Lorena, but she had her back turned. "I'm sorry for that. I wish things had worked out differently."

The men all shook their heads.

"But I want two things from you before I go to Meek with a deal. Number one, I want ninety days notice of a strike, for arbitration and to let hotheads cool. And number two…"

I stood up and pointed out the Revolutionary. "I want that man on the next train for Denver. No more professional agitators. No more socialists and seditionists. We are not going to have another Cripple Creek up here with gun thugs and bomb builders. Remember Harry Orchard? I won't live in another Cripple Creek. It's not worth the nerve-racking aggravation. If I don't get your okay on those points, I'll drop the whole thing and take the next train myself. It's him or me."

They didn't take long to decide.

"Now one more thing, boys," I said smiling and holding up a leather satchel. My confidence came back full, and I knew Miss Lorena would like this. I tried to find her blue eyes but could not. Even still, I liked what was coming next.

"I got a little surprise yer going to enjoy, boys. I'll give you a hint."

I paused to let ideas circulate.

"Now I won't tell you what is in this bag, except that it's about twenty-six pages of the most glorious words you'll ever read. If Meek takes the deal, I'm handing these pages over to him."

I waved the leather bag for three minutes amid cheers and whistles.

Operations at the Colorado-Yule Marble Company resumed within a week. And Colonel Meek didn't have me arrested.

Now, there was just one more thing I wanted.

Chapter Fourteen

"MISTER CLARK, YOU'VE BEEN in to see me twice in the last two months," Doctor Rosen puzzled. "You obviously don't need spectacles. Your visual acuity exceeds 20/15. There's no milky eye, no bloody trauma, and you're not cross-eyed." He lifted his own spectacles and scratched his head. "Is there some special optometric service I may perform for you?"

I finally answered his curiosity, "Doctor, have you ever seen a person with especially bright eyes?"

"I suppose. Every eye is unique."

"What causes that?" I asked. "Scientifically speaking."

"Causes what? Bright eyes?"

"You know... eyes with sparkling qualities or an extra brightness, and you can't stop staring at them? Is that actual crystal in their eyes?"

"Blue eyes?" the doctor asked, forming a perceptive smile.

"Well any color, I suppose. But yes, blue eyes in this case."

"I know just the eyes you're referring to," he said, smiling. "And yes, there is a scientific reason." He pulled out a hand-drawn chart of his own design.

He pointed. "The iris is the part of the eye that's colored. It controls the aperture for which light enters the pupil. That's the little black circle in the center. The iris is composed of at least six layers from the anterior to the posterior. Oh sorry... from the outer surface to the inner one, like an onion I suppose. Within those layers are muscles and pigments. About one in every ten thousand sets of eyes have extra pigmentation definition, right here on the anterior pigment epithelium. You see the deep crevices? They form facets of sorts, like little mirrors to reflect light, as you might see in a cut jewel. Like a diamond or emerald. Understand?"

He checked to make sure I was still following.

"Hundreds of these deep faceted crevices give the appearance of tiny embedded crystals. You see this very clearly in the micro-glass at fifty times natural size."

"So, one in every ten thousand, huh? Seems like one in a million to me."

"I know what you're saying, Jeremiah." He smiled and whispered. "Every man in Marble has noticed. I avert my eyes when those irises come up the sidewalk for I fear I might stumble into a drainage ditch. And then my wife would beat the tar out of me right there on Main Street!"

"The effect is spellbinding, wouldn't you say?"

"And delightfully arresting," he added, inhaling with wide eyes, and slapping the desk.

"Arresting, yes!" We agreed.

"Glad I could be of assistance. I hope you see things from a new perspective, if you know what I mean."

"Okay gotta go, Doc. Got a meeting over at the Colorado-Yule with the Colonel." I ran down to the mill office with the new information sucking ninety-eight percent of my brainpower. It was only eight blocks, but with only two percent brainpower I could stumble into a drainage ditch of my own and not know it til next week.

Those brilliant crystals worked on my emotions. There had to be more to it than deep crevices and facets on 'anterior whatevers.' Not the way they made me feel.

I sprang up the steps to the office and popped open the door. Colonel Meek was deep into it but brightened up to see me. I always liked working with him.

We shook hands and I sat. He had something on his mind.

"You won't need Lorena at those meetings," Colonel Meek said, rising to his feet with great excitement. "There is no way we'll lose the Denver Post Office deal again, not with these new contracts." He held up the russet folder I had brought back from Washington. "It's a surety. And I should add, you have saved the Colorado-Yule again. Thank you for that famous 'gantry speech' as it's come to be called. I misjudged you, Clark."

He pulled sheets from the portfolio and began reading titles with a big smile.

"Metropolitan Museum of Art, in New York City."

"U.S. Customs House, in Denver."

"Memorial to President Lincoln, in Washington."

"Memorial to the Unknown Soldier, in Virginia, at Arlington Cemetery."

"Those are not hard commitments," I interjected. "We could wait years for those to materialize. It's just a handshake for now. I only got verbal commitments."

Colonel Meek assented. "True, but I was thinking we could go back out to Denver and get that Post Office deal, now that we have these in writing. That deal is worth a half-million dollars." He drew breath. "And I don't think you'll need Lorena on this one, although I know she's willing."

"Oh, I will," I said. "She is the best stone sculptor in Colorado. Maybe the world."

Colonel Meek got inventive. "Take one of the master carvers. How about Giorgio?"

"Wops don't speak the language, and don't know the culture. What happens when the commissioners start asking stupid questions and Giorgio thumbs his nose and walks out. They do that, you know."

I gestured obscenely. "Sei duro come il muro,' is what they say right to your face. And then they thumb their noses and walk out. Garlic-eaters don't abide ignorant Americans."

"I know, I know, but maybe he could be coached. Plus, women don't travel well. They're fragile and fresh, and the common means of travel don't agree with them."

He covered his mouth and whispered. "There are days they cannot travel at all."

He had a point there, but it seemed easier to coach Miss Lorena on the hardships of travel than extract centuries of intolerance to idiots out of Giorgio. Giorgio, or any of the other stonecutters from the Old World could spot idiots a mile off, and had little patience for them. I was afraid we'd encounter a passel of them in the government offices in Denver, and had no assurance we'd come out alive, let alone with a deal they'd already turned down twice before. Idiots proliferate in government.

But on the other hand, could the government toads turn down a pair of brilliant blue irises with deep facets on the anterior whatever-he-said? And so talented and well-spoken?

Not likely.

"She may not even care to go," Colonel Meek added askance. "You know, on account of that incident, you know…"

But she did go, which surprised me and the Colonel, and every other citizen of Marble. Of course, Colonel Meek insisted that the Three Blind Mice: Marley, Anson, and Tolbert negotiate the deal. Lacking Mortimer Mathews who was previously engaged in Butte, Montana on that day, they were the true professionals. Miss Lorena and I were just their industrial experts used only to fill in esoteric details the mill managers had little interest in understanding. Maybe we had our own idiots.

Marley had pitched the Denver politicians on a grand marble Post Office back in Ought Eight, but it didn't take. They dismissed him like a child. Anson gave it another try in Ought Nine. That didn't take either. Nobody trusted Tolbert to open his mouth, so I wasn't sure what his role was.

So, there we were on a sweltering July day on the Denver & Rio Grande with a new tactic. Marley and Anson would alternate with carrot and stick until they wore the pinstriped dimwits down. Tolbert would take their signatures and assure them that Colorado-Yule marble would suit their plans for the new post office in every regard.

I settled on a different plan.

"I need to stop here," I announced, and stood to pull the cord and notify the conductor. "Please stop the train up here at the Denver Union Stock Yards. I need to call on some old fellows."

"That's not a scheduled stop, sir," the conductor informed me. "Plus, we usually gain speed through this section of track. You notice the um... odor?"

I glanced at my railroad pocket watch. "You're ten minutes ahead of schedule and I'll make it worth your while."

Moments later every patron reached for their handkerchiefs. Masticatable vapors filled the car from the floor to our nose hairs.

Tolbert hollered, "It's a lake of wet manure." He pointed out the window, and his estimation of the place was not unfounded. There was nothing but floating turds out to the distant horizon.

"Why are we stopping, Clark?" Marley complained. "We're dying here!" He stuffed two linen tissues into his nose, which reduced his complaints to coughs, puffs and tearing eyes.

Miss Lorena politely raised an embroidered linen to her nose. She had been distant and uncaring for the last four hours, offering little or no pleasantries to the trip. Perhaps she was too tender and fresh for travel, as the Colonel advised. Or just biding her time until the thing was over. Females were sometimes so hard to read, so I spent little effort trying.

"Will you be long, Mister Clark," she asked between petite gags.

I laced up a pair of long leather boots, jumped into the lake of manure, and assured her. "I'll be back before you miss me."

"Conductor! We're ready."

"Haha," I said. "See you soon!"

The Denver Union Stock Yards occupied some sixty acres, just off the main line of the Denver & Rio Grande, only three miles northwest of the city center. It stunk up the entire city on hot and breezy summer days but brought in so much trade the city fathers refused all demands to tamper with it. Every business within fifty miles traced its profits back to the Denver Union Stock Yards in some way or another. Miners fed off its beef. Leatherwear, straps, boots, and gloves came from it. And Denver had the best colloid adhesives in the world. So, no one messed with the Stock Yards, regardless of how rotten the stench became or how deep the manure flowed.

Manure was a cow-town's cash crop.

Heck it was only calf-deep anyway and the office was only a hundred yards off. I could tolerate it. Plus, it reminded me of Randalls Flats, back in Missoura. I might have liked the rich aromas just a little too much.

I emerged from the office fifteen minutes later to shrieks from the distant train.

"Get back up here, Clark!"

"What is wrong with you?"

"Can't you see we're dying?"

Knee-high russet boots with seventy-two eyelets were made for this muck. I praised their efficacy and trusted the sheet of beeswax I had layered onto them yesterday. Solid leather soles. Snug and watertight. And stiff enough to act as splints in the event of slippage, averting any possibility of tumbling or sliding into the stirring slurry. What an invention. What a marvel! I would be sure to mention the acme of their performance at the next Marble barbeque I was invited to.

"You're not getting in here with those," Miss Lorena warned.

Turns out, I was prepared with a bucket of rinse water. I got about half the muck off and stashed them into a painted canvas bag.

I laid a burlap sack on the wooded train seat, and jumped in. "Let's go!"

"What's in the sack?" Tolbert asked anxiously. "A bag of dead rats?"

I smiled. "It's my secret weapon."

Miss Lorena's eyes lolled up. She doused the linen with rose oil, pushed it in tighter, and gazed out the window at the hazy piles and pens and cows and cowboys, thankfully now escaping into the distance.

I tapped the bulging burlap sack and smiled. "Secret weapon. You'll see."

The commissioners made us wait an hour past our scheduled meeting time. Punctuality and promptness was evidently not in their government purview. And just like the year before, they evaded Marley's new attempt to pierce the government shield. Anson and Marley were no equal to the wily government tricks, and had little idea what they were up against. Do governments actually practice frustrating the populous, I wondered, or was it just incompetence?

Fortunately, I had just come back from Washington.

I finally grew weary of the cunning maneuvers and pulled out the burlap sack.

"I knew we smelled something," one of the nitwits said.

Anson mocked, "Mister Clark is our transient muleskinner and cattle herder."

"He comes prepared to shovel," Marley added, snorting through his covered nose.

I ignored them. "Fact is fellows, the Denver Stock Yards are getting Colorado-Yule Marble. I just signed them up."

Tolbert jumped in with a gurgling snicker. "Clark polishes baby headstones back at the mill." He pointed to the burlap sack. "This must be all the little skulls he's collected." He looked expectantly for a big reaction, but everyone just grimaced and shook off the creeps, so he shut up.

Miss Lorena just puffed.

I wanted so bad to know Miss Lorena's thoughts, and the little puff didn't help. Was she siding with the mill managers? Did she take me for a transient muleskinner and cattle herder? A temp worker on the baby headstone line, like the fifty transients before me? But like before, I could not read her – her breathing, her hands and shoulders… her eyes. Nothing gave her up. She might have allowed her eyes to connect with mine for less than a second, but certainly no longer. I think she knew how dangerous that could be, and marshalled every muscle against that possibility. I just knew that if we met long enough for the soul to engage, those warm feelings would return. Her well-crafted defenses would fall, and she would take my hand and confess her need for me and be helpless to my words.

That was a satisfying fantasy for the moment, and it handily dismissed any fears of the powers ordered against me.

I reached over and turned down the burlap sack. Loose cash tumbled out. "Turns out," I said. "The Stock Yards pay in big piles of dirty cash. They're getting Greek columns on our next production run. Have you seen the enormous drum saws and column lathes in our finishing mill? Or the fluting machines?"

Anson could not hold himself back. "Ha! Imagine fluted Greek columns rising out of a lake of manure! All splattered with cow dung and crawling with maggots." He got up and danced around in minstrel blackface style.

"Lookz at us stock herders." He winked at Marley. "Knowz what we got?"

Marley played along. "I givez it up, Anson. Whatchoo got?"

"We gotz a black lake o' excrement, and da whitest marble on de planet!" He bared his teeth.

Everyone laughed again. Heck, I even laughed. The little minstrel show amused me, and the images they conjured could not be easily dismissed.

Even Miss Lorena eased into smiles and stopped ironing her dress.

Manure jokes tumbled out for another ten minutes, which amused the pinstriped politicians to no small effect. They had long-ago sidestepped the proposal of marble for their own treasured post office edifice, and evidently felt at ease to burn the afternoon in leisurely dismissal of the whole ridiculous notion. Anson and Marley had merely provided an hour of entertainment, and the government morons might just as well call out for sloe gin fizzes to cap off the relaxing day.

A post office of marble? Not in Denver. Not anywhere near Denver. And not on their commissions.

I broke the dying laugher with a new idea. "Gentlemen, it is now 1910, and a new age of prosperity where even cow pens get marble. Ponder that for a minute. What happens when rank stockmen do business in polished marble offices, but affluent citizens still pick up their mail from a wooden shack?"

The three Blind Mice must have thought it was another joke. They piled on new gags about the humorous differences between cattlemen and mail carriers, but soon found the mood changing beneath them.

"Word of that gets out!" I said, holding up the sack of cash, still tumbling onto the desk before me and stinking up the room. I recounted images from the dirty little stockyard offices: stacks of cash against the clapboard walls, half covered with cobwebs, cowboys kicking muck all over it, trade sheets piled six feet high on wire nails, and busy as a railyard.

The images poured out like steaming manure.

"The Denver Stock Yards are now the richest business from New York to San Francisco." I said. "And I mean richer than the Cresson Mine up in Cripple Creek. Richer than the Paris importers. Richer than Tiffany's."

"Richer than you, Clark," Tolbert ventured, but fizzled and popped. No one even glanced his way.

"Here's the thing, gentlemen," I half-whispered. "When Denver gets so rich that stockmen get marble, what's the average citizen going to ask for next? They read newspapers, you know."

I paused on each stunned face.

"Gentlemen, we're right up the hill past Glenwood Springs. We can have sixteen Greek columns down here in eight months. Each column is constructed of twelve 16-ton fluted drums, for a total of one hundred and ninety tons each. That's three thousand tons of marble just in columns alone!"

Miss Lorena came alive. What had triggered her? The manure or marble?

She reached into her bag and pulled out miniature columns she had hand carved, and went on to explain how certain types of marble sparkled and how that was found principally in the quarries of the Colorado-Yule Company. It is the hardest in the world and over ninety-nine percent carbonate of lime, which is where the glossy finish comes from. She smiled at me, and her eyes flashed like the sparkling miniatures. Just like the little charts in the doc's office.

I turned to the politicians with renewed zeal. "And snow-white Corinthian capitals to match. And twenty of those long marble steps leading onto a grand portico." I marshaled the little columns on the desk before them, which prompted Miss Lorena to extract another half-dozen miniatures from her purse. I assembled those with the others, and shook my head at her thoughtfulness and ingenuity. Finally, three more little marble parts emerged from the purse with a shy look, which earned her a jaw-dropping stare.

What else do women keep in purses, I wondered.

With all the pieces assembled, it resembled the grand portico I had just prophesied about only seconds earlier. Every piece was perfectly designed, cut, matched, and polished to sparkling perfection. Not a crooked angle. Not a sloppy corner. Not a detail unfinished. This was the kind of exquisite work her little marble curiosity shop produced – the finest in the world. And evidently from one of the most thoughtful and caring hands in the world.

I noticed those fingers again. Lean and muscular. Smooth and white, and sensual to the eye.

I had to break off.

My arms went up with great effect. "Gentlemen! I give you Solomon's Grand Temple. Pure as the Colorado Rockies, and just as solid. Tell me if you can… what Denver citizen would refuse a trip into your city to gather their mail at a temple like that?"

I crossed the finish line. "And word of that gets out too."

Handshakes flew across the desk.

Clumps of dirty cash tumbled to the floor.

The eager pinstripes kicked the crumpled cash aside in their efforts to get to Miss Lorena and me, to explain how they had been thinking along those very lines just days earlier. All our eyes connected in a flashing network.

"It's a sign!" they declared. "We're more than a cow town. More than a weekend stopover to the mining camps. More than a train station on the way to Los Angeles. We are the Midwestern hub of commerce. Hey, businessman! You want to do business anywhere from Kansas to California, you come through us. And bring your millions! We've got the

Brown Palace Hotel. We've got the Union Station. And now we've got the biggest marble post office you've ever licked a stamp in."

Their nib pens nearly tore the contract asunder.

And Miss Lorena twinkled at me.

Chapter Fifteen

THE DRAFTING OFFICE OF the Colorado-Yule Marble Company may have been the most luxurious place in the whole outfit, if luxury was ever a term to describe the marble millworks. I would upgrade from the baby headstones to this in an instant. It might have been even more elaborate than Colonel Meek's office where not an excess dollar was ever spent on appearances. Or even the finishing mill foyer where investors came in from far-flung locales like Kansas City, Chicago, or New York to spend thousands and get small percentages of the company in the form of paper stock certificates, or nothing at all in the case of bonds. Not a parson's penny had gone into those offices, so they must have spent the wad here.

I'd never actually seen it until today.

Levi and I got pulled off the line and marched up there. The Three Blind Mice were not happy. You could see that in their footfalls.

Marley pointed. "Leo Bergmark wants you two polishers. Git in there."

Levi spoke up. "Who's Leo Bergmark?"

"You'll see. Sit over there, lad."

The office consisted of one square room measuring fifty-by-fifty. Varnished tongue-and-groove red oak covered the floors, walls, and ceiling. Sort-of like a hardwood cigar box. A very luxurious cigar box –

waxed to a luster – and so professionally crafted that any one of the finishing mill Dagos would give up a pinky finger to do their shifts here. Enormous windows flooded the drafting tables and expansive floor with pure Colorado honey. But even with all that light, special electrical receptacles in the ceiling accepted plugs for electric lights. I'd never seen the likes of it. Ever. Long white wires with electric bulbs hung from forty receptacles over the tables and cavernous floor space. And you could move them from receptacle to receptacle just by pulling them out and reattaching them.

I suppose with only four hours of direct sunlight in January, lights were more than just a luxury.

"Oh heavens, it's a ballroom floor!" Miss Lorena exclaimed, entering the room behind us.

"Actually, it's where we lay full-sized building plans," a man explained in a thick Swedish immigrant accent, shaking our hands and spinning around to Miss Lorena. "I am Leo Bergmark, and Levi is here to see me today. You will excuse my accent, no?" He smiled but waited for no reply. "What a talented son is he. I can tell you two love each other oh that much, and it echoes... Echoes? Reflects? It is echo's, no?" He searched for the words in English. "In a fine son you have bringed to us." Mr. Bergmark held Miss Lorena's hand with both of his, tilting his head in admiration, and heaped on more praise for a disciplined and well-mannered young man for which the world needs more of, but which America has no shortage, and how America was the greatest land because of talented and well-mannered boys like our son, Levi.

"This not my native land," he explained.

I just smiled and waited for Miss Lorena to wiggle out of this one.

She blushed. "Oh, but–"

"I am new to Marble City, myself." Mr. Bergmark interrupted. "The office... and I are new."

"It's just Marble, not Marble City," I said. "I made that very same mistake myself."

Mr. Bergmark objected. "But sir, you have the Marble City Hotel, and the Marble City Pastime, the Marble City Times, and the Marble City something else, no? " He raised his hands in obvious conclusion. "To me… it is Marble City."

He turned back to Miss Lorena without pause. "We are questioning your son for drafting employment. Talent, discipline, and detail attention are the requirements only." He smiled generously. "How old is your son? The boy, Levi. His age, please…"

Miss Lorena answered. "He's fifteen. But sir, he is not–"

"Age is no concern. I will learn everything I need to know this morning from the boy. Mother and father, please stand against the wall." He swept his hand over the dance floor. "The photographer is capturing images today, and I want this floor wholly exposed."

We leaned against a far wall, deep into a corner. I smiled and teased, "So I guess you are my wife for the day." I leaned in. "I wouldn't mind–"

"Mind your manners, Mister Clark," she scolded and lifted a hand.

Six draftsmen, including Mr. Bergmark took places next to their tables, which seemed little more than boards thrown over some old sawhorses. If there was one improvement, it would be those quickshod tables. But I supposed them to be temporary and scheduled for replacement any time. And even with the simple wooden stools, most of the draftsmen chose to stand and lean into their detailed drawings – every man in bowties, vests and white collars. Every man a professional.

Henry Johnson raised his voice, "Everyone, please be natural. Don't look into the lens. Don't make any sudden motions. Shutter speeds are half-second today. Just keep working as you were, although very slowly. I will take several photographs and move the camera from time to time. This may take an hour or more. I appreciate your patience. Please move very slowly, and don't look at me."

Mister Johnson pulled out a chart and held it to the light, then adjusted his lenses. He moved from window to window, evidently looking for the best light and the best shots. Miss Lorena and I tried to stay out of his way. Actually, that wasn't hard in our quiet little corner Mister Johnson didn't find interesting enough to venture into.

The dark corner invited my passions for opportunity. "Well, well,

Mrs. Clark–"

Miss Lorena lifted a hand. "You know I can do it. Now just behave."

I pulled back with a big smile. "And you're man enough to do it!"

"Uh! Mister Clark!"

"Miss Lorena," I asked. "How did you arrange this?"

"Arrange what? Meeting in a corner with you?" She lifted her chin. "I'll never know."

"No, this interview with Bergmark. It sounds like Levi could get this job. Leo seems to like him, and it sounds like he could get off the rubbing beds and into a professional position. How did you arrange it? You must have influence somewhere."

"Never mind how I arranged it. A woman never reveals her methods. But 'why' is a better question."

"Okay, why?" I asked, surprised by her thoughtfulness, and pleased just to look at her without being taken for a lecherous gawker. Why would she go to such lengths for a boy on the rubbing line? And the son of a man who evidently held the life of her brother in such careless regard that he perished in his very arms? And then had a ready list of other ways he could have perished. Why?

"Levi will not marry Adelaide in Cripple Creek until he has prospects."

"How do you know this? Does he confide in you?"

She just drooped her tongue like a retard. "Uhhhhh."

I felt a little cross. "Isn't the finishing mill good enough–"

"No, it's not. It's for transients, and it's dangerous. And I'll tell you another thing, Mister Clark."

My eyebrows went up. Miss Lorena seemed to know more about my own son than I did.

She continued. "Levi doesn't know the smallest thing about women. For instance, he doesn't even know–"

She reddened and adjusted course. "He doesn't even know how to court Adelaide. He doesn't know what she likes or dislikes. Last time they met in Cripple Creek, Levi thought they should dig a privy. He

136

doesn't know how to treat her, or even how to be around her. He does not know how to provide. Where they might live. How they would live. Someone should explain these things to him."

"Don't those things just work themselves out?"

She assented. "Yes, but a little guidance couldn't hurt. And yes, he confides in me."

My passions sparked. "I have an idea. A wonderful idea!"

She said, "I was hoping you would–"

"Let's come up with some fresh ideas for Levi." I looked into her crystal blue eyes, those very eyes that normally rendered me a dumbstruck leering gawker, but today induced a completely new boldness. "Together."

She nodded. "Okay."

I smiled devilishly. "We're married, right? Like Mister Bergmark said. So we could–"

A doeskin glove cracked my cheekbone. "I warned you!"

Some of the draftsman and cameramen turned to locate the disruption, but soon returned to their drawings. The cheek skin smarted a little longer than most good slaps you might receive from a mother or schoolmarm, but tolerable, and oddly invigorating, especially to my newfound devilish nature and swelling inclinations.

Miss Lorena said smugly, "I will correct Mister Bergmark after Levi–"

"I'd kill kittens to marry you!"

She raised a finger. "I told you to mind your manners, Mister Clark."

"Actually, I enjoy our little slapping episodes. How about another?" I offered my other cheek to the leather and nuzzled up to her. I figured, hey… I'd either win her with boldness, or get another hard one, knocking me into next week. And that might be equally enjoyable.

Her glove flew up. "I will… and you won't like it, Mister Clark. I swear!"

"I might!"

She huffed and turned away.

"Okay, here's my idea. If we pretended to be man and wife it might inspire us to help little Levi with his... um... you know... his relations with Adelaide."

She jerked around to face me. "I will not play your little games, Mister Clark."

"Hear me out." I almost touched her wrist, and then thought better of the risky play. I'd already gotten the doeskin; I could end up on a gurney. "You know how play-acting helps to get into an idea? It might work for us if we–"

Miss Lorena pointed to the drafting tables. "See Levi on that stool? You should go sit by him during the interview. Go on, right now." She turned and folded her arms.

"He'll be fine," I said. Levi fidgeted in the stool at Mister Bergmark's drafting table next to the big windows on the south side. Henry Johnson continued snapping the shutter, and glancing over at us from time to time as if some entertaining act might erupt at any moment, for which he didn't want to miss.

I wondered aloud, "if we played married, like Bergmark said, we could get some ideas and help little Levi out. We could give him and little Adelaide advice."

"Have you always been a naughty schemer?"

I slid around to her other side. "I don't know anything about the female mind. You know that. I'm an ape in dungarees. A caveman. Without you, Levi and me is just a pair of bachelors living down on Roebuck Row. Dago Town. We're transients and hobos in the finishing mills. Can't you see? Levi needs you. Those two kids need you. Levi and Adelaide."

Her eyes rolled. "Alright, I'll play your little game, Mister Clark. But only until this interview is over."

My eagerness peaked. "I figured we could pretend we're Levi and Adelaide ourselves... and see what great advice we come up with."

"I understand, Mister Clark. Okay, little schemer. You start." She said, with a hand on her hip and a funny little grin. Haha, she was hooked. I could tell. She liked the idea and wanted to play, and I liked the idea too. Gosh, I was good at this!

"The way I figured it, Levi and Addie ought to start married life with a secret getaway."

"Like a little bungalow in the mountains?"

"We could pay for a day off work so they could... well you know. In a little hidey-hole somewhere."

She giggled. "Secret. Oooo. And never come out for a whole day! Have food brought in and not cook. Just get taken care of."

My eyes darted in thought. "My uncle could get one of them little wedding night-dresses for a wedding gift."

"What?" she asked. "A dress?"

"Wedding frills. You know. They're special little dresses, just for the wedding night."

"That doesn't seem practical. A dress for just one night? I've never seen anything like that in the Montgomery Ward's catalogue." She said.

"They're French."

"Oh!" She shrieked and kissed the wall. "I am sure I do not know—"

"I think they only sell them in New York. Or Paris. Uncle Olin could get one."

Miss Lorena peeked back around. "Are they... um... silk?"

"I suppose any fabric."

"Any but wool," she laughed. "Know what I mean? Haha."

I laughed.

"Do they reveal the ankles?" she ventured, hiding whispers from the draftsmen at the other end of the room, but not well enough to prevent the occasional glance and scowl.

"I believe they do. Not everyday gingham, if you know what I mean."

"Mister Clark!" she shrieked in a suppressed whisper. "You are a naughty man and I don't know if I like this game anymore." She would not face me. "Naughty and devilish. How did you talk me into this?"

Yep, I was good at this.

I circled around Miss Lorena and lost my words on account of certain thoughts barging onto my conscience intentions. In that instant, I began wondering what Miss Lorena's own ankles might look like under that long white dress. I pictured them slender and muscular, with deep creases over toned muscles, like the rest of her body I'd never actually seen but imagined so clearly in my mind. Tight skin. Smooth. Almost hard. White and unexposed to sunlight for a single minute of her life. That single image overtook my intellect so completely that I could no longer form another rational thought. Truth was, stuff like that happened nearly every time I stood in her presence.

In other words, I got so stupid I couldn't talk.

One morning on the rubbing beds I began gliding half-numbed fingers over spinning marble and wondered if that sensation might closely approximation the touch of her tight legs. I closed my eyes and took sweeping strokes over the hot slab with nothing but the thinnest trace of marble dust between my fingers and the whirling stone. Two-thousand-grain sanding discs produced the most luxurious surfaces known to man, except maybe the notable exception of a woman's tight skin with rose oil poured over it. I calculated the similarities to be more than a few.

That single notion now worked ruinous confusion on my mental concentration.

"What are you looking at, Mister Clark?"

I snapped out of it. "Oh, I just had a thought…" But I didn't tell her that thought.

"We gotta do this!" I touched her elbow. "We gotta help these children with all our years of tender experience."

She giggled and buried her face in the red oak. Probably because her face steamed up. She could not suppress the little giggles and halted breath that evidently arose from her own mental images.

"We're going to be found out, Mister Clark!"

She was probably right. It wouldn't be long before Mister Bergmark came over and asked us to leave. But I didn't care. I just wanted to play. I didn't care if we got caught or what gossip it might invite on the avenues that afternoon.

I needed a little risk in my life.

More risk than flapping overhead belts and screaming saw blades.

Her nose reappeared from the corner. "Are there little ties in front? You know… on the little dress?" She drew a risky breath and giggled, then buried her face again.

"You're the naughty one!" I slapped her wrist. "You need to be punished. We need to get back to the advice-giving and stop this naughty talk, or you'll have to be punished."

"Mister Clark!"

"I'll slap your naughty wrist again."

The photographer's shoulders fell.

Then two draftsmen's.

I giggled. "Now this is serious, Mrs. Clark."

"Mrs. Clark?" she sniffed, tossing her chin. "Really? Where's my wedding ring?"

"Get those gloves off!" I pulled a copper electrical wire from my pocket and wrapped it around her ring finger. "There! You are now Mrs. Clark. Naughty Mrs. Clark who needs to be punished."

She puffed up her hair. "Shall I rise while it is yet nighttime like the wives of Proverbs 31? And buy lands and plant a vineyard? Would that atone for my naughty sins?"

"Only if you cooked porridge and packed meat pies for my lunch. Then you could go back to bed and dream of me all day long. And ache for my return each night."

She whimpered. "And then drain the last of your energy in kissing?"

I slapped her wrist. "Oh… you are naughty!"

"Will Adelaide do that for little Levi?"

"Only if we teach her how."

Miss Lorena got quiet and stuttered. "Um, Mister Clark…"

"Yes, Mrs. Clark" I smiled.

A serious thought had struck her. "I couldn't…" she shied off. "I couldn't teach them anything of the sort. Do you know what I mean?"

"Why, Mrs. Clark. We are legends in the arts of marital relations. We could–"

Her eyes grew larger. "No, Mister Clark. I don't know those things either. I'm so… embarrassed… I don't–"

I just laughed and tugged her sleeve. "Maybe they could teach us.

After the bungalow in the mountains. And the little wedding frill."

Her mouth popped. "Mister Clark!"

Except for a few snickers and faux slaps, the risky chitter-chatter gave way to serious talk of Levi at the drafting tables, and how his talents might aid the Colorado-Yule Marble Company, and if Mr. Berkmark might find his talents employable.

We watched Leo Bergmark lay full-sized plans on the drafting room floor for the camera. And learned how he could design them in such ways that no tool would be necessary in their assembly. Exact measurements must be taken, and retaken, and checked, and rechecked there on the drafting floor. Down to the smallest measurement, at every curve and angle – with the expert application of beziers, tangents, and arcs. Calipers and calculus. Such that when blocks arrived at the job site, whether it be post office or state building or monument, no worker need touch them except for the thinnest application of mortar. They would simply fall into place like the blocks in Solomon's Temple. Bergmark said that if they could do it a thousand years before Christ, we could do it today. Especially since we had modern slide rules, and all Solomon had was ancient Chinese adding apparatus, brought in from the Orient.

After all, what did the Chinese know about math?

Miss Lorena's face never did lose the glow. The game had thrilled her more than all of Mister Bergmark's drafting plans. She wanted to know how to be married, and what it felt like, and what went on between a man and woman in the bonds of matrimony, even though she said she had ideas. And she wanted to know about Patricia, and how she had passed, and if I was sad and if I would marry again. But then noted that her and I were already married for the last hour on account of her new copper ring, which she held aloft for frequent inspection. She apologized for not knowing anything about "the subject," and not having any advice for the young married couple, except Proverbs 31 where the virtuous wife rose early to care for her family, and how that made her husband known in the city gates. I told her I might be ruined for marriage until another woman like her came along, and that there was so much more to married life than "the subject" and that "the subject" would take care of itself. Levi and Adelaide would figure that out for themselves.

The copper ring never left her finger. She rubbed and eyed it, and listened to my stories of Patricia and Caleb and Micah, and coming out of Missoura, and fighting anarchists in Cripple Creek. And how I loved being married, and was so deeply depressed at Patricia's passing, but new thoughts were now forming.

Her bosoms budded in passion and fancy. She drew stilted breath, and tilted and swayed, and opened her lips to speak, but held back and exhaled. Something within was stirring.

You can't hide certain things, no matter how you try.

I looked at her and realized Miss Lorena was the only person who had ever listened to my feelings for Patricia, or who had even asked. It was the first time I had spoken of her death without crying. I loved Patricia. Every word had invited warm and wonderful memories.

But I soon guessed the interview was over.

Levi stomped over and voiced his displeasure. "You embarrassed me, Father. Giggling and scooting around. We all heard you. I thought Mister Bergmark was going to kick you out. And then I would be even more embarrassed. Can't you behave?"

Then he turned on Miss Lorena. "What were you doing with him, Miss Lorena? Don't talk to him anymore. He embarrasses me!"

She laughed. "Your father tickled me, is all."

Levi just shook his head.

"I'm sorry, son," she said.

He folded his arms and groused. "Gosh, are you two eleven? Now I'll never get the job."

Chapter Sixteen

A T 5 A.M. GRAY LIGHT barely crawls up the Maroon Bells, ten miles east of Marble. After scaling the massive fourteeners, it first touches down on the little mountain village of Crystal City to the east, but then must again assault Sheep Mountain and Hat Mountain before finally flooding the Crystal River basin and the town of Marble with the first rays of glorious summer light. And filtering through gentle white clouds of drifting cottonwood.

That gave me fifteen minutes to pull on a pink chiffon dress, white gloves and wool cape, and get down to the Crystal River with Bible in hand to witness the glorious event my God had set to pattern thousands of years ago when He spoke the words "Let there be light."

I had the perfect spot. Pure solitude.

I'd been using the same wide spot on the Crystal River for my morning scripture reading for two years. It was just across the tracks from the finishing mills at the end of West Third Street, right under a little waterfall spraying over the edge of Mill Mountain and collecting in the river. All I had to do was go south two blocks over State and Park, jump over a new ditch where a six-inch clay water pipe and a square wooden telephone wire conduit was being installed, and then skip west three blocks over First, Second, and Third.

They should make special shoes for that.

But they didn't, so I did my best in stiff black leather, slipping and skidding along on the early-morning dew.

But I discovered my scripture reading spot was taken. Voices from two men came out of the misty gray light. One of them was little Levi, so I assumed Mister Clark was with him.

Didn't they know this was my spot?

Levi ran up to me in the semi-darkness, also skidding on the dew-covered grass on his own leather soles, hand-me-downs from other men in the finishing mills, worn out and used up, such as they were.

He seemed eager. "Miss Lorena! Miss Lorena!" And then skidded like a newborn calf to my feet on his back, feet in the air. He looked up and smiled. "I really liked Mister Bergmark. Did you like him? I hope he remembers me. He thought you were my mother. Haha!" He got up and brushed himself off.

"But don't talk to Father any more. He acts like a child around you."

A small fire was glowing along the bubbling river, but there was no sign of Mister Clark. Of course, the light was too dim to positively identify any figure over ten feet away. But I thought I heard him splashing. Or was that just the rushing current against the rocks?

I squinted for a look.

"We're cooking up some trout and biscuits," Levi informed me. "Want some?"

I squinted again. "This is my scripture reading spot. Didn't you know that?" Mister Clark was over there for sure, but not recognizable. He must have been in the water. I wondered if he'd be swept away.

"It's so warm we thought we'd clean up here in the river before work. See the little beaver dam? The water's deeper and slower there. I like it when it's warm. I don't' think Pa's decent yet, but you could come over anyway. He prolly don't care. We gotta get up to the mill at six. Did Mr. Bergmark say anything about the job? I like Mr. Bergmark."

I got my first glimpse of Mister Clark's true form. "Oh heavens!"

"Mister Bergmark taught me how to draw on the drafting table. I drew up some ideas of my own. And he added some good stuff to them and–"

I ignored Levi and peered into the river's edge. Mister Clark was almost visible. "Mm-hmm." A few rays snuck through the canopy of elm trees and struck the beaver pond. One thing Marble had no shortage of was beavers and beaver ponds. It threatened to turn the whole east end into marshland.

"What tree makes acorns?" Levi asked. "Elm trees?"

He fidgeted in the gray light. "Mister Bergmark says... yeah, that's Pa over there." He pointed into the rising vapor.

Mister Clark came up out of the water with a big block of Crystal White soap in hand, scrubbing his scalp, eyes closed, and hands working the soap overhead.

"Acorns? Oak trees... I think..." but couldn't form a competent thought at the moment.

The undulating river water just covered his lower parts. Then suddenly the first full rays of morning struck his wet body, dripping and running with white soapy lather.

Levi hopped on one foot, extracting a stone from his shoe. "You know that new Denver post office–"

"Uh-huh... Hold that thought..."

Mister Clark dunked his head three or four times. He shook it out, and then scrubbed his breasts and shoulders.

"Oooh..."

The sponge released generous streams of lather, which he worked into his chest, which tapered down to a tightened gut where stiff bundles of muscle tightened and loosened with every stroke of the sponge.

This was my first sight of such anatomy. I almost lost footing.

"I guess Pa's still cleaning up. Sorry, Miss Lorena. You can come back if you want."

"Oh, noooo!"

"Pa's real slow, I guess on account of he's so old."

I liked slow.

Mister Clark scrubbed the tight stomach bundles for a time, and then fell under for a final rinse. When he came up, rivulets of water streamed down his face and body, and down into the little gut muscles, which he rubbed once more.

Then he walked out.

"Oh dear heavens!"

"What's wrong, Miss Lorena?" Levi rushed to my side. "Do you feel flush?"

The boy hit it on the first try.

I turned my back on the river scene, drawing Levi around to my aid. "Are you getting the vapors?"

"I'm just flushed like you said." But I had to fan myself... and turn around for another peek.

"Would fish and biscuits help? We have butter." He pointed to the riverside where Mister Clark was still pulling on trousers. The fire and food were clearly visible, along with some other items of personal nature. A Bible. A satchel. A comb and tin of tooth powder. "Father's done. Come over; I'll get you a tin plate. That's all we got. Not real China. Not like you."

Mister Clark noticed my approach. "Oh good morning, Miss Lorena! How are you this fine morning? Sit with us, will you?"

"Oh no. That would not be appropriate. If we were spotted–"

"Just for a minute." Mister Clark opened his Bible, scanned the page, and closed his eyes. Then he looked up with a smile. An old-fashioned daguerreotype photograph tumbled out of the pages.

The curious word "Monkeyface" was scratched at the bottom.

I nearly fainted.

"Miss Lorena is flush," Levi explained. "Have a seat next to Pa. I'll bring fish." He handed over a plate of freshly buttered biscuit with filleted and grilled trout – a little sandwich I could eat without silverware, which to me was such a novel idea the lower classes had evidently invented some ages back. Of course, I never ate without proper silverware, but this morning I began nibbling, and could not pull my eyes from the Monkeyface tintype long enough to check my manners or decide if eating with my hands was okay or not.

The photograph was a boy, Levi's age and a sweet little girl by his side.

Heaving breasts and erratic breath came next.

Where was my little bottle of Dr. Shiloh's System Vitalizer when I needed it?

"Who's Monkeyface?" I finally asked. The words nearly failed. "That's a... curious name. Is it... a... a name?" I did get those words out, but just barely. And fortunately, Mister Clark did not see my face in the dim light or know my thoughts. If he had, he would have leapt to his feet, dumbstruck and stupefied. Nobody knew what I was thinking.

"You are flush," Mister Clark agreed. "Pull up to the fire. How's your fish?"

"Very tasty. I like the butter and salt. You make a good biscuit." I tried to think of anything else, anything but the photograph, but failed within the minute. "Who's Monkeyface?" I blurted out.

Mister Clark lifted the daguerreotype and stared into it. "I've been carrying this around for nearly thirty years. Almost forgot I had it. Monkeyface is the little girl on the left. This is me in Leavenworth City, Kansas. Back in–" He lifted his eyes and turned away. "Um, back in '79. I called her Monkeyface, and had the photographer scratch that into the emulsion. It's permanent. But I'm afraid the tintype has seen a little too much mishandling. Guess I've been carrying it too long. See all the scratches?"

"What was her real name?"

That question stunned Mister Clark. He shook his head and laughed. "Strange you should ask. I never knew. Everyone just called her Monkeyface, even her sister and mother, so I called her Monkeyface too. That was her name to me. I never knew her real name. She was the daughter of a Yankee house-mother."

"That is strange. You never knew her name? Why get a daguerreotype with someone you didn't know?"

"Oh, I knew her. I just didn't know her name."

"You're a strange man, Mister Clark."

"You see, a friend named J.T. and my Uncle Olin and me and Cousin Buford all roomed at this woman's house. And this girl waited tables and changed bedsheets at the rooming house."

"Who?"

"This Monkeyface girl," he said, lifting the daguerreotype.

"The one with no name."

He tilted his head and lifted a hand. "Of course she had a name, but I didn't know it."

I nibbled. "You must have cared for her, to get an image struck like that. Look at her. She's holding your hand. Was that before Patricia?"

"Patricia was eighty miles away in Randall's Flats, Missoura. This was Leavenworth City."

"But wasn't Patricia your childhood sweetheart?"

"She was." He pulled the tintype closer and studied it, then let it fall by his side. "Patricia was my childhood sweetheart, and I always knew I'd marry her. Right from the cradle, I knew. By the age of two we thought we were married. She had her babies named by the age of six."

"Caleb and Micah?"

"Uh-huh."

"So, what's the story with the little girl?" I couldn't help myself.

Mister Clark didn't have an answer. He just took up the photograph again and studied the image deeper and more thoughtfully. Some images capture subjects so perfectly that you cannot mistake their feelings, even decades later. This one did just that.

The little girl loved that boy.

A belly-laugh was still escaping the girl's mouth, and she was wiping errant hairs from her little eyes – color unknown. She was on one tippy-toe trying to match the boy's height, and turning a shoulder into his. The other foot flew backward, carefree and foot-loose, as if she might climb onto his shoulder, wrest him to the ground and try to make him eat grass.

This was all plainly visible in the faded and scratched daguerreotype.

She could have spoken from the tintype, "Jeremiah Clark loves Monkeyface. Haha!"

Mister Clark finally spoke. "There's no story. I just liked her is all. We played together. I was fifteen and she was eleven. I didn't love her. I loved Patricia."

I just smiled. "Didn't love her, huh?"

"We just played together is all. That was a hard time for me. Did

I ever tell you about Leavenworth City? And my grandpa?" He paused and looked away, then back again. "He was hung there. Hung for murder. In Leavenworth City, Kansas. That was hard for me. And this little girl–"

"Monkeyface."

"Yes, Monkeyface… we played together."

He brightened up. "Here's one thing we played! Want to hear a story?"

"Sure."

"Okay, you asked for it!" Mister Clark smiled and raised his index finger for me to observe. "I offered to let her bite my finger as hard as she wanted. I said I would put my finger into her mouth and she could bite it."

I laughed. "So this was a game you played? Did she bite it?"

"Well, it was a trick, you see. I offered to let her bite my finger… so she let me stick my finger into her mouth…" Mister Clark began giggling and staggering about. He finally continued. "But then before she could bite, I gouged the roof of her mouth with my fingernail." He rolled over laughing, accidently kicking the fire. Sparks flew.

"Oh how awful!" I yelled. "You were a bad boy! What a terrible game."

"But she played it more than once. I swear she did. Somehow I was able to talk her into it. And she always played as cheerfully as the first time."

"You know what that means, right Mister Clark?"

"No. I guess it just meant she liked to play. I tricked her a hundred times, and she just liked it."

I just shook my head. Sometimes men are so stupid.

He giggled and began another story. "Here's another you'll like. I offered to swordfight her. I gave her a broomstick, and supplied a butter knife for myself. I explained that my little butter knife could never reach her before she whacked me with the broomstick, so she had the obvious advantage."

"You rascal. Did she take the bait?"

"Oh yes. She would do anything with me. Anything. Any game I invented."

I laughed. "Like… let's pretend we're married?"

"Yeah, like that. Any game," he crowed.

"So how did the swordfight go? Did she whack you good? I hope so!"

"It was another trick, just like the finger thing." He laughed and tumbled into a tree. "I just snuck right in and jabbed her with the butter knife before she could even bring the broomstick up. Jab, jab, jab. Quick, like that. I got her a dozen good ones before she threw the broomstick down and ran inside to her mother. But the funny thing was, she always came back. She played every game I invented. Always cheerful, and always there for me, always ready for another game. In my darkest hour, there in Leavenworth City, she was there."

"And you didn't love her?"

He looked away. And I think he sniffed.

"Of course you did. You can't hide that."

"Okay, maybe I did. Maybe I loved her." He sniffed, and this time he could not hide it. "But I was never unfaithful to Patricia. I loved her too."

"Fair enough. She lived in Leavenworth. And you were born in Missouri."

"Yes."

"And she was a Yankee and you were the son of a Southern rebel."

"Yep. A states-rights, Bible-toting, fire-breathing rebel. A traitor to the Glorious Union."

"Now, I have a question. Would you have married a Yankee? I mean… if you hadn't married Patricia?"

"I would."

I laughed. "Oh really!" I jabbed him in the ribs with a handy stick, like he had done to Monkeyface. "Would you marry a Yankee now?"

"It doesn't mean as much as it did back then. But yes, I'll play your game. I would marry a Yankee right now." He shook his head with flourish. "I would marry a hell-fire Baptist abolitionist Yankee!"

"Did you um… kiss… Monkeyface," I asked.

"Absolutely not! You didn't do that back then. I never even

kissed Patricia until our wedding night. Talk about Levi not knowing anything. I didn't even know how to kiss a girl."

"You didn't kiss?"

"No. Patricia was my girl, and I would not touch another."

"So you were faithful to Patricia."

"To the letter of the law, yes."

"Did you hold hands? I mean with Monkeyface. Did you hold hands?"

"Nope. Because that's like kissing, right? It means you have feelings for a person and you're sort-of giving yourself to them. I would not do that. Not with anyone but Patricia."

"Hmm. So you were a good boy." I shook my head. "In a naughty sort of way."

"Of course her mother saw to that. Her mother... I'll tell you a story about Patricia's mother, Mrs. Branson. One day when they were castrating calves on the farm in Missoura, she called me over. She laid a hand on my shoulder and she sez, 'I like you, Jeremiah, yer a good boy.'"

"What else?"

"Nothing. That was it. She just sez, 'Jeremiah, you're a derned good boy.'"

I was confused. "That was it?"

"Yep, that was it."

Mr. Clark raised a finger. "Now... she had that castrating tool in her hand. You know the one they use on bulls. She just sez, I like you boy... and swung that tool by her side and grinned."

I nearly fell over. "So Mrs. Branson looked after her daughter. I like that!"

He laughed. "I'm glad you're amused. I'll tell you, I wasn't. Not at the time. I believed her."

I took up the daguerreotype. "Hmm, okay... so that's Monkeyface. And you loved her."

"I guess. Can a boy love two girls?"

"Of course. But I'm happy to hear you were true to your first love."

"But oh, boy... we played a lot. Me and Monkeyface." He

giggled like a girl.

"More games? If you say yes, I'll hit you!"

Mr. Clark pulled back. "Maybe I shouldn't tell you."

"Tell me what?"

"Oh, gosh. I did all manner of mischief to her, as I recall. I pulled her hair, gouged her mouth, stuck her with butter knives, poured oil in her hair, gosh... every bad thing you could imagine." He just laughed and shook his head.

"And she kept coming back?"

"She did." He said.

"Did she love you?"

"I have no idea. Maybe. How would I know?"

"She kept coming back. Doesn't that tell you something?"

He just shrugged. "Are women some kind of wizards? How would you know?"

My eyes rolled involuntarily. "Where is she now?"

"Oh, long gone, I guess. Prolly a gentleman's wife... a banker... or politician... I don't know."

"Not a common man?"

He pulled the daguerreotype close. "She was too wonderful for that."

Chapter Seventeen

"HEY, CORNPONE!" CAME AN old familiar voice when Levi and I stepped out of Shop Three, whipped and beat from a double shift, and layered in eighth-inch coats of white powder. It was so thick I could taste it. Not only was the voice familiar, but the salutation too. It was Uncle Olin hurdling off a Crystal River & San Juan boxcar. Cousin Buford and J.T. juggled a half-dozen carpetbags behind him.

"Hey, you old chicken thief. It's yer favoritest uncle, Olin!"

"Who's that?" Levi asked.

"Your uncle... actually, your great uncle from Missoura." I smiled. "Watch this, I'll give him some dog food."

I repeated my old line from Randalls Flats. "Oh, it is you, Uncle Olin! I'm sorry; I mistook you for a hobo coming to beg bread off us." Uncle Olin tried to slump in disappointment, but instinctively sprang into my gut for a spectacular take-down. Two minutes later he was as white as me.

This particular month, every corner of the load-out and mill grounds was strewn with marble chips and an inch of white powder. A hearty hog-wrestle could ruin any garment laid to its disposal. When we finally stood erect for hugs and handshakes, Uncle Olin's traveling duds were shot.

"Hey, Uncle Olin," I smiled. "You gotta meet your nephew,

Levi."

"And who is this, Mister Clark?" Miss Lorena asked, just emerging from Colonel Meek's office next to the east end. "A younger brother?" She eyed Uncle Olin curiously as he shook out his long hair and swung his head in a two-foot circumference to let the silky mane free to the wind. White powder drifted with the breeze all the way up Mill Mountain it seemed. The long black strands settled on his slender frame and waved generously for her visual inspection.

Uncle Olin swept in with a ready hand and kiss. "Indeed ma'am, I am this miserable whelp's younger brother. May I kiss your hand, my Belle?" Uncle Olin seemed to glide to one side of Miss Lorena, and then to the other in smooth advances and retreats he had evidently practiced many times. I guess that sort of thing worked for him.

"And what a surprising young sibling you are," she giggled, then turned to me with a bounce. "Mister Clark, you must introduce us."

"He's not my younger brother," I explained. "He's fifteen years older–"

"Oh, yer jes jealous cuz I can still nail yer hide to the woodshed wall." Uncle Olin seemed to move like a silky black cat, and turn everyone's eyes back on him.

I turned to Miss Lorena, still trying to explain, but feeling petty and foolish. "He's my uncle. My mother's brother from back in Randalls Flats, Missoura. Miss Lorena, please meet Mister Olin Cantrell."

Uncle Olin added, "The greatest living outlaw of the Confederate Nation." He paused and studied Miss Lorena. "You do look familiar!" Uncle Olin said. "Do I know you?"

"I can't imagine how," Miss Lorena stuttered.

"Did we spark in one of those cow towns? Missoura maybe? Or in that dark Yankee abode, Leavenworth?"

"Absolutely not, Mister Cantrell!" She giggled and tried to fend off his charm. "Please mind your manners. This is a Christian community." She looked around in hopes that that very notion might become obvious and convince him to slow his advances.

It didn't.

"Well alright, sister!" He kissed her hand again, sweeping kisses up her arm, completely forgetting J.T. and Cousin Buford who stood waiting for the scene to invite them in.

J.T. spun around on one foot at the three-hundred-degree view of mountains, with waterfalls cascading off Mill Mountain, and then up into the four-mile mountain draw leading to the quarry and Quarry Town above it.

"Top shelf of the whole house," he exclaimed.

I slung an arm around J.T. and dragged him up. "Miss Lorena, please meet John T. Martin. He was a good friend back in Leavenworth City and Randalls Flats."

J.T. looked cross. "Was?" And then smiled widely with a beautiful set of glistening teeth. His manners had refined in the decades since we last spoke. A little age and a few crow's feet had crept in, but his obvious access to skin treatments and manicures had evidently whisked away what lessor men could never hide. He had aged well. And he was still my dearest friend, maybe with the exception of Uncle Olin who was more like the younger brother Miss Lorena pegged him as. "I am so pleased to see you well, Jeremiah. We have a lot of catching up to do." He smiled and laid a hand on my shoulder.

J.T. extended a gentle hand to Miss Lorena and bowed. "I am enchanted, Miss Lorena." He lifted a hand to the skyline. "But this hamlet has nothing on your beauty and poise." He gestured to Whitehouse Mountain. "The natural beauty of this place takes second prize to the serenity of your own."

Miss Lorena took breath. "Oh, bless you, Mister Martin. Pleased to meet you too."

Cousin Buford seemed happy to pull a stretch of fabric through his hands, and flick his eyes so rapidly I expected a seizure. He never spoke, except in mutters. "Seventy-eight thousand, nine-hundred and fifty-one. Minus four. Minus four." Then again, "Seventy-eight thousand, nine-hundred and fifty-one. Minus four on the ground. Four on the ground."

Uncle Olin stepped in. "He does that. Jes ignore 'm. It's just retard talk. It don't mean nothing. He likes cloth, is all. He's my retard son. Jay's cuzz."

J.T. explained. "He's designing a garment as we speak. With mental cyphers only."

"Nope, just retard talk," Uncle Olin shook his head.

"Actually, he is," J.T. insisted for Miss Lorena's sake, who seemed mystified by the odd numbers he repeated. "He'll do this nearly all day, and then suddenly an entire men's suit is ready for seamstresses in the space of one hour. He does it every day. I'll explain later." All eyes turned to Cousin Buford, except Uncle Olin, who was evidently already visually scanning the corners of Marble for entertainment or a ready source of what he began to call Rocky Mountain spring water.

Cousin Buford never would touch people, and would probably fall on the ground and flop around if Miss Lorena endeavored a handshake. Fortunately, she did not, and he just kept pulling on his length of white linen and looking into the looming mountainsides, which he must have considered confining and threatening rather than majestic as they were.

"We're from New York," J.T. announced. "Sorry for the surprise visit." He spun around on a heel. "These mountains are taller than any building on earth. Nothing like New York. I love this! But I'm afraid they might totter over and come down upon us. What a wondrous place!" We all acknowledged the splendor of towering mountains surrounding the little valley.

Miss Lorena smiled. "What do you do in New York, Mister Martin?"

"Hey, let's get you checked in," I suggested. "Are you at the Larkin or Marble City Hotel?"

"We're jes here, nephew," Uncle Olin said. "We'll stay at your place." He threw an arm around Levi. "How'd dat be?"

"The Larkin is very nice," Miss Lorena offered. "They have good rooms and 'A-number-1 meals.' See the tall white building? It's up on West Third and Park. Just a short walk, one long block up that way. You should stay there."

I'm glad Miss Lorena offered the accommodations of the Larkin Hotel. Our little company houses over in Dago Town would probably not appeal to the tastes of New York gentlemen, as austere as they were.

And I did not relish the thought of bunking with Cousin Buford who would likely keep me up all night with talk of mountains falling on us. I had spent enough time bunking with Buford in Randalls Flats and Leavenworth to know that much.

Workmen pushed a large automobile and motor-bicycle off a boxcar and whistled to us.

"Let's take the Packard," Uncle Olin offered. He trotted over and handed the men a nickel each, and pointed up to the Larkin building, then fired up the enormous auto-car. It eased up next to Miss Lorena with its rakish and eager-to-go lines.

"Such extravagance, sir," she fawned and drew breath so hard it lifted her frame up and outward, corset and all.

"Fleet of foot and capable, my Belle."

"My door, kind sir?"

J.T. smiled and gestured. "We'll walk. Young Levi can show us the way." He guided Cousin Buford to the big Larkin Hotel on the corner. I jumped into the back seat of the "fleet of foot" Packard, melted into the brown supple leather, and instantly hated it.

And so began the fastest automobile ride I had ever been on. And perhaps the fastest moving vehicle on earth.

"She'll hit sixty on a long stretch," Uncle Olin offered, with Miss Lorena shifting eagerly in the long leather bench seat. I occupied the back alone. "I rebuild the engine every six months. Packard men come in with new pistons and rings, and try all their fancy new notions on me. Cams and valves and such. This ain't no factory job. I 'spect you can tell."

Miss Lorena pulled fingers across the polished wooden dashboard and supple leather seats. "I can tell."

"I have to curb its tendencies to buck and snort and climb telephone poles!"

I rolled my eyes and gazed into the Crystal River as we sped down its length in the general direction of Redstone and Carbondale. So much for the Larkin Hotel, only two blocks from the train depot. I guessed we were taking the long way.

Uncle Olin finished a beverage and tossed the glass bottle into the rocks. It crashed on the discarded marble rip rap alongside Crystal

River. He pulled another out and laid a hand over Miss Lorena's shoulder. "Wanna go fast, sweetheart?"

She shrieked. "I do. I want to go fast!"

"Alright, sister. I'll git 'er up to forty. Let's see how you like that!"

"But won't that burst our lungs?"

Uncle Olin grinned. "Let's find out!"

Miss Lorena raised her hands and opened her mouth to the wild winds of forty miles per hour. Her breasts lifted and peaked with the undulating dirt track, and it took her breath away. You could barely hear her screams in the rushing winds.

"That's torque." Uncle Olin crowed. "Can you feel it in the seat of your pants?"

Miss Lorena shrieked. "Uhh! Women don't wear pants!"

"Yep, torque. It's a science thing." He explained. "You wouldn't understand. It just means how fast the car goes when you pull the throttle back. See this lever?" He engaged Miss Lorena in the mechanical workings of the elaborate Packard. "Go ahead. Pull it! But don't say I didn't warn you!"

Miss Lorena pulled the nickel-plated lever and the machine lurched forward even fleeter of foot. She shrieked again and grabbed Uncle Olin's neck.

"That's torque. Understand now?"

"I do, and I like it!" she bounced back into her seat, with winds blowing her eyelashes back.

Uncle Olin cleared his nose into the wind then jerked back around. "Did I get any on ya, Jay?"

The test of man's piety is the list of words that come to mind at times like this. The best I could do was sit back and watch brownie's jump for flies, and picture myself in gum waders pulling out five pounders, and cooking them up by the riverside. Anything except torque.

The joyride ended only after Uncle Olin had extracted four more beverages from under the seat, drained and smashed each one on the rocky edge of the river as we sped by. We could have plunged into the rapids six times. Uncle Olin didn't seem to notice the front tire lifting off the rocky precipice at close edges, and bouncing back onto the dirt trail. He just whirled the machine like a spinning tool for Miss Lorena's obvious delight, edging her further and further toward female elations – wind and vibration, daring and danger, yet safely in the hands of a skilled operator. He must have practiced that a million times too.

The Packard finally skidded to an angular stop next to the Larkin, setting four horses to panic. Uncle Olin's motor-bicycle laid up against the clapboard, evidently delivered by the baggage stewards. He leaped from the Roadster without unlatching the door, then staggered around like a carnival clown, laughing and stumbling about. The poor engine pinged and knocked to an undignified end, with a geyser of steam blowing out the brass radiator. Uncle Olin just waved off the racket and steam gusher as nuisances in his haste to lift Miss Lorena from the leather cabin.

"Did you get a little female thrill?" he cried.

"Oh, heavens," Miss Lorena let out. "That is one powerful machine. Did we hit forty?"

"Fifty, I reckon," Uncle Olin offered. "Along those straight downhills. Fifty, for sure." He pointed to the motor-bicycle along the hotel wall. "I can do fifty on that. On the board tracks of Saint Louis. That's an Excelsior. Fastest in the world. Want a little ride into Glenwood?"

"I don't believe my heart would tolerate it," Miss Lorena said in heaving breaths.

Uncle Olin pulled up his trouser leg to reveal a nasty burn. "Got that from the exhaust off that boardtracker. Ain't got no pipes. Raw flaming gasoline, right out them exhaust ports. That's how I get fifty out of 'er. But I'll put a pipe on it just for you."

"Maybe when my wild heart calms." She skipped into the hotel under Uncle Olin's arm.

I trailed behind like a baggage boy.

Cousin Buford and Levi had become true friends in the space of the hour it took us to ruin the Packard, lay piles of smashed glass along the riverside, and scare off all the wildlife in the Crystal River valley. I suppose you could have called them cousins, although Buford was really my own cousin, which made him Levi's first cousin once-removed. I don't believe I had ever seen Buford warm to anyone like Levi. Buford didn't shriek and flap his ears when Levi laid an arm around him. They played and joked, like me and Uncle Olin. Surprises never cease.

The Larkin Hotel was a busy place in the summer of 1911. As was the Marble City Hotel, the rooming house on Main Street, and every Marble citizen's spare rooms to let. Would-be marble investors occupied every available room in the Crystal River basin, out through Crystal City, Redstone, Carbondale, and even into Glenwood Springs. Quarry Town was probably the only vacant housing, if you could call it that. The Colorado-Yule Marble Company was sponsoring two full weeks of meetings with daily trips to the quarry, complete with an assortment of bond offerings the bright-eyed investors might be attracted to. After all, marble was to become as ubiquitous as coal. It was the building material of the next century.

Maybe that explained J.T.'s sudden interest in this little cut in the Rocky Mountains. For whatever reason, it was good to see him and Uncle Olin again after two full decades. I just wished Miss Lorena had not been assigned the task of investor liaison under Mortimer Mathews, and to one of the most powerful investors in the United States, John T. Martin – my own dear friend. But she was, and so the three of us spent a good deal of time at the Larkin Hotel.

"I'm going to be honest with you, Jeremiah," J.T. said. He looked back and forth between me and Miss Lorena and Colonel Meek. "From what I've seen, the Colorado-Yule is a little overleveraged. Your startup costs are still not covered."

I objected. "How long has it been since founding? Eight or nine years? Isn't that to be expected?"

"It is, but–"

Colonel Meek added. "And those new contracts Clark secured last year will cover all those costs."

J.T. drew a long breath, tilted his head, and squinted. "Are all those contracts secured? I mean those government contracts from Washington. The Lincoln Memorial? The Unknown Soldier?"

I spoke up. "I have Taft's assurance. Teddy lined those up, and William Taft plans to honor them. I have full confidence that those contracts will–"

"Fair enough. I know you and T.R. are friends from Cripple Creek. I trust him. And I trust you. I'm just a little uneasy about the debt-to-equity ratio. You've been aggressively financing growth with bonds. That's admirable, but risky."

Colonel Meek assented. "Very astute. But everyone knows marble is America's building blocks. Everyone wants it. It is luxurious and visually pleasing. In a hundred years you will see it on every street in America."

J.T. head-dipped and blinked. "That's a tall bet. God forbid, what if something should happen?"

Colonel Meek smiled. "Happen? You Eastern boys are always skittish."

Every meeting with J.T. followed those same lines. What if war broke out in Europe? What if granite or slate should overtake marble as the fashionable building material? Or for monuments and headstones? What if something should happen to Colonel Meek? What was the company's risk management plan for each of those unlikely possibilities? Did they even have one? Or was the entire enterprise based on the incredible popularity of marble, and the fact that the finest supply in the world came out of Marble? He asked a lot of questions.

But then, Miss Lorena had some of her own, and they weren't all investor related.

"How did you and Jeremiah meet? I understand it was in Leavenworth, Kansas, right?"

Uncle Olin burst into the room and laid a hand on J.T.'s shoulder. "No it weren't. I dragged this double-wrong Yankee blasphemer into Randalls Flats on a generous length of hemp rope, is how! Two minutes later, he was to be paroled to Jesus for his crimes against all Missoura and her glorious sons."

"What?" Miss Lorena turned to J.T. for confirmation.

Uncle Olin stood wild-eyed. "I'd a hung the man within the hour."

I shook my head and agreed. "That is true, Miss Lorena. In my granddaddy's barn, with all Uncle Olin's rebel mess-mates as judge and jury."

Miss Lorena laughed skeptically. "No…" She shook her head at J.T.

"It's absolutely true," J.T. admitted. "The God's Honest Truth. I had my prayers said."

"Yet you sit here today. In the Larkin Hotel." She rubbed his shoulder and smiled deeply. "I must hear this story. Do you have time?"

Miss Lorena spared no questions about Missoura and Leavenworth City and my grandfather's crimes and punishment. And about me, how a boy of fifteen could witness such daily horrors and not be his ruination. She had deeply emotional connections to the stories, and asked the most private and painful questions without breaking into a sobbing mass.

I sat listening, like it was somebody else's life. And somebody else's horror.

But it was mine.

"That is how Olin and I became business partners," J.T. concluded. "We just expanded my father's New York clothing business into a worldwide corporation. We are known all over the globe, and our fashions are the finest in the world, even besting Paris."

Miss Lorena turned to Uncle Olin. "And you agreed to this? To live in the land of Yankees?"

Uncle Olin retrieved a fourteen-inch blade from his boot and grinned. "My enemies breathe no more."

J.T. waved him off. "He's just kidding!"

I fixed on the ceiling and whispered, "Or maybe not…"

J.T. laughed and nodded to Cousin Buford, who sat facing the corner with three bolts of cloth and a block of soapstone. "Buford is actually the reason for our success." He was jabbing and slashing at the fabric like it was his mortal enemy. Piles formed and then disappeared, over and over again. He hissed and argued until the lengths of wool complied with his wishes, whatever they were.

"Buford designs all our suits. And every businessman and sophisticate in New York owns a Buford Cantrell suit."

Uncle Olin added grudgingly, "But he can't hardly tie his own shoes. Danged retard."

"He counts threads," I added, trying to stick to the conversation. Miss Lorena and Uncle Olin were so familiar by now I felt like a lump of coal next to him, my 'younger brother.'

"We've made millions from his designs alone," J.T. said. "But I do believe Buford is the richest. He won't touch a paper dollar – insists on gold coin – and then just stacks it in steamer trucks in the back room. It's becoming a nuisance!"

Miss Lorena laughed. "Steamer trucks of gold are a nuisance?"

"That's one of the reasons we're here. I'm hoping to talk him into investing." J.T. turned an eye toward Cousin Buford and laughed. "He won't wear the same suit twice. There is a new design every day. I'm not exaggerating, we have to take his cloth into the factory every single day."

"Even on the Sabbath?"

J.T. clucked. "Twenty-one seamstresses cannot keep up with him. Every day they produce a new suit and we all wear them." He tugged his own lapel. "This is from two days ago. There are two dozen seamstresses down in Glenwood Springs right now awaiting their daily shipment on the Crystal River & San Juan Railway. God forbid a boiler blows in Redstone."

Uncle Olin blurted out with a snarl. "Paris suits is for grandpas now. New York is top cock."

J.T. agreed. "Every millionaire owns a Buford Cantrell."

Uncle Olin bragged. "I jes wear a new one into them Yankee dance halls every night, and we get a hundred orders the next day."

J.T. tried to explain that it was a little more complicated than that, but finally agreed that word got out mostly just from wearing the suits around town. And he had to admit that fifty orders had been placed in the short time they were in Marble. Even Kobey's wanted one.

But Uncle Olin jumped right back in. "I inform them Yankees how I killt a mess of their granddaddy invaders, and how I took off their top-skins and sold 'em to the Injuns, and hung them carpetbagging invaders on Missoura fence posts fer the crows to eat. Crows gotta eat too, I sez. I inform them that the Cantrell family is wanted in every Northern state of the Yankee Nation, and if you want a thrill, just throw a loop over my neck and bring me in. Them abolitionists turn white as lilies, but they keep coming back askin' for more of them Buford Cantrell's every time. That's how we sell suits."

"Uh! Mister Cantrell. Are you really still a wanted man?" Miss Lorena feigned surprise.

"Come to New York with me and find out. They want me bad out there." He stood up and twisted the Bowie knife. "I'm a dangerous fugitive."

"Oh, you are not!" Miss Lorena giggled. "You're a stuffed teddy bear. And I like you." She stood up and hugged his arm until he nearly toppled over. "A little rebel teddy bear."

Chapter Eighteen

WHAT IS A HELPLESS FEMALE to do when she arrives home in the dusky hue to find her home being plundered by obvious opium fiends? Glass breaking and furniture thrown about? Grunting and screaming? Kerosene lamps smashed to the floor? And one of the very perpetrators flying out the door with greedy hands filled with your possessions?

Oh sure, a man has no such dilemma. He calmly enters the house, pulls his revolver and burns the criminals down in a hail of bullets and cloud of white smoke. The sheriff just drags the carcasses out, and the dried blood lays on the floorboards as a curious conversation piece for future entertainment. But a woman can take no such action.

Unless she carries the new nickel-plated Colt five shot rim-fire revolver.

Yes, I had one, but it was broken and no man could fix it. Actually, just the wooden pistol grip had fallen off the right side and was lost, and that trivial defect alone prevented my carrying it. Millicent and Blanche would laugh at the marred device. They'd pull theirs out to show how perfect and polished they were, how ugly mine was, and how you could look in and see the mainspring and rusty dirt. But I had also heard that if you winged an opium fiend instead of killing him outright, it might only make him mad and invite further acts of criminal retaliation. But still, it was worth the risk. You can't live in fear.

So where was my little purse pistol? In the house with the other opium fiend of course!

Then I looked a little closer, and come to find out it was only little Levi. He came scrambling out and stumbled on the dirt berm along the street. A stack of postcards skimmed into the wind. The postcards were his, not mine. And he had none of my prized possessions in hand. Just the postcards.

The youth of Marble had begun employing postcards as their sole means of conversation, even when living in the same town as their recipients. They didn't pick up the telephone and instruct the friendly operator to connect them with their friends and loved ones. They didn't sit down and draft a proper letter on proper stationery and walk down to the post office on First and State to post it. And they most certainly did not jump on the train and make personal visits. Not the youth. Nope. Postcards were their choice. A line of text one day. Another phrase of text the next. And maybe a picture-postcard on the Sabbath. Sending and receiving the daily dispatches, and using the United States Mail as their personal messenger was their choice.

That was the youth in 1911. And that was little Levi to a T. Postcards every day.

And I knew who the postcards were from. Little Addie Burns from Cripple Creek.

"She's coming to Marble! Miss Lorena! She's coming tomorrow!" Levi cried, still erecting himself from the fall and dusting off his threadbare trousers. He scrambled for the evidence in the blowing pile.

"Isn't that good news?" I asked, approaching. "And what were you doing in my house?"

"Looking for you. I need you! Gosh, where were you?"

Men are so helpless. And babies. For instance, let one come down with a little head cold and they cry out like they'd been shot. Come to think of it, maybe that was the very effect that the little .32 caliber rim-fire Colt had on them as well. If so, it was best not to shoot them. Or if you shot one, make sure to hit the heart on the first try. Otherwise you could get a bawling opium fiend with a bad head cold coming at you for revenge.

"What is the problem, Levi?" I strained my neck for signs of damage.

"She's coming to Marble on the morning train. It's only a twelve hour trip."

"And?"

"They'll be here by 5 P.M. tomorrow! What should we do?"

"Bake some pies?"

"You don't understand. Her father is coming!"

"Get a slab of bacon from the Marble Meat Market?"

Levi shook his head and stomped around, gathering up the postcards into a tidy handful. He had thirteen other stacks like it at the bachelor shack. Then he composed himself enough to explain. "Miss Lorena, you don't know him!"

"Who?"

"Grrr. You don't understand! Plus, I want Addie to… um. I want to ask her… um. But her father is coming. Don't you know anything?"

"You want to ask her to marry you?"

"Yes, gosh." He shook his head. "And her father is coming, and I can't ask her on account of I'm still polishing baby headstones in that dirty mill, and that's work for transients and wops. And her–"

I nodded. "And her father would not approve. That is a dilemma."

"He's a doctor, and–"

"I have an idea." I suddenly adopted some of Levi's panic, but decided it was too late in the day for any actionable plans. "Let me check on something tomorrow. But for now, why don't you come back in and have a little dinner and fix my house back up. I thought I heard glass. I'll make you a fried cheese sandwich, and you can take one back home to Mister Clark. The Lord will find a solution; He always does." I patted him on the head and we started in.

After cheese sandwiches and leftover fried potatoes with salt and pepper and a little basil and sprinkled sage, it was decided that Levi should buy a new suit at Kobey's, get the drafting job, get cleaned up from a week of marble dust, and become an overnight professional – all in one day. It was either that, or his chances with Miss Adelaide would be forever sidetracked. The boy sure had ambition. Problem is, all those tasks fell to me, or so Levi lobbied hard to convince me with fear and trembling. Men are so helpless. And babies.

"You have to help me, Miss Lorena. I don't know what to do, and—"

I just nodded thrice. "Take a sandwich home to your father, and I'll see what I can do."

"But only you can—"

"I'll see what I can do, Levi. Sweet dreams."

After all, it was eight o'clock, and boys out that late were either into mischief or shot by mistake, bursting out of homes in the dusky hue. Mister Clark would be tramping up Park Street any time. Best get the kid home to his father.

The next day I did what I could, and met Doctor Burns and Miss Adelaide at the Marble Depot – if you could call it that. The Marble Depot was still just a little covered platform next to the finishing mill on the Crystal River & San Juan Railway at the end of the line. But it would likely become a majestic marble railway hub in years to come, with Greek columns and a grand portico where travelers would come and go at breakneck speeds. At least that's how I saw it, and most other loyal Marble citizens too, plus the Marble Booster foretold as much. We might become the new capital of Colorado if things worked out like Colonel Meek said, and we'd need a polished marble depot to match the rest of the city.

"I am so pleased to meet you, Doctor Burns." I extended my hand, which he took with a gentlemanly two-finger grasp and a bow. I turned to his daughter. "Adelaide, I presume. What a charming little travel suit and tie." All the young girls liked the men's style tie on stark silk, revealed behind a wide travel lapel. It was so daring. So bold. And there was the fifteen-inch waistline, if ever I saw one – corset tightened down, boosting the breasts up and out. Bold and daring, and so youthful. I would never dare venture into such fresh fashion, but it looked perfectly stunning on her, even with her sweet little-girl face. She looked so grown up for a fifteen year old.

Doctor Burns was no transient himself. The best dressed

gentlemen always sported tightly-woven black wool, with derby, and white gloves. Glossy patent leather shoes completed the picture of a highborn gentleman, or at least a man of means. He lifted a monocle from his eye.

Levi's panic swept over me. This was the man we had to satisfy.

"Oh goodness, look at the time." I pulled my timepiece from its perch on my breast. "You must be exhausted. Left Cripple Creek at 4 A.M? It is now almost dark."

Doctor Burns spoke up. "We telegraphed ahead. Rooms are available at the Marble City Hotel. Could you escort us? Or should we procure a taxicab?"

"Let's walk! It's only eight blocks, and the evening is so pleasant."

"Is Master Levi nearby?"

"I believe he is disposed for the evening."

"A shame. I am a man of few deferments, and should like to learn more of the boy's occupation and prospects. He is courting my daughter. I'm sure you understand. We'll make a point of meeting for breakfast."

I didn't tell him that Levi's breakfast was biscuits and trout by the riverside.

And I didn't have a good excuse for Levi's absence at breakfast, except to say, "I am so sorry, Doctor Burns; Levi and Mister Clark were called in early and could not partake." Which was not exactly a lie, as I knew full-well that all liars shall have their part in the lake which burneth with fire and brimstone. The truth was that the mill whistle blew at 5:45 A.M. and workers were expected to be on the job by six. It was already 7 A.M. now, so it wasn't exactly a lie.

Doctor Burns did not look happy. "May we visit his place of employment?"

I did not tell him that by now Levi was a ghost, with hair so full of marble dust I could carve a mountain scene in it. And that his overhauls had more shreds than a battle-torn flag, and that it took no effort to get a glimpse of his red underdrawers. That is, if you brushed away a layer of marble dust from his trousers. I don't think that was the image Levi wanted to leave his future father-in-law.

"I'll check on that toot-sweet."

And so began a day of dizzying misadventures and athletic challenges.

First, I headed off on a straight line for the drafting office next to the mill. After three blocks down Main Street to State, I remembered Kobey's. Levi needed a suit if he were any gentleman. Back I went up toward Main and Center, but only got one block. There was no point in buying a suit if he didn't have the job. So I turned around again and stepped lively for the mill. All the red blood must have been draining out of my stupid little head, because I realized the suit could take hours to tailor, and I should order it first so it would be ready by afternoon. My hips twisted instinctively back in the direction of Kobey's. And then back again. Wait, Kobey's didn't sell tailored suits, only suits on their shelves, and I didn't even know if those would fit Levi. I could strain a hip by indecision alone. Should I check first? No, best make sure he actually had the job.

"Oh, Mister Bergmark!" I slumped before him at the drafting office.

"Yes, Miss Lorena?" His eyes snapped in three directions, wondering what the emergency might be. "May I assist?"

"I wondered..." I placed a hand on his shoulder for support while the thin mountain air took its leisure filling my wearied bones.

"Yes," he asked impatiently.

"Have you heard word of Levi Clark's post in your office," I finally sputtered. "Has Colonel Meek authorized his employment? In your office, I mean."

He explained in his newly mastered English. "With him you must speak, Miss Lorena." He waved a hand over the drafting room tables and floor. "I am architect only. You see my drawings–"

"I understand. I'll drop in and speak with him."

Down the steps to the Colonel's office. And then back up. "He's not in the office."

Mister Bergmark replied, "Colonel Meek is in New York. He is at the Biltmore Hotel."

Brainbusters. Grisly grimy brainbusters. And pollywogs. Brain...

brat… braaaah. "New York, you say?" I smiled, but felt a growl escape.

Back to Doctor Burns at the hotel. I took his hand. "A visit at 3 P.M.? What a wonderful idea!"

Back to Mister Bergmark. "Do you have the phone number for the Biltmore Hotel?"

"The Biltmore is not built yet, Miss Lorena," Mister Bergmark informed. "Colonel Meek is only meeting at the proposed building site. There is no telephone."

Back to the Marble City Hotel. "Operator, may I be connected to the Colorado-Yule Marble Company in New York City?"

"Is this Miss Lorena?" the switchboard operator answered. "This is Myrtle Linda. You're in Marble now, sweetheart! Why call New York when everyone you need is right there? And how are you feeling after that awful head cold you had? I'm praying for you, sweetheart."

"I just need to. Can you connect me?" I learned you can sweat a gallon in fifteen minutes. Or at least soak a perfectly dry petticoat. I guessed they didn't call them petticoats any longer. Chiffon underslips? Whatever the girls called them now, mine was feeling a little sticky.

"I'm so sorry, Miss Lorena," Myrtle Linda came back on. "I'm told Colonel Meek is at the Biltmore Hotel. But they don't have a telephone installed yet. It's not really ready for—"

"Can you leave a message for him?"

Back to Mister Bergmark. No, back to Kobey's. "Do you have a suit that would fit young Levi Clark?"

Back to Mister Bergmark. "Do you know how I might reach Colonel Meek?"

Back to Doctor Burns. "Have you visited the Marble hydroelectric power plant? Nine-hundred-thousand watts of electricity. What a marvel!"

The neighbors had taken to setting out on their porches just to watch me march past, leaning into my mission with all the fierceness of a suffragette. Even Mister J.T. Martin sat watching from the Larkin Hotel porch with the Marble Booster under his nose. He nosed up with raised eyebrows. "You have a fine stride, Miss Lorena." He tilted his head for a long look. "Fine stride!"

Back to Kobey's. No, Mister Bergmark. "Expect a telegram from Colonel Meek forthwith."

Now back to Kobey's. "Oh, that one is perfect. Do you have it in black? And a nice derby? How about some good shoes?"

Does my timepiece always lie? 2 P.M. Impossible.

Back to Doctor Burns. "3 P.M? Sounds perfect to me. Let's meet at the east end of the mill."

Back to the mill. "Levi, get your work finished up. Oh hello, Mister Clark."

Back to Kobey's. "It's ready now? I'll take it. Six dollars? That's a crime!"

Back to the mill. The Three Blind Mice came out with Levi in hand. Marley said, "I don't know who you know, buster, but they want you up at the drafting office right now. You better get cleaned up. Don't make us look bad, buster, or you won't be working for us tomorrow." They handed him over to me, shaking their heads.

"He'll make more money than you, Marley," Tolbert mused, which earned him a slap on back of the head and a shove into the S. J. & C. R. steam engine.

Back to my house. "Use my bathtub. Get cleaned up and put on this suit. We've got ten minutes."

"Ten minutes for what?"

"Just do it!"

The boy came out a different person. His hair was slicked down with an overdose of rose oil. The loose suit hung off his skinny frame, and the trouser length was suitable for fording high waters. I pushed his shirttails in and shook my head. "It'll have to do. Follow me!" I jerked his arm out of its socket.

Back to the drafting office. "Levi! Levi!" Adelaide called from Park Street with her hands in the air. "Levi, I'm up here!" She came running down West Third, leaving her father up near the Larkin Hotel to trundle down the hill alone. He huffed but allowed the youthful breach of etiquette. What fathers won't allow for their daughters. Plus, it gave me twenty seconds to spit on my handkerchief and clean the boy's ears.

Doctor Burns finally stepped up and admired the massive mill structure tucked under the shadow of Mill Mountain, barely a shack in comparison to the monolith above it. The Crystal River splashed and roared nearby. "Is this your place of employment, Master Clark?" He said above the roaring. "You don't own the place, do you?" He grinned and patted Levi on the shoulder. "Nice suit, son."

Levi looked at me. "Ummm–"

"Let's go into the drafting office," I said. "It's right here." I pointed to the new addition on the east end of the enormous finishing mill. Steps leading up to the second floor landed us where I had been a dozen times that very day. Mister Bergmark must have feared my arrival and fled for the far corner where a hundred new drawings lay stacked. He buried his head in the corner.

"Not that insane female again," he must have said. "Where are those column dimensions?"

I showed the troupe around, pointing out the glassy varnished woodwork, electric light fixtures and ballroom floor. "Lookie here, now." I pointed out the various plans carefully positioned on the fifty-by-fifty floor. "Watch your step, Miss Adelaide."

Mister Bergmark never moved.

Bad sign.

I itched my scalp and breathed. "Here are the drafting tables, right next to the southern windows. Isn't it nice exposure?"

Still no movement.

"They may be laying out plans for the Denver Post Office right now. Or is that the Metropolitan Museum of Art?"

Bergmark buried his head. I'm in deep trouble; I'm sure of it.

Just then a uniformed boy entered the room. "Telegram for you, Mister Bergmark!"

Bergmark lifted his eyes from the stack of drawings long enough to decode the yellow slip. He turned to Levi with a widening smile. Then winked at me. "Master Levi Clark sits at this table. It is his table. Sit, boy."

Doctor Burns smiled and nodded. "Show me what you're working on, Levi."

Levi looked up in stunned panic.

Mister Bergmark must have read our panic flashes and figured out the ruse. He snatched a drawing labeled 'Metropolitan Museum Elevation' in front of Levi.

Levi's dazed eyes didn't help but the drawing seemed to satisfy Doctor Burns.

Mister Bergmark said, "You will finish this drawing, boy. Then you are discharged for the day to be with your family. Do you understand? Now draw it right, boy."

Levi came out of the drafting office an hour later tripping over marble blocks and hollering into the nexus of Whitehouse Mountain and Mill Mountain. "Miss Lorena! Addie! Hey, you guys!" Heads popped up in the Crystal City mill, six miles up the mountain.

"Levi?" I whispered. "Don't you have something you wished to speak with Doctor Burns about?" I nudged him in the back. "Miss Adelaide and I will take our parasols out on State Street and tease all the menfolk. I'll show her the wonderful sights of Marble. We may stop by the Crystal River and watch the trout jump, so we may be an hour." I leaned in and whispered in his ear. "Do you know what I went through for you? Do it or I'll murder you."

"Umm, Miss Lorena," Levi said later, after the doctor took Adelaide back to the hotel.

"Did you ask him?"

Levi looked into Mill Mountain, as if some curious monster were coming over the forested slopes. His eyes wrinkled and he tugged on his new suit.

"Did you ask him?" I repeated and raised my hand. "I swear, I'll…"

He clenched his teeth and lifted his shoulders. "I chickened out. I'm so dumb."

Chapter Nineteen

EVERY NOW AND THEN you have a real pleasant dream, like today. It is late summer on a Sunday afternoon. Levi is off the rubbing beds and on the drafting job – a true professional man. Adelaide and her father have left for Cripple Creek. J.T. and Uncle Olin are gone but will return for the quarry road opening in March. I'm laying in the summer sun with hot rays on my eyelids, thinking of someone. Someone so special I could ponder her qualities forever. Her fingers and neck. Her little mouth and the fine hairs on her cheeks. Her bounce and lift, and those perky little curves that leave me short of breath. And of course, her sparkling eyes. Her eyes alone could fill a hundred satisfying dreams in the hot afternoons by the Crystal River.

But I suppose even the summer sun fades. Cooler temperatures sweep in and a little mist brushes my face. But still, I like it here on the river bank. I'll just pull up my coat and rest a while longer. A little shivering; sure… that happens. Plus, I have to pee. And the privy is fifty feet down Park Street. So I'll just hunker down for now. So what if a little mist turns to snow and then to an icy gale. I like it right here in my satisfying little dream. I guess they don't call it the Crystal River for nothing. Ice Crystals is what I call it about now, but I'm burrowing in and ignoring everything but the sound of gurgling water.

"Father, wake up." Levi shook me. "It's snowing."

"I know. I'm fine. I like it right here."

"But it's snowing inside!"

"What?" I forced an eye open for a lazy look. And soon found it filled with icy flakes. Then I opened both eyes, which filled again. I jerked up, shook my head and snow flew across the cabin. Six inches of powder had covered me in the night!

"Pa look, there's a hole." He pointed up at a collapsing roof.

I jumped for the door. Frozen solid. So I climbed out a window into a six-foot drift of new-fallen powder. And they said Quarry Town was bad. Then I sucked breath at my first look at Mill Mountain. Thirty-foot cornices now hung over the skyline ridge, the work of sideways wind and snow. Last night must have been a whopper. And it wasn't letting up. I nearly fell over from the gusts, but then, how can you fall over when you're waist deep in a snowbank?

Levi crawled out the little window after me. "Do you think Miss Lorena is okay?"

"Of course, she's got a solid house. Her roof is just fine. That ain't no Sears and Roebuck she's got. It's carpenter built." I climbed up onto the roof. "But we gotta—" And then I got my first real look at the massive snow ledges hanging over the Crystal River – a million pounds of stored energy just sitting there wagging in the wind, like a mountain on a mountain.

"Did you see that?" I pointed into the ridgeline. "Up there!"

Levi's brow turned in. "She's at the mill this morning. Miss Lorena is. Do you think—"

"What?" I shouted in the howling squall. "Look at that... that mountain! Do you see what I'm seeing?" Wind and snow lashed my skin, but that sight could not be dismissed. Maybe when you stand on a rooftop things just look bigger. But still... I mused at the force that must have amassed behind those cornices. A million pounds? Yes, a million or more. And the Colorado-Yule finishing mill sat right below it.

"Gosh, that's big!" I said with a hearty shake. "What did you say?"

"Miss Lorena." Levi cupped his hands against the blizzard. "Miss Lorena is at the mill."

"Right now?"

"Didn't you know?" He got mad. "She was the night telephone operator."

"No… Myrtle Linda is the night–"

"But Miss Lorena took her…" His words faded into the wind, but I got the message.

I turned for one last look at the trainload of snow, and jumped back into the snowbank. "You stay here. I mean it, Levi. Stay here and fix that roof. Shovel it off and fix it."

Now… how do you get from West Park Street to the mill office? Easy, you cut crosslots down West Fifth and then under the traveling crane. Nope, blocked. Okay, then you go down West Fourth and around the crane. Blocked again. Six-footers filled every narrow lane. That only leaves West Third. And while I was at it, I figured I'd pick up Uncle Olin and J.T. at the Larkin. Yep, they had returned for the quarry road opening, and just in time for the worst snowstorm in Marble history. It took sixty minutes to slog four blocks through waist-high drifts. Wheeu!

"First day of spring, fellows. How do you like it!"

Uncle Olin shoved me. "I'd like it better if you'd let me sleep for another hour."

"Sorry fellows, I need your help. We got a problem!" I pointed up at the crest of Mill Mountain. "See that?"

"It's snow, Jay," Uncle Olin said sleepily. "You got us up for snow? We got that in New York."

"Holy Moses, that's big," J.T. gritted. "The entire length of the mountain."

I nodded. "It took me an hour to get over here. Drifts are six feet–"

And then before our very eyes, Mill Mountain erupted. All along the ridgeline cornices broke loose and spilled down the near-vertical slope toward the mill.

"Missssss Lorenaaaaa issss upppp…" I shouted, but could not hear my own voice in the roar of crashing snow. A thunderous white cloud sped out in front of the collapsing cornices. It swept a mile into the sky in the space of three seconds. Alternating gusts and vacuums toppled us over.

What followed oddly reminded me of an old goat back on the farm chewing dry twigs. It was the sound of crumbling and grinding wood – churning like a corn grinder on tree branches – cracking and smashing and busting. Within the time you could roll a cigarette all the trees on Mill Mountain were gone. Swept into the wall of snow, fifty-feet high. Coming as fast as a Sioux arrow.

The speeding wall skimmed over the frozen Crystal River and slammed into the south wall of the finishing mill. One second later, as if fired from a shotgun, wood splinters peppered the front porch of the Larkin Hotel where we stood, a full country block from the now demolished mill. Fifty little cuts opened up on my face and chest, which sprinkled my coat red. I couldn't have looked up if I wanted to. And I didn't want to because I knew exactly what the scene below meant.

But you have to look. Nature demands it.

We all leaped off the Larkin porch just as the wall of snow slid up onto it. It filled the porch to the eves like a poke sack with rice. The six-foot drifts on the way to the finishing mill were now twenty. All the little shacks on Park Street were smashed and covered. Trees mowed down and carried with the slide. Buggy wheels floated over the snow. Bricks, clay pipes, chimneys, window glass, marble blocks, shoes, boots, road graders, chains and hooks, and every article made by man landed on the Larkin lawn within arms' reach. We could have been swept over ourselves, save for the diminished energy in the wave. It was played out.

And then I squinted into the mist.

The mill was gone. Flattened. Just gone from sight, as if it were never made. As if Colonel Meek had never discovered the Crystal Valley in 1904 and thought, "Hmm, we could quarry a little marble out here. I wonder if anyone would buy it."

It was all gone. Everything.

And Miss Lorena?

I now knew how the lunatic asylum is filled. It happens in an instant. Men lose their minds, not from decades of abuse, but in a single instant. Something cracks. You hear it. Physically, you hear your mind snap. You go into an uncontrollable rampage that no sane man can harness. You watch yourself from some distant place outside the body.

And you marvel at the perfect rage within you.

Under such rage, I dived into the settling snow on a straight line for the mill.

"She's gone," J.T. hollered. "You can't get there from here."

"Get back here," J.T. bellowed. "You're gonna freeze out there. Nobody could survive that."

They finally caught up with fifty feet of hemp to stop me. But I never stopped. Even a lasso didn't help.

"Ya danged fool," Uncle Olin shouted. "If yer gonna kill yerself, the least we can do is join ya." He hung onto the hemp and got pulled. "Dang it, Jay. Hold up, will ya?"

They both tied on so that we represented little black pearls on a string in a sea of swirling foam. I didn't listen to a word, and did not hold up. I just kept pushing. It was only one long block down to the mill, I told myself. And I would not let a mere thousand feet stop me from her. She was now my only occupation. That is how the raving lunatic thinks, and why no man can restrain him. He thrashes and gnashes and fights for that one thing he must have.

For this lunatic, that one thing was Miss Lorena.

But twenty feet of snow is even more than the lunatic can abide. It means your feet never touch ground. Your waist and chest are submerged in light powder, making forward motion somewhat akin to treading water in half-frozen slush. Occasionally, a foot struck upon a ground-up Ponderosa Pine the girth of an oak barrel allowing some leverage in the forward direction. But it was mostly just thrashing and flailing in some insane way with just one obsessive goal in mind: to save the only precious thread holding me to this earth and to this little mountain village, and tell her that I would do any penance for her brother Thomas, and to weep over my awful negligence and beg her understanding, and to say that I would make any allowances to prove my worth. I was a foolish and careless person, but I could change. I could be the man she wanted, if only she could forgive.

I would get there, and I would save her, even if it killed me.

Problem is, a mere thousand feet can kill you. That is, when you are swimming in freezing snow, buffeted by winds that blow windmills over, and sideways snow that slits your lips and eyes like razor blades. Your breath fails, and you slip into nods of exhaustion and fall limp from frozen blood vessels. Sack coats are not made for this. Neither are ankle-high boots that pull off when you posthole into the abyss and hook them on unseen tree branches and clapboard slats. So yes, a thousand feet can kill you.

"We gotta go back!" Uncle Olin shouted at the end of the hemp tether. "We can't make it! And yer pulling me half the way. Slow down, up thar!"

I'll cut the rope, is what I thought. I won't slow down. Not when my mind got flipping images like a bad film reel at the picture show gone off-frame, jarring until it snaps – images of Miss Lorena pinned under rough-hewn timber, or slung into a snow cache and buried under ten feet of ice, or crushed by fifty pine trees. Not when my only chance for life and happiness lay motionless under smashed piles of saws and rubbing beds and pulleys and belts. J.T. and Uncle Olin would just have to keep up or get dragged. I didn't even look back.

That's what lunatics do.

But I should have looked back and realized my link to reality because my mind got sucked even deeper into the black world of madness and lunacy. Between blackouts, images flipped. They flipped like stereoscope photographs you hold up to your eyes in those little wooden boxes. Each image more disturbing than the last. Jarring, snapping, flashing, and pulling my mind into places it should not go – where no sane man should go.

And then everything went bright and yellow. Yellow, like when the picture-show cellulose melts and burns under a hot arc lamp, and finally bursts into flame and flickers white.

There in distorted frames before me was the body of Miss Lorena, naked, blue and lifeless, as though carved in marble like those Italian statues on the Greek isles. Smooth and crystalline, shrouded in deep blue mist, and encased in glass for display. It floated just out of reach in some dream-like vision. My legs and hands slowed to a stop. The winds abated, which gave me the longest look I ever had of her. Hours of looks.

Problem was, she was cold and blue and dead.

I thrust forward and smashed the glass, releasing blue mist into the angry sky. My hand landed on her cheek and I recoiled at her temperature, so far below freezing. The fine grain blue marble itself could have been glass – the work of pumice and emery, the painstaking toil of a master carver ruining his fingers to leave a legacy to the world.

I tilted my head over her cold blue body and traced my fingers over her cheeks and eyes. My fingers tested the hard blue marble of her neck and breasts. Polished marble. Statuary. Glassy and ice cold. Tight skin, lean muscle, taut breasts, now peaked and hardened – an unblemished shell for the sweetest spirit I had ever known on this earth, save my own Patricia who had also gone into eternity to ever be with her Maker.

"Why did you take her?" I asked Him, the Almighty, losing tears over her hard blue lips, and breasts and down to her navel. "I only wanted to be with her. Can't you recall your Holy word?"

The one good thing about being a lunatic in a spell is that you can linger for hours. Nobody stops you. Nobody says, let her go. Stop crying; she's gone now; we'll take it from here, Mr. Clark. Being a lunatic means you can lay your face over hers and lose more tears than you have in you. You can forget time examining her skin, and her tiny pores, and those little puckers in her cheeks, and milky skin stretched over little collarbones. No one pulls you off as your heart ceases beating like hers.

I just wanted to go back to yesterday and sit with her. And read books. And smile with her.

But time does not go back. Not for the lunatic, and not for the sane man. Not for Patricia who succumbed to pneumonia on a warm spring day with all the promise of a new decade before her, and not for Miss Lorena who was now rendered in statuary marble for eternity. Blue marble. What is gone is gone, until that day we cross over Jordan and meet on the other shore. So I will give her one last kiss and return to my earthly burdens until that day.

My own mother's plaintive voice came softly into my mental concentration, singing her favorite ballad beside the fireside with a hand-stitched shirt in her hands. I had heard the words many times as a child, and knew them intimately.

"The years creep slowly by, Lorena.
"The snow is on the grass again.
"The sun's low down the sky, Lorena.
"The frost gleams where the flowers have been.
"But my heart beats on as warmly now.
"As when the summer days were nigh."

I laid my cheek on Miss Lorena. My nose grazed her lips and lingered for one long bitter kiss.

My first... and only kiss.

"I loved you," I said, and set her body adrift into the blue mist. I watched her leave me. She drifted out of sight, and out of my life forever.

Just then the angry weather crashed in again. Sideways snow shaved my frozen face. The vision left just the outline of a smashed and derelict structure ahead. It was the mill. My face was as cold and hard as the blue marble statue, and legs just as stiff. Nothing operates in such conditions. Not even your mind.

Yet the shop lay directly before me.

I tore off a layer of windswept planking, then a wall of rocks and brush. I dug into the morass to find Miss Lorena huddled under a smashed telephone switchboard. She had no coat, no wraps, and her dress was torn and whipping. Her skin was black and blue like the statuary marble so perfectly rendered for eternity. And just as lifeless.

She was gone. This time for real.

I touched her blue lips and laid my own on hers. And lingered long enough for a frozen tear.

"Oh God, can you recall your Holy word?" I whispered. "I loved her."

He answered, and miraculously her eyes opened to mine.

She coughed and breathed, and looked into my eyes. "Mister Clark, you saved me!"

Chapter Twenty

Same day, 4 P.M.

"LAY HIS BODY HERE." The men gently laid the body of Jeremiah Hiram Clark on my front room carpet, for his final resting place, at least for now. Everyone backed up and peered down, shaking their heads with quivering lips and draining tears. The room went silent for the longest time. No one looked up. No one moved, not even to shift from foot to foot. Levi lay at his father's side, sobbing. I could not even talk to the boy. He just cried and hit me when I reached in. The winds had finally calmed, and all you heard was Levi's sobbing and the tall Ponderosa's dusting the sky, two sounds created for each other. Night was not a minute off.

Blanche sniffed and tilted. "He saved you." She covered her eyes and swayed in disbelief.

Doctor Swift turned to me. "He will be gone by evening. We appreciate you allowing this irregularity in your home. I know he saved you, and I know you wanted him here for that reason. With this weather it is physically impossible to get him into Carbondale. Telephones and telegraphs are down. Tracks won't be open for a week. And..." he hesitated, "the mill is completely gone. This town is gone. Industry is finished. Not another marble block will ever ship. All is lost, I fear." The doctor could not contain his emotions and fell into his handkerchief — for the fate of the mill or the man I could not tell.

A rap sounded at the door.

"I'll stay with you," Blanche said, still sobbing. She went to the door. "He might—"

"I'm afraid not," Doctor Swift interrupted. "Both lungs are collapsed, filling with fluid. There is nearly no blood pressure. He can't hear anything we're saying. Can't open his eyes. I'm sorry; he will perish."

Blanche protested, and opened the door for me.

A distressed voice sounded in great volume. "The mill is demolished! Did you know?"

Blanche slammed the door on him and turned back to the doctor. "But maybe—"

"No. He has two hours left, maybe four if he's kept warm. Stoke your fireplace and stove, and throw that bear robe over him. That might give him another hour or two. Every man must make his peace with The Almighty."

I knelt before the man – the wonderful man who had saved me just hours earlier. I pulled the bear robe over his weak and shivering body, as white as the thin muslin he was now clothed in. His eyes were closed but I wanted him to hear me. "Sleep well, my dear. This day you will be with Jesus in paradise. He knows what you did for me."

Pastor Brian bid everyone leave. "I have one final word for Miss Lorena, and Miss Lorena only." The mourners reluctantly slipped into the darkening night for a hateful trudge home. Surprisingly, even obedient little Levi heeded the pastor's request and dragged himself to the door, but only after hanging on my shoulder and kicking the furniture enough to earn him a little smack in the head and then a long hug and kiss. Plus, I had to promise to call him in when the pastor finished. Within minutes, it was only me and the minister standing over the poor man.

"Miss Lorena," the pastor said softly. "There is one thing you could try."

"A sleigh?" I asked. "But wouldn't the horses freeze before they hit Redstone?"

He touched my shoulder. "Something else."

I headed for the chifforobe. "I have four quilts."

"I probably shouldn't even say this…" he sniffed and fidgeted. "But yes, get the quilts. He needs all the warmth he can get."

"Shouldn't say what?" I returned with the quilts and laid them on. No movement.

"There was one Biblical remedy that worked for King David. You can find it in the first Book of Kings."

"Oh good! Some ancient medicine? Do you think it might work?"

The pastor shook his head and smiled. "Nobody knows the future. It might. But I tend to agree with the good doctor. I believe he will die."

"But we should try everything, don't you agree?"

"Maybe… I'll let you decide." He shifted and broke contact. "I hesitate to mention it, and no one would fault you. I would not fault you. God would not fault you. The man is likely to pass. I don't believe there is any question of that."

"Tell me… I will try it!"

"Umm, do you know the story of King David when he was advanced in years? You know… before Solomon became king?"

"I'm lost." I looked down at Mr. Clark, then back at the pastor. "What should I do?"

The pastor walked around and sighed deeply, but finally spoke. "In the story… the story of King David that is…" he stopped and peered out the window.

"Yes?"

"In the story, when King David was old and could not get heat, even with blankets piled on him… they brought in a young girl to lay with–"

Slap! The pastor reeled back and favored his now-smarting cheek. "I don't even want to hear the rest of that story. And you're the Baptist minister? I'm switching to the Methodists!"

He tried to apologize. "I completely understand. The man will die. And there is no remedy under heaven likely to revive him. Not even the one used on King David. It's not your responsibility to save him. The men will pick him up tomorrow morning. Nobody will fault you – one way or the other."

"I guarantee you, there will only be one way." I threw up my arms. "There will be no other."

"I understand. And I agree with you. Your conscience must be clean."

I looked at him. "Is yours?"

"Yes ma'am. I know exactly what I'm suggesting. It's probably not what you're thinking, but pretty close. And I know that probably doesn't align with your—"

"Does it align with any Christian woman?"

The pastor tried to reverse his suggestion. "Perhaps not. I probably spoke out of line. But I prayed and was not moved to advise otherwise. Perhaps that is happening now. I apologize. I too am a forgiven sinner and sometimes get a little wrong-minded." He extended his hand and bowed.

"Well, now that you brought up the sinful subject..."

He raised his head. "What should you do?"

"What could I do? And still be pure before The Almighty?"

"That is in your own heart. The Apostle Paul explained a similar issue. He said that some men eat meat offered to pagan idols, but others cannot because their conscience doesn't permit."

I flicked a finger. "And Jesus said, any man that looks upon a woman for lust has committed adultery in his heart. I assume that applies to women as well."

"Yes, that is a label, not a gender."

I pulled up the corner of the bear robe. "What if I look?"

"Don't look."

"What if I accidently—"

"Don't accidently anything. You're a grown woman. Control yourself."

I started for the door. "Okay, Pastor, I understand. But I'm probably not going to—"

"That's understandable. And no one will know either way. Not even me."

"God will know."

The pastor nodded, took his hat and kissed me on his way out.

"I will see you Sunday, Miss Lorena." He rubbed his cheek and smiled. "The Methodists don't have a pew for spirited souls like you."

I sat down next to Mr. Clark, then lay across his chest and stroked his cheek. "Do you know what the pastor wants me to do, Mr. Clark? Is this another trick of yours?" I laughed under my breath which soon gave way to long exhaling whines and sweeping slaps to his face and blows to his chest. "Why did you die here? You should be in Missouri with your mother." Tears now wet his nose and cheeks, and I wiped them with my hair. He didn't even know it. "You should be playing with Monkeyface in Kansas. And teasing her. And tempting her to hit you while you scoot around until she gives up in maddening frustration. You should be with your mother, Mr. Clark." I finally just pounded his chest and lay across it. "Why did you die here?"

Sobbing overtook me.

I finally dragged myself to the window for a look, still on my knees. Black as pitch. "Did you even hear that pastor?" I looked back at Mr. Clark. No movement. "He wants me to lay next to you. To warm and revive you." No answer. "I won't do it, Mr. Clark. You're not going to trick me this time! You'll just have to be a man and get up yourself." I laughed and sobbed at the same time. "You're all such babies sometimes." And then I lay over him again and cried.

I brushed his hair, and then pulled it and yelled at him again. "You should have stayed home."

Minutes passed. No change.

"Okay, I'll do it. I don't care. If you're going to die here on my front room floor, I'm going to make you work for it." I stripped off my clothes and slipped under the bear robe beside him. Mr. Clark shivered in short halting breaths. His muscles shook and twitched. But I was able to strip him and throw the wet muslin garment out in front of the fireplace.

We were now skin to skin. Bare and bristling.

Which left me short of breath.

"Your trick is working, Mr. Clark. What do you think of that?" No answer. Not even a blink. I pressed my back into his chest and pulled his arms around me. I fit like a little doll in his arms. My little shoulders folded into his ample breasts. I wiggled in and wrapped my legs around his, then pulled the robe in over our heads.

He did breathe, but so shallow I could not feel it on my skin. I had to wiggle around and lay my lips on his to tell. I was back and forth, front to back every ten minutes.

Was he breathing? Roll over and check. Yep, still breathing. Roll back and wiggle in. Then repeat. Eight hours of that left me hot and exhausted. So much for the four hours Doc Swift gave him.

"You're flat wearing me out, Mr. Clark!" I puffed into his mouth.

"What's wrong with your stupid lungs anyway?" I puffed again, not sure if I was doing more harm than good. But the man was dying, so I figured it couldn't hurt. Plus, I liked it. I played with his mouth and remembered the Hang Man game when I bit his lip, and he still didn't let me down, and I didn't let loose. I found the little scar I'd left him, touched it and fit my teeth into it again. Then I gave him another smart bite. "That's for dying on my living room floor." I bit him again. "And that's for wearing me out all night!" My lips went for his again, and a slow breath escaped. This was more exciting than I expected, or terrifying, I couldn't tell.

I slapped his shoulder. "They say you can lift two-hundred-pound marble blocks, Mr. Clark. But you don't seem strong to me. Show me your muscles, Mr. Clark," I teased, beating his chest. "Even a girl can beat you up. And you're making me do all the work and making me hot and sweaty!" I punched him in the stomach. He didn't seem to care, but I found that I liked that too. I dragged my hands over his sweaty chest and shoulders. I was now just as wet.

I yelled at him. "Wake up!"

But Mr. Clark didn't move so I rolled over and tried to sleep. It turns out, you can't make yourself dream. It's like trying to make yourself sneeze. I tried a few satisfying formulas but nothing worked, and I finally fell asleep in his arms, hot, wet and exhausted.

There must have been a knock at the door, but I didn't hear it. But I did hear the rap on the front window and Levi's desperate voice. "Miss Lorena, Miss Lorena. Did the pastor leave?"

Oops, forgot the boy.

True panic struck only when I realized I was naked under a bear robe with his father. And Levi did not always knock. I skinned out from under the robe and ran into the kitchen with nothing but my toenails covered. I blinked and realized that was stupid, and scooted back through the front room and into the bedroom. Just in time, because Levi came right in without another knock.

Wheeeu!

"Good morning, Levi." I emerged from the bedroom, bright-eyed and barefoot, and lucky to have a nightshirt. It was inside-out but mostly covering everything a boy of sixteen would blush to witness. "Your father is still right here." Levi was already bent over Mr. Clark. I snatched up a sock and slid it into my nightshirt.

"Is he…"

"Alive? Yes. Barely. He has shallow breath and he's still sleeping." I bent over next to Levi. "Put your mouth down near his. You can tell he's breathing. Feel that?"

"But the doctor said—"

"I've been nursing him." But I didn't say exactly how. "I'll fix you breakfast." With that, I escaped into the kitchen to brush my hair and check my face. And breathe. And laugh. And breathe some more. Did I look like I had just come out from under a bear robe with a naked man? Any black hairs? Carpet threads? I found my heaving breasts still glistening. After a blink, I yelled, "I've got scrapple, eggs and sourdough. It's just scraps and heels. Is that okay? I'll make you a scrapple sandwich."

Levi finished a third sandwich next to his father. "If father gets better, I'm going to ask Adelaide to… umm… you know…"

"You don't have to be shy. I understand. Do you love her?"

Levi hid his face. "Miss Lorena! Gosh!"

"I'm sorry, Levi. That was not so subtle. How many postcards have you sent her?"

He brightened up. "Do you think I could do it with a postcard? You know… ask her in a—"

"Absolutely not!" I grabbed his face. "She's going to remember that day for fifty years. Take her by one hand, kneel before her and ask for her hand in marriage the proper way."

"I'm too afraid. You know what happened last time."

I looked over at Mr. Clark. "Your father will have some advice." But I still didn't believe he'd make it. He didn't look good and there had been no improvement. He still shivered and shook, and breathed in little puffs. I pitied him, and only wanted to lay next to him again and warm him and have him whisper into my ear, and take soup. I could make potato soup with melted cheese and bacon, and hand-feed him and ask him if he was feeling better, and yell at him for dying on my carpet. He would say he was feeling better and wonder how he came out of it. I would just smile and hand him another spoonful and ask if he dreamed of me and felt me in his arms, and did he want to feel me again, because I definitely wanted to feel him again.

Snap out of it, Lorena, I thought. You're not getting under that robe again, you sinful little tart.

I turned to Levi. "He'll be fine," I lied.

He sighed with relief. What a trusting boy.

"Why don't you go down to the mill and help the men shovel; it's a disaster down there." The self-admonition didn't work because what I didn't say was that the moment he left I would probably throw off the nightshirt and slide under the bear robe and ask his father to smother me in his arms. I would press into his breasts again and make him squeeze me, and then abuse him for saving me and then dying without a word.

Instead, what I said after Levi reluctantly left and I slid under the bear robe was, "You could have married Monkeyface." No answer. Not a twitch, except the shivering. I wrapped his arms around me like before, but then wiggled around to face him. I lifted an eyelid and peeked in.

"No answer?" I pulled his eyelid and let it snap back with a little slurping sound. "Then I'll answer for you."

"You could have married Monkeyface," I repeated.

"She was only eleven," I imagined him saying. "You know that, Miss Lorena."

"You probably broke her little heart, don't you think? I mean when you left for Missouri."

"You pronounce that wrong."

"I'll pronounce it any way I like! I'm not the one dying here." I repeated, "Don't change the subject. You probably broke her little heart, don't you think?"

"How should I know?" he said, but not really because he could hardly breathe let alone talk. But it's what I thought he'd say if we were sitting under the big Ponderosa's next to Crystal River on a warm morning with his biscuits on hot coals, and the cutthroats were jumping, and cottonwood tufts were falling like big flakes of snow.

"I bet she cried," I said, sliding my lips over his and getting nervy and sweaty all over again. I puffed into his mouth and massaged his chest. Then I blew into his mouth and pressed on his stomach and chest. "You probably made her cry."

"You coughed! Mr. Clark, you coughed!" Not only did he cough, he sucked breath and bucked. "You're breathing, Mr. Clark. Ha!"

"Don't get your hopes up," he said in my imagination. "I'm leaving for Missoura."

"And I'll cry like Monkeyface when you go?"

"Who says she cried?"

"Come on, Mr. Clark. Don't be stupid. Of course she cried."

"Nah, probably married with a dozen kids. Prolly don't even remember me."

"Don't be so sure, Mr. Clark. You may be her hero still."

No answer.

"Oh, you positively exhaust me. Cough again or I'm biting you!" I slapped his chest and rolled him over to face me. Then I climbed on top and arched into him. "I swear I'll bite you!" No response. But I guessed the bear robe over our heads didn't help.

"Give me your hands, Mr. Clark."

"What for?" he said in my wandering imagination.

"Oh, be quiet and let me have them." I pulled his hands to my face. He stoked my cheeks and hair with passion, dragging fingertips over my wet skin, then pressed deeply with little teasing motions.

And then headed for my neck.

"Mr. Clark!" I protested. But he didn't stop. He pinched my tightening neck and shoulders, and ran his hand over my wet collarbones and over my ears and hair. He took a clump of hair and pulled, which peaked my breasts into him.

"Jeremiah Clark!" I slapped his hand, which fell as limp as always. I took it up again.

"You are a mischievous man. This doesn't mean we love each other. I'm only doing this because the pastor told me to. I don't love you. Now go to sleep, bad boy." But he didn't sleep; he just kept pinching my hot skin and sweeping my face with long rapturous strokes. I had to slap him four more times and bite him smartly, but that only encouraged him into further acts of mischief and merriment.

"Mr. Clark!" I wailed to no avail. His passions could not be dissuaded by any means.

All the wriggling under the bear robe made me so hot I could no longer tell which sweat was his and which was mine. After another hour of hot wriggling and slapping Mister Clark for mischievous acts, I started drifting into dreamy thought, or maybe sleep. I could not tell.

I saw Mr. Clark slowly ambulating through a misty rainforest, covered only in wet muslin, and me waiting on a bed of slick green leaves under the canopy. Hot rains drizzled over my tightened skin as a rivulet of warm water washed over my bare stomach. Hot steam and the squawks of forest creatures lulled me to heavenly rest. My heaving ribs slowed to a calm.

Mr. Clark lay down beside me... and didn't die.

I don't know if Levi came back or not. I must have dreamed all that day and half the night. It was 2 A.M. when I finally scampered out to the privy in a half-sleep.

The moon was bright and little shadows danced over the hardened crystal snow. Everything was silent under snow-laden pine boughs – a winter wonderland you would never know existed unless you ventured into the Colorado backcountry where breathtaking scenes came with every turn of the calendar.

I looked back at the house where Mr. Clark lay fighting for his life and prayed.

Then I raised an eye to heaven. "Okay, okay, I will tell him if you bring him back."

No answer.

"I said… I will tell him."

"Tell him what?" God said, smiling.

"You know what."

Chapter Twenty-One

THE ONE SURE THING about Colorado weather is that it can kill you one day and delight you the next. Within weeks all evidence of the snow slide was gone. Twenty-foot snow caches, gone. Eight-foot wind-swept drifts, gone. True, broken trees and ruins of smashed buildings littered the valley, but that wicked snow was gone. There was talk of a fifty-foot marble wall on the Crystal River to prevent this from ever happening again. I just wanted to forget the whole awful event. Today was sunny and bright, perfect for strolling the avenues of Marble.

Mr. Clark was still too weak so J.T. offered. "Your parasol, Miss Lorena? What a day for a stroll!"

I smiled and curtseyed, a dreadfully old-fashioned act in modern times, but then J.T. was an old-fashioned gentleman with all the graces and manners the last century had amassed. J.T. may not have been as nimble and swift as Olin, but every word and movement was calculated to please. J.T. knew how to treat people, and women in particular.

"I knew I recognized you," he said. "I sort-of knew it that first day we met last year at the train station. Olin and I figured it out back at the Larkin after your automobile excursion along the Crystal River. He said you looked familiar, and we figured it out together."

"Thank you for your discretion."

"Jeremiah and Levi don't know?"

"Little Levi wouldn't, of course."

J.T. nodded. "How is your mother?"

"She passed."

"And father?"

"I never knew him. My true father, that is. You know I'm an orphan, right?" We turned and headed up the hill toward Silver Street. J.T. was unaccustomed to the altitude.

He stopped with hands on his hips. "That explains why you and Levi get on so well." He exhaled deeply. "Wheeu, this is a climb! Where are you taking me? Up the Maroon Bells?"

"Just up to Marble Street. You'll like the walk down. And the views from up there are ooooh." We turned and gazed across the Crystal River valley, higher now than the remains of the Colorado-Yule finishing mill next to the river. In fact, five-hundred structures were now below us, and even a few tents along Mill Mountain, which had been stripped of every tree during the avalanche. "We're standing at eight-thousand feet above sea level. Isn't it grand?"

J.T. huffed. "It's something!"

I smiled and headed up again. "Just another block."

"How did you end up here, of all places? In Marble?"

"Thomas came out first. He was here with Colonel Meek in the beginning when they blasted the first holes from a boson's chair, hanging off the white cliffs." We stopped and looked up at Quarry Town where the Pea Vine railway had been, but was now replaced by the electric tramway.

"We heard about Thomas. I'm so sorry."

I sighed and turned my face into the sunny sky. "I came out next, in 1905. I was only going to stay the summer. I had other plans... other ideas... But those plans suddenly changed, and I stayed."

J.T. stopped again. "Do you mean with the marble shop? Those were your plans?"

"No, Thomas set me up with that... but that's not what I meant—"

"Miss Lorena, this is rough. I'm not used to this! The avenues of Manhattan Island are so different. Now those are grand."

"You must tell me!"

"Well first off, the shops. There are hundreds. You can spend an afternoon on Fifth Avenue alone. Shops of every kind. Clothing shops, hats, shoes, candy, bicycles and even automobile shops."

"They sell automobiles in stores?"

"Uh-huh, in stores!"

Automobiles in stores? And shops of every kind? That alone was enough for a good fantasy. I saw myself on the crisp avenues of New York, strolling in the early evening, smelling salt air. J.T. bounced ahead, pointing into shop windows, joking and hand-feeding me fried bread and honey bought off a hand cart for a penny. Every smell wonderful. Every sight brilliant and perfect. No mountains, only views of the East River and society folk strolling or riding new bicycles. Even the women rode. Men approached J.T. for his business advice, and he gave it cheerfully and abundantly. All the shop owners invited him to their homes and said, bring your lovely wife Lorena, won't you? J.T. bounced and spun, breezing my hair and leaving kisses on my cheek. He replied to the shop owners that we would come, and we continued up the avenue in the soft glow of a dying sun. All silly thoughts, but that was the way my mind was working lately. I wasn't sure why.

I turned to J.T. "My grandfather was from back East. Eli Thayer. Have you heard of him?"

"Eli Thayer. I have. Everyone has. And if Eli Thayer was your grandfather then you know that the most convivial society originates in Manhattan Island."

"I don't doubt it. But I've never actually been."

"Every man tips his hat. Every woman tilts her head and nods. It's almost a law. But the curtsey is out, I'm afraid."

I blushed. "I feel so silly."

"Don't. Living out here, you may not be acquainted with recent fashion and etiquette. It's my business to know those things. I'm in the garment business, you know." He paused, but not because we had reached Marble Street, or that the view across the valley had expanded into another picture postcard. You couldn't really talk. It was that good. But he wanted to, real bad. He had a thought trying to escape, but his sensibilities blocked it. I almost laughed.

I added, "We never had high society in Kansas. That was rough country. Mother and father were emissaries – missionaries almost – into Free Kansas before the war. We never had anything finer than whitewash. I never learned real etiquette."

"I could teach you." He mused. "I mean, you could pick it up. Just mix with the right company and you're a practiced professional in no time." He smiled. "There are society parties every night. Teas and balls. Soirees and mixers. Even Sundays!"

"Do you partake?" I asked.

"On occasion." He drew breath. "But there's no one to share it with. I mostly work."

"Even on Sundays?"

"Absolutely not! Not the Sabbath." He shook the parasol with a faux scowl for my amusement. "I think you'd be a New York hit."

"I'm more of a 'work with your hands' type of girl. Where would I sculpt?"

"Are you joking? Manhattan Island is the very center of culture and art. Forget Paris. Your marble sculptures would be in every gallery. And if they weren't, I'd see to it myself. I know people." He smiled and lifted an eyebrow. "But, you know we're leaving soon."

"No! Why?"

"We're finished meeting with Colonel Meek."

"Are you investing?"

"We are. And mostly because of Jeremiah and all he has done to advance the company. Olin, Buford, and I made a five percent investment in the company. The deal closes next week."

"Is the Colorado-Yule Marble Company sound?"

He smiled and lifted a finger. "As a dollar!"

Then he added, "Although I would say that the mill operations are far too big for the orders coming in. That makes getting orders easier, but I fear the company may be a little over leveraged, over capitalized, over built. You've got 150,000 square feet of floor space with three enormous firewalls between shops, stretching over a quarter of a mile! You simply do not need all that mill space."

"They're talking about more mills down the valley. Marble is filling up, so there's no more room. It'll be like back East, with textile and paper mills all along the riversides. Rain follows the plow, they say."

"I understand; the goose hangs high. But I fear more building would be a mistake." J.T. said, pursing his lips. "Mortimer Mathews and I agree on this point. This marble mill is already the largest in the world. The craneway over the block yard is thirteen-hundred-feet long – the longest of its kind in the world – a quarter mile."

"And they need more temporary yard space because it's so hard to keep the quarry road open all winter."

J.T. grimaced. "If orders ever slowed, the operation could be in danger. How could the bonds be paid? You know, when they come due you either pay or go into receivership." He paused and smiled uneasily. "But I like what I see now; we're investing."

"How else could contracts like the Lincoln Memorial be gotten without that mill space? That will be a million-dollar contract when it comes through. We can handle 500,000 cubic feet of marble a year. And the geologists say there's enough to keep the mill running full-handed for a hundred years."

"You're absolutely right, Miss Lorena. We're happy, for now."

We walked in silence, thankful for the bright sun and cooling breeze.

JT. spoke. "Did you know Jeremiah was offered an executive position? In New York, to work with J.F. Manning on West 33rd Street."

My heart fluttered. "Ohh… I did not. Is he going? To New York?"

"For some reason he turned it down. Said he's content polishing baby headstones in the mountains of Colorado." We both mused at the interesting choice of occupation and wondered at his true motives.

Heading downhill, Silver Street, Main, and State passed in a blink. Especially with a society gentleman on your arm, fawning and completing your sentences. I wondered, maybe I could enjoy the avenues in New York. Throw in a confectionary and millinery, and I might be enticed. Gloves. I'd definitely want white leather kid gloves for the winter. And silk for summer. And long walks on the avenues. Maybe I could enjoy New York.

"Olin needs a doctor, you know. Pain in his back." J.T. remarked.

I laughed. "You wouldn't know it! He's been speeding around on his Excelsior, inviting me to ride behind him. He loves to race past the meat market because old man Mackerel raises his fist and shouts profanities. 'Hold on!' Olin says. 'let's buzz him again!' But the Packard is closer to my danger limits, so fast and luxurious. I love it! And Olin is a daredevil with it."

"He is a good ol' rebel. Always has been."

We arrived at Park and West Third. Time for me to change into work clothes and put some emery powder and tin oxide to the nearly mirrored surfaces of a new cross with the robe of Jesus lifting into the wind. "He is Risen," the inscription would read when finished. "He is Risen Indeed." I experimented with red dye. The marble soaked it up nicely, but lost most of its color within a month and turned dirty red, so I quit that. I'd leave it snow white, and bring the 99.97 percent carbonate of lime to a high gloss by hand rubbing.

Jesus would like that.

J.T. shifted from foot to foot. He inspected a few discarded marble blocks along Park Street and bent down as if to examine their grain. Then he exhaled nervously.

"Come to Manhattan Island with me, Miss Lorena!"

"Mister Martin!" I nearly slapped him for his forward notions, but allowed it with a fake scowl and a wide smile.

"I'm serious. Yes, I'm a little older than you. But I will treat you right. I will cherish your presence. You will be the essence of life, the spirit of joy and happiness. And I will love you and provide your every desire. I have the means, and the fire within. You will see."

"I don't doubt it." I touched his face. "You are a virile and attractive gentleman, Mister Martin."

"And I will exercise that virility every day for you. Every secret pleasure is yours to own and explore. Work when you want. Play when you want. And fulfill your passions in between. You will find an eager and fiery devotee in me."

He knelt before me, right there across from the Larkin Hotel. "Miss Lorena, would you accept my earnest invitation to be my wife?

And experience wedded bliss wherever we wish to explore?"

"Mister Martin!" I stumbled back and tried to pull him up. But he pleaded all the more earnestly, with elaborate verses from paradise, with oaths of commitment and fidelity. He could not be dissuaded. He had given this more than a single thought, and practiced it; that was clear.

I whined softly, "remember that plan I spoke of?" I finally said and sat down beside him. Forcing the man to swallow his pride and return to his feet felt too cruel. I laid a hand on his, and we both leaned back into the tall grass. "You see, I still have this thing in my mind. It's been with me for a long time."

He sat up. "I understand. But ohhh, I would stroll the avenues into eternity with you."

"And I with you, J.T. If not for... it's just..."

He patted my hand and smiled. "I understand." He took my hand and lifted me up.

It took some doing, but we parted with a mutual understanding.

As it turned out, Olin really did need a doctor. Maybe all that motor-bicycling on rocky ground did it. He ended up on his back on the Larkin Hotel porch, practically paralyzed. Mr. Clark was too weak to haul him over to H.H. Swift's office, so we called the doctor in.

"Probably just pulled a muscle," the doctor said. "He'll be fine in a few days."

"It's a Minnie Ball," Olin protested. "Left over from the war."

"You fought in the Cuban War, Mr. Cantrell?"

"The War of Northern Aggression, you fool. The Civil War. Do I look twenty-five to you?"

Doctor Swift shrugged. "Maybe. Sure!"

"You idiot! See them holes?" Olin moaned. "Them two still got bullets under 'em."

The doctor examined the six scars, pressing and pinching until Olin straightened up with a shriek. "I don't believe it. It's muscle pain from all that hooliganism. The whole town knows and now the chickens have come home to roost. I prescribe Mexican Mustang Liniment for such—"

"You ignorant Yankee fool," Olin shouted, and then stiffened up in pain. "Country doctors."

Doctor Swift knelt to examine further. "You could try Denver. They got a machine that can 'see' under the skin. But it's more dangerous than surgery."

"Dig it out," Olin demanded. "Dig it out!"

"Have you got the constitution for this?"

"Doc, I got shot in the corner of my eye, and three lead parts came out through the roof of my mouth twenty years later. I got whatever."

"But right here? I couldn't possibly."

"I swear, I will slap you as soon as I'm up." Olin turned and raised his head. Angry eyes made his demands clear. "Them other four bullets was done on the back of a horse, and then the horse was shot out from under me not one hour later. I don't much care where it's done. Here on this old porch or in yer fancy office. It's all the same to me. Jes git 'r done."

"You'll lose a lot of blood."

"I got plenty."

"You might be paralyzed."

"I'm already that. Now git that pig sticker and commence."

"This is not exactly a Boston surgery bay—"

"I swear, I'll slap you this instant." Olin began swatting the air and wriggling like a flipped crawfish.

Buford started kicking the doctor while he probed. "I'll slap you. I'll slap you," Buford yelled and kicked until Mr. Clark pulled him into a corner where he flapped his hands and continued muttering, "I swear, I'll slap you!"

"Alright, alright," the doctor reluctantly agreed. "I can probably do it here. But don't blame me if you're paralyzed in the morning."

"If I am, yer a dead man," Olin grouched. "Best take a drink first. Steady yer nerves. And give me six or eight shots too. You ain't digging into me with less than a fifth of popskull between us. Check my boot."

Sure enough, pulling off Olin's boots revealed two tin flasks of dubious origin, three knives, a boot pistol, and a deck of cards, none of which were necessary or useful in the city of Marble.

"Where did you get this? The sale of alcohol is prohibited in Marble. Been so since Ought Eight. We're a dry city."

"Are you all fools? Thar's a feller around the corner what sells it out of his boot leg every night. And did you ever wonder how a jailed man with no visitors can be dead drunk by morning? He sucks wood grain liquor from of a macaroni straw through the window bars. Now give me a dozen belts of that spring water. And git one fer yerself fore you take up that skinning knife!"

"Wood grain alcohol will make you blind or cotton-eyed." But the doctor didn't wait for Olin's response; he just took a deep swig and coughed until he nearly bled. "Is this elixir ingestible?"

"I will slap you. Now hand me that nerve medicine!"

The doctor gave Olin a dozen snorts, which he imbibed without effect.

Buford stepped up. "Give me a dozen snorts of that nerve medicine!" Mr. Clark pulled him back.

"Now commence, Saw Bones." Olin buried his head in the porch planking.

"Better get a bucket and some rags. This is going to get messy."

An hour later Olin was standing, and he didn't slap the doctor. He just danced around like there was a jubilee on, shaking hands, and occasionally favoring his bandaged back and grimacing. "That's been forty-five years a comin'. I ain't never felt so good. Where's that popskull? Let's have a fandango!" He started dancing with me and singing the words to 'Kingdom Coming'.

"De massa run, ha, ha! De darkey stay, ho, ho!

It mus be now de Kingdom Coming, an' de year ob Jubilo!"

Olin soon fell back onto the porch floor in fatigue. "Okay, maybe not just yet." He smiled up at me, winking and gesturing as though I might like to lay next to him.

"I hope you go blind, Mister Cantrell," I said, rolling my eyes, but failing to suppress a little smile and then a little chuckle at the silly man. Here he was dying of a bullet wound and still sparking me. What a little rascal, I thought.

"Getcha some of that woodgrain and we'll both go blind!"

"You're drunk, Mister Cantrell."

"I could dance a reel with you!"

"You can't even stand. And you're misbehaving."

"Lay next to me, sister, and I'll show you misbehaving. You and me'll finish off that sugarhead."

I just folded my arms and rolled my eyes. "Lips that touch alcohol shall never touch mine."

"Marry me tonight," he slurred, and then passed out on the porch planking. He didn't wake up for two days.

A week later the sheriff had Olin in manacles, leading him up Park Street. He stopped at the Larkin Hotel and shouted from the street. "You three are out on the next train. Git your kit and clear out! You all hear me in there? You're out on the next train!"

Half the neighbors came out to witness the disturbance, including me. It was nearly 5 A.M. just before light began sniffing around the edges of the mountain, looking for a way into the Crystal River valley. It would wait another two leisurely hours for full appearance, but I could see the two silhouetted figures on Park Street, loud and agitated, one in chains, the other with a shotgun in the crook of his arm.

The sheriff tugged the chain leading to Olin's restraints. "We ain't havin' yer kind here no longer! Get yer kit. Yer out today!"

J.T. and Buford emerged from the hotel in sleeping caps, rubbing their eyes and hair. Olin protested incoherently but without effect. The sheriff was resolute in whatever he demanded. He cuffed Olin in the head and yanked his chain whenever the prisoner got vocal.

"Is you them? This man's comrades?"

Buford paced a little in confusion. "I need milk. Milk for breakfast. Milk for breakfast."

"Is that you, Olin?" J.T. shouted from the porch, still bed weary and adjusting to the dim light.

"They got me, this time, friend." Olin confessed.

"Buying bootleg whiskey?" J.T. asked.

"Bootleg whiskey," Buford repeated from the porch rail. "Milk and bootleg whiskey for breakfast."

"No, they got another crime up here I ain't never heard of."

"Lewdness," the sheriff added. "Lewdness and cohorting with a minor."

"I was jes showing her my bullet holes. I thought she liked 'em." He chuckled and danced a little hop-skip. "But I guess her daddy didn't. Hehe. But that ain't no crime, ere it?"

The sheriff yanked the chain. "Shut up, prisoner. Yer on the next train. Right now." He started down West Third on a quickstep.

"Hell for leather, boys!" The sheriff yelled back. "You're on the 5:40, or you're walkin' to Redstone at the end of this scatter gun."

I sent a boy to fetch Mr. Clark and Levi. "Tell them to get over to the depot, quick. Don't eat; don't bathe; just come right away." I handed him a penny. "Hurry, now! Do you know where he lives?"

"Dago Town." The boy scampered off and I headed after the sheriff.

Minutes later, Mr. Clark came skidding up. He had recovered from near death weeks earlier, but still had no idea I was involved. I know he craved familiarity with me but seemed to fear what animosity I might still harbor. So he kept a civil distance until a mischievous notion overcame it from time to time. Today was not that day. He tipped his hat and searched my face for signs of approachability. Was I so hard-hearted that such protocols were required? I hated that about myself. Even a warm smile and "Hello, Mister Clark" didn't help. He waited for signs he seemed to read in my eyes for which I had no conscious control. Perhaps a gentle touch would help, so I extended my hand and we touched.

"Uncle Olin," Mr. Clark said, turning. "What is going on?"

"These three is on the 5:40," the sheriff answered. "Deported."

Uncle Olin mocked. "Lewdness with a minor," he said. "As if that were some kind of law."

"It is in these parts," the sheriff asserted. "Get aboard or walk." He waved the shotgun.

Sad goodbyes were exchanged. Handshakes. Back-slaps. Touches and kind words. Steam rushed out the boiler and pistons, flooding the depot with white mist, and then the whistle blew. That only rushed an already confusing and hurried departure.

J.T. took my hand. "I so regret we didn't have more time. I wanted so much to–"

"I have my plan, you know. This silly idea of mine..."

J.T. looked deeply into my eyes with longing and sensitivity, ready with new words on his lips. I glanced at Mr. Clark at that very moment, the very moment J.T. would have left a silky fragrance of poetic verse for me to consider. That one glance ruined everything for him. J.T. made the mental connection and nodded understandingly. I felt so bad for him.

J.T. smiled. "You had better tell him," he said, releasing my hand and stepping onto the train.

"I'll try."

Olin danced a little Ozark flatfoot jig, "See ya at the hangin!"

Chapter Twenty-Two

"MISS LORENA! TEACH ME to drive it!" Levi shouted, bursting into my house while it was still dark. Or, I guessed it was still dark at 5:15 in the morning. What a good alarm clock the boy made.

I shuffled from the bedroom in a new Kobey's house dress, those new ones you wrap around and tie in the middle. I tightened it around and tugged it to fit. Ooh, nice! Then rubbed my eyes enough to find Levi going through my icebox and coming up with what he believed was the best choices for breakfast: left-over Johnnie cakes and chocolate pudding. "After work, teach me to drive it!" He blurted, with ground corn flicking off his lips. Mister Clark stood outside with two black metal lunch buckets, politely bobbing his head and looking around.

Levi smiled and added. "I'm getting better at belching? Want to hear?"

I shook my head. "Drive what?" I managed in a mind-fog, but still noticing the cornmeal crumbs falling onto my waxed floor. And wishing Mister Clark might come in, yet knowing he was too polite or too afraid. Still, wishing he might come in and look through my icebox.

Levi ducked back into the dark opening and yelled. "Miss Lorena, I had a dream last night, one of them that last about four hours."

"Oh?" I said, sweeping up the crumbs.

"I climbed up Whitehouse Mountain and built a marble finishing

207

mill up there. All the Austrians worked for me, but then they all quit and went back to Europe and the mill went out of business."

"You're a silly boy—"

He tilted the pudding crock up to let the contents drain in. "They hated me and fired guns at me, not the Dagos, just the Austrians." He turned around with a big chocolate smile. "But I didn't die. Instead, I started a pencil factory and made a million dollars. Then I woke up. See!" He stretched out his arms. "I'm not dead!"

Chocolate pudding dripped onto his shirt.

"What are you talking about? Pencils? And drive what?"

"You know… it's still up at the Larkin." Levi shoveled in another Johnnie cake. "You got better food than Father," he remarked, with the icebox still open and now dripping cold water onto the floor. "Plus, she comes tonight, and I don't know what to do. And you know I'm no good at nothing. You gotta help me, Miss Lorena."

The big steam whistle sounded, which prompted Mister Clark to remark, "We gotta go!" He tipped his hat and headed for the mill with both barrels.

Levi grabbed a bottle of milk and ran for the door. "I'll bring it back!"

What do you do when that happens? Go back to a warm bed? Or pick up a sanding block and remove another ounce of rough marble from Moses with the Ten Commandments coming down from Mount Sinai with his face shining from his meeting with Jehovah God? My brain said, go back to bed. Then it said, what was up at the Larkin? Then it said, Levi, you really must learn to knock. Then it said, who was coming in tonight? Then it said, Mister Clark might like my icebox. Then it said, Haha! Now you're too wound up to sleep!

The note on Olin's Packard, still at the Larkin Hotel, read:

"To my faverist nefu Levi. Retard the spark befor ya start her or she'll brake yer rist. I'll git anether in Detroit. Marry that girrl. I bot the William D. Parry house next to the bank fer yall two. Move in when yer hitched. Heres a hunred dollars. Dont by no popskull."

Oh! That's who was coming in tonight! Was her father coming? Or was she alone? Did they have reservations at the Marble City Hotel?

Which train? What time? Silly boy.

Turned out, she was alone and had no idea where she'd stay that night. The two lemonheads had not thought to make arrangements. And her parents were due in two days. There was evidently to be some big surprise, but she didn't know what. And now she was standing at the Marble train station with no place to go.

"You can stay with me, Adelaide. You know… until you and Levi are…"

"Are what?" she asked shyly.

"You know… umm… didn't you and Levi?" Then I realized he had chickened out again! The poor girl still had no idea what Levi had planned that might require both her father and mother to travel all the way into Marble. After all, it was two hundred miles through the Rocky Mountains and over the Continental Divide. Travel through the backcountry was no small undertaking.

"Wait here at my house, Adelaide."

I walked straight down to the temporary drafting office.

"He's not here," the men said. "Maybe at the mill. The old part that's still standing." Sure enough, Levi was in the column shop getting told how to properly design a Corinthian capstone in a shotgun mixture of Italian and Austrian languages, and probably wondering if they were going to quit the mill and start firing guns at him. I walked up and snatched him by the shirt collar.

"What did you tell that girl?"

Even with the clatter of fifty overhead belts, the thunder of twenty-ton blocks coming off the overhead crane, a man losing a finger on the gang saws and hollering his head off, and the whirl of fluting bits biting into statuary-grade marble, he heard me. And so did twenty Italian workers within trumpet range. They all shrunk back to their jobs. They knew: don't mess with a female with her blood up.

"I was too afraid. You know that!" Levi clenched his jaw.

"But her parents are coming in two days."

"I wired eight dollars. So they could be here for–"

My hands landed on my hips. "For what? So they could be here for what?"

"It's Sunday in two days. I figured we could... you know..."

"Get married? Were you going to tell anybody? Do you even have a ring?" I gnashed my teeth. "Levi!"

"I don't know how to–"

"You're doing it right now. Come with me, Buster Brown." I grabbed him by the wrist and marched him up the hill at a pace even a sixteen-year-old might soon tire of. He stood before Adelaide, who had a pretty good idea what was coming. Her little eyes widened and her hands jiggled at her side. She bounced on little toes at his arrival.

"Hi Levi. I'm here from Cripple Creek!"

Her hands mechanically flew up to her hat and to fix her hair, and then down to straighten her dress, then back up to her hair ribbons, and then back down to the little gray travel dress for straightening and random tugging. Then more bouncing and jiggling and tugging and fixing. Her perky little breasts arched up.

I whispered in Levi's ear. "Remember what I taught you. Kneel down. Take it slow. Step by step." He nodded and summoned his nerve. I stood there knowing what a flood of emotion would emerge from Adelaide's tender heart. When the words, 'will you take my hand in marriage' finally did come out, every passion within her would flow like living water out to him. She would give herself over. She would forget her own bodily functions and belong to him. Those were the words I wanted spoken up to me, so I knew what she had prayed for so many nights. I longed to stand in Adelaide's place, and lose my own bodily functions, and give myself over.

I fantasized over those very words.

I closed my eyes and saw the man I wanted before me, like little Addie in gray chiffon and frills, with nervy hands and bouncy toes. I felt my own constitution flowing out of me, and saying 'yes' before the question was even posed. I saw it all from above Sheep Mountain, swooping in like a white dove on hot winds, and landing right here on Park Street where the two children now stood.

"Miss Adelaide Burns?" Levi began nervously.

"Miss Adelaide Helen–" He tried again.

"Miss Adelaide Helen Burns, will you take... umm..."

Mister Clark walked up. I whispered, "Will you take my hand in—" Mister Clark almost answered.

Levi snapped back to little Adelaide, who had already begun to dip. "Miss Adelaide Helen Burns, will you take my hand in holy matrimony?"

Adelaide couldn't even speak. She just breathed out, "ooo, ooo, ooo" as a baby dove coos in the morning mist, and she smiled so widely no words could possibly emerge. Her emotions emptied out exactly as I knew they would, and weakness blocked any verbal response. Her knees dipped to where Levi had to help her up.

"Yes, I will," she finally said. "I will, I will!" She shrieked. "I will!"

Levi leaned over to—

"Uh, uh, uh," Mister Clark warned. "That's for the wedding night. You know that. When I was your age, I never even—"

"Father, it's modern times." He leaned in for his first kiss, which Mister Clark reluctantly allowed. Little Addie melted in his arms.

Three days later I stepped up next to Mister Clark at the exit of the Marble Episcopal Church. The crowd cheered as Levi and Addie broke into the hot sunlight and braced for a rain-shower of white rice and cheering applause. Trumpets went off.

I smiled. "Congratulations, Mister Clark. Your son is now a married man. What do you think you'll do, now that Levi is married and you're all alone?"

Mister Clark winced. But then Blanche sauntered past and he blinked.

"I'm sorry; I just meant, will you be lonely? I mean, do you think you'll stay in Marble? Or go back to Cripple Creek? You probably have so many friends." As hard as I tried, the sting never left Mister Clark. Some things you cannot unsay.

"I hadn't given it much thought until you mentioned it," he said a little teary, and still grappling with what must have been a swirling cloud of scenarios and emotion of giving over his last son. "Maybe take a trip back to Kansas."

"Kansas? I thought you were from Missouri."

"Oh, just a wild thought. It's nothing." He smiled dreamily and tilted his head into the bright rays of the morning. He half-whispered into the sky, "Have you ever been to Kansas, Miss Lorena?"

"Umm, well I've been to Kobey's new dress display. Do you like what I got for the wedding? Just look at these new cuffs and collars. They change every year and I simply cannot keep up. And…" I peeked up at him. "You won't believe this. Every dress down there is over a dollar now. They even have one for two dollars from the American Ladies Tailoring Company. It's price-fixing. I won't pay it, but Blanche doesn't even care. All she does is spend money. How do you like the new cuffs, Mister Clark?"

He touched the one-inch cuff treatments leading to bloused sleeves, hugging my wrists tight enough to prevent blood flow. I felt his finger through the fabric, that electric connection that stimulates in ways you don't expect, and you still like it. And you close your eyes and it lasts.

"I miss the cicadas," he said.

I lifted my eyes. "Oh… I know…"

"What? There are no cicadas in the Colorado mountains. How would you know?"

Oops, said too much.

I glanced at Blanche, who had been stealing peeks at Mister Clark. "Are you going to marry Blanche? She likes you, you know."

Mister Clark nodded her way, which prompted a little shoulder-shake and a smile. He'd glanced a few more times, which only encouraged the little tart. Ooo, she made me so mad. Her, and her tawdry little American Ladies Tailoring outfits.

I probed further. "Are you and her close?" Mister Clark just frowned and clucked his tongue.

"I saw you walking yesterday. She seems to–"

"Yes, and you walked with Mortimer Mathews. And with J.T. too."

"He told me you turned down an executive position at the mill."

Mister Clark scanned the mountain ridgelines. "It's just… there is something I've been thinking."

"You're leaving, aren't you?" I demanded, maybe too strongly. "You don't like Marble, do you? It's too small-minded. Too remote. Not like the big cities… Cripple Creek and such. Denver."

Mister Clark frowned. "Did J.T. tell you I also turned down the executive position in New York? What's that tell you about my interest in big cities?"

I eyed Blanche again. "That you have something else in mind." The little flirt started fingering pine needles and laying them on her lips like some wanton hussy in a hoochie show. She pulled them over her scarlet lips, and touched them with her tongue. Where did she get such antics? The French magazines? Definitely not in Marble.

Mister Clark sniffed. "You're a little ill-tempered this morning. Let's play a game; that will cheer you up! I got a new idea just for–"

"Does it involve pine needles?"

He frowned. "What has gotten into you?"

Blanche lifted her dress to adjust her stockings, and accidently revealed some ankle skin. She blushed at will, "Oopsie daisy," and smiled at Mister Clark. He didn't miss the hoochie show. Men are like boys; show them a piece of chocolate and they want the whole box.

I turned a lip. "Someone you'd rather play with?"

"Where do you get that?"

"You act like it."

"I do not."

"You're fidgeting and talking about Kansas and–"

"I've had schoolmarms less interested in my behavior. Are you going to slap me again?"

I crossed my hands and gave him a shoulder. "Psst."

Levi called out. "Father… Miss Lorena…" He waved. "It's time for the photograph. Mister Johnson is here. Stand over here next to me and Addie."

I said, "Levi, you're going to have that photograph for the rest of your life. Are you sure you want me in it?"

"Come on, Miss Lorena! He's going to make our image!"

"Your father may not want–"

Just then Blanche bounced in. "I'll stand there!" She slid in next to Mister Clark and fixed her hat. "I'll stand next to Mister Clark." Mister Clark glared back at me but was forced to stand next to bouncy Blanche.

213

The French tart laid her hands on his shoulders and settled in on them.

Before anyone could object, the powder flashed and the shutter clicked.

It was done.

Of course, they looked so perfect together. Her in lurid red silk and flowered hat silhouetted against the mountains and Ponderosa pines. Him, with broad enough shoulders to lay her chin on and collect her ruby red fingernails. Glossy lips and painted eyes. Slender hips nestling in perfectly.

She bounced and scooted around, fixing his hair and tie, and whispering in his ear.

I exhaled in fuming frustration. End of that junk.

I kissed Levi and Addie, and headed up Park Street kicking rocks and yelling at God.

"No, I'm not telling him. Not now."

"But you promised," God said. "Remember, back when–"

"I don't care."

Chapter Twenty-Three

C OLONEL MEEK WAS THE kind of fellow a man like me could lose hours with. But we didn't have hours. It only took one hour to descend from the quarry transfer station to the Colorado-Yule Marble Company finishing mill on the electric trolley – a distance of four miles. And that was when the brakeman felt nervous about his load. You could do it in forty-five minutes on an empty trolley.

Our trolley was not empty on the morning of August 10th, 1912.

In the middle of the electric trolley rested two twenty-five-ton blocks, which were to be a Denver man's monuments for him and his wife. The stones would likely be cut and polished into tall blocks with inset inscriptions – the type you stand and admire when strolling the grounds of any nice cemetery. That precious load meant we leaned a little on the turns, and only occasionally went up on two wheels when the brakeman wanted to give hardened men a little hair-raising thrill.

"Rotary Station ahead. Hang on to yer britches fellas! We're on a hot one this morning!"

We flew around Windy Point where Yule Creek comes into view, and four-hundred feet of empty canyon suddenly appears below you. The thought of shooting right over the edge and into the thin blue horizon comes across every man's thoughts. It doesn't matter how hardened. But I put that out of my mind. I wanted a little time with the

215

Colonel, and I knew he'd be busy once we hit ground again.

"There's one thing I don't get," I asked the Colonel, exerting my voice over the noise of the rattling car. "You organized The Shredded Wheat Cereal Company, right? The Colorado Coal and Iron? And The Colorado Fuel and Iron. Now the Colorado-Yule Marble Company."

"Right. Those were my companies. In former lives, of course."

"What does a cereal company have in common with fuel and iron? Or marble?"

"Jeremiah," the Colonel replied. "I guess I just enjoy organizing new companies. Some fellas enjoy mechanical inventions or engineering. I like engineering companies."

I shook my head and smiled. "I never heard it said like that!"

"Hey I understand you ran a pretty big operation back in Cripple Creek too. Wasn't the Black Jack Mine as big as the Colorado-Yule? So you've done some engineering yourself."

I nodded. "Maybe. And I suppose things worked out as well as they could, given the circumstances. But I never engineered much of anything. Just tried to keep the wheels on. You know... with all that Western Federation of Miners hooliganism."

Colonel Meek grimaced. "That was some nasty union business. Jeremiah, I don't like to leave things unsaid, even if it takes a while. Life's too short. People up here just did not know what you boys went through. The Western Federation of Miners is a terror outfit, in my opinion. I don't want them anywhere near this mountain. And I appreciate you heading that off when you did. I don't know if I truly thanked you for that. But I am now."

"Oh, that's—"

"Fellas, we got a problem!" The brakeman hollered. He jiggled the air brake lever with horror on his face. His jaw clenched, and eyes widened.

W.F. Frazier said, "What's wrong?"

The brakeman burst into good cheer. "We're all missing the Marble Tea and Social Hour at the Elks Lodge!"

All the men laughed and shook their heads.

There were seven men on the dead-end rattler, actually just an old CR&SJ flatcar converted into an electric trolley to haul blocks down from the quarry. And that was an engineering marvel if I ever saw one. Motorman cabs were installed at each end, leaving the middle for freight – a capacity of about seventy tons if you were man enough to operate it.

One does not 'drive' an electric trolley. As with any large piece of equipment, one 'operates' it. Fifty-gallon compressed air tanks actuated the brakes, which had to be bled and flushed yearly. One ounce of water in those lines would kill you in about eight different ways.

That was nothing to mess with.

But still, the New Boots on the electric tramway were given faux maintenance tasks like being handed a kerosene can and told to top off the fuel oil, or told to shine up the rails with emory cloth for better traction. When a poor fellow came back to the shop perplexed, everyone laughed and shoved him around. So the mood on the old bone-rattler was light and jovial. Plus, it was a break from hard labor. All you had to do was enjoy the ride into Marble and the view over Yule Creek hundreds of feet below.

Colonel Meek asked, "Won't you reconsider that executive job, Jeremiah? You got dirt under your fingernails. I need good men like–"

The brakeman hollered again. "Confound it; I'm serious this time, fellas. We got trouble."

The men all shook their heads and chuckled, then went back to idle talk. That is, until the car jolted, bucked, and we nearly went overboard. At twenty miles per hour, you did not want to go overboard. You could break a leg or a collarbone. It happened every week, and nobody wanted to be laid up for four weeks without pay.

W.F. Frazier yelled at the brakeman. "You locked up the brakes, Johnson. Come on!"

The brakeman pulled the lever, released, and pulled it again. "Consarn it! You rolling junkyard." Only after six more tries and another run at profanity did the brakes release and we were rolling free again.

"Learn your job," a quarryman yelled. "Yer going to kill us!"

The brakeman ignored him and kept at the lever.

Somebody quipped, "If Sylvia Smith died in a railway accident today, the Marble City Times would get its news from Hell tomorrow!"

Everyone roared and piled on even better Sylvia Smith and Marble City Times jokes. Like, "What's the Marble City Times headline when Colonel Meek gives free marble to build a church? BLESSED IS THE MEEK. FOR HE SHALL INHERIT THE WORTH."

Laughter spread freely from man to man, except the brakeman who ran from end to end pulling levers and rapping pressure gauges and valves. He even dropped to his belly and threw his head and shoulders over the edge of the car for a look at the underworkings.

The car picked up speed, which brought another ration of grief from the men.

"Slow it down, you imbecile. You'll kill us all."

"I'm not joking, boys. We got problems," he said. "No air pressure. No brakes. We should jump while we still can. There's a seventeen percent grade coming up after Rotary Station. And then we got Smelter's Curve." He slapped a pipe wrench to an air value fitting to no obvious effect. Golden aspens whipped by. Slap an aspen branch at this speed and you'd lose a finger.

"What about the hand brakes?" W.F. Frazier hollered.

"Not working," the brakeman shrugged. "Try the brakewheel yourself."

Frazier twisted the brakewheel without effect and growled. "Brakes are probably hot from all that skidding. Shot, by now."

We rattled past Rotary Station and picked up speed on the sudden downgrade. A worker jumped out of the depot shack yelling his head off. "Fools! You gotta stop here for cool-down and safety check. You'll roll over into the old slate quarry!" His hands fell, and he shook his head and went back in.

Another try at the hand brake made no change. Seventeen percent grades are real. We doubled speed in five minutes, which makes your stomach drop and your hair burn, all at once.

"I tell you," the brakeman yelled out, still wielding the monkey wrench with terror on his face, "We gotta jump. We gotta go before we hit Smelter's Curve." He pointed down the track at a turn on the lip of a three-hundred-foot ledge. The Yule Creek tumbled over train car sized boulders jutting out of the canyon walls. And that turn flew up on us faster than it ever had.

I never saw track come at me so fast.

Homer Knouse threw out his arms and leaped into the crisp air. Time stopped for one desperate moment as the man hung suspended in the wild blue horizon, with his eternity in the hands of the Man who spoke it into existence. Homer Knouse had guts. He had faith. He was prayed up, read up, and his mind made up. A second later, he touched down, rolled a half-dozen times and came up on his feet like a circus acrobat. Homer raised his arms with a big smile. "I'm okay!"

"Lucky cuss," I yelled with a smile.

The quarryman went next, followed by the brakeman and an Italian marble grader.

Only Colonel Meek, W.F. Frazier, and I lingered. And I don't know why.

The rattling flatcar reached sixty miles per hour. It was time.

Colonel Meek yelled out and leaped. "I'll see you here... there... or in the air!"

Just as the Colonel entered the air the load shifted and the rich man's monument slid off the flatcar and landed only moments after Colonel Meek, nipping his heels like a yappy terrier. The Colonel went one way and the block went the other, smashing down four aspens before stopping.

Meek landed on his feet, but hard and bad. He catapulted twenty-five feet with hands and legs flailing for purchase but finding nothing but open blue sky.

W.F. Frazier yelled, "Even the load is jumping ship!" We both went next.

When the Colonel finally came down again, there was another hundred feet of rolling, scrambling and sliding over rough ground. And it was just in time; the trolley rounded a curve and flew over the cliff wall. A burst of smashing trees and dust gave evidence of the crash below us.

Colonel Meek didn't rise.

Every able man scrambled to the Colonel. "Walk it off," W.F hollered. He grabbed the Colonel and worked to erect him. The man was crying in manifest agony, in great pain but perfectly conscious. "Leave me be!"

"Are ya busted up?" Homer skidded to the Colonel's side. He pressed Meek's legs and arm. The other men probed his ribs and skull.

"I don't believe he broke a single bone," W.F. said, surprised and happy. "Guess it wasn't your day!"

"I… I… I can't," the Colonel eked out. "Can't get up."

"But you ain't busted up," Homer informed him. "You gotta get up. Come on!"

"He's just shook up," I said. "Leave him be. We'll get another trolley."

Evidently the Rotary Station man had already called down to Marble for another trolley. The Number Six was trundling up past Forest Lawn even as we worked on the Colonel. The Marble men could have missed the signature brake squeal, or witnessed the crash from the depot and sent a car in response. In any case, a new trolley came in as fast as able men could deploy it.

"Let's get him up to the tracks," W.F. said. All the men grabbed an arm or leg or head and managed him up to the waiting trolley. "Can you stand now?"

"Absolutely not," came the answer from the ailing man. "Something's wrong."

And the answer was still the same when we reached the mill, so we loaded Colonel Meek into his Model T Ford, which must have been a considerable comfort to his ailing body compared to the bone shaker he'd just come off. Doctor H.H. Swift met us at Meek's home on the hill.

"You are all correct," the doctor confirmed. "No broken bones. But I cannot say why he ails so. There must be something ruptured inside, but I do not know what."

"You are a surgeon, aren't you?" W.F. asked. "Why don't you—"

"You can't just cut into folks. I will check on him Monday. That should give him a few days to recover on his own. He may be just shaken up inside. Terribly shaken up, is my guess."

That must have been the wrong guess because Colonel Meek spent the next two days in great pain. We checked him again for broken bones. Not a thing out of place. He just felt like dying is all, the pain was so bad.

W.F. couldn't stand another minute of pacing. "Call in a specialist from Denver. We can get someone out here by tomorrow, or Wednesday at the latest. Somebody has got to figure out what the pain is from. He can't just lay there in agony."

"I agree, call them up."

But the specialist wouldn't be in until Wednesday morning, or maybe after noon. And that was probably not soon enough.

Colonel Meek called us together around ten in the morning, Wednesday the 14th, while his strength was still up. "Fellows, I feel myself leaving this earth."

"Don't talk that way," I said, rubbing his hand. "The Denver doctor will be here on the Twelve 'O Five. We'll have him up here by twelve-thirty. And you'll be feeling better–"

"I appreciate your optimism, Jeremiah," he said. "But if this accident should not turn out right I want the work to go on just as I have planned. That is why you are here." He looked up earnestly at W.F Frazier and me. "Promise me the work will go on."

"Of course… but–"

"I'm going to give you full instructions for the mill, and then turn the daily operations over to you two." Every word seemed to extract another ounce of strength from the man, and he didn't seem to have that many ounces left. But he kept on. "You must bring in new contracts, and those contracts must result in profitable employment for the men. We are not here for ourselves. We employ men who provide for their families. Your first priority is to get those government contracts signed and in the mill. We have invested heavily for that very outcome and have not yet seen evidence of their promise. Without them, the bonds we've carried will come due and there will be nothing to cover them. You must not default on those bonds. Do you understand?"

The clock on Colonel Meek's bed stand was slowly approaching the twelve o-clock hour.

"The specialist will be here in less than an hour," I reminded him. "We've got men with instructions. Maybe you should sleep until he–"

"I'm leaving you all, Jeremiah. And I…" he exhaled and labored for new breath. "This will be my last hour with you. Please listen to my words." He gathered up more breath. "The time for new investments in the mill and new equipment…" The words came more difficult every minute. "Are ended. Turn your attentions to contracts and profitability and…"

The clock struck twelve.

And just like that, Colonel Meek was dead.

I waited for more, but knew it was over. And fell to the floor in disbelief.

"That is not possible," I whispered. "It can't be," I muttered about eight times in a blank stare, with Frazier standing over me in the same state. It just was not possible that the man who built this enterprise, and who had so much more to accomplish was gone. Does that happen to people? How? Cut short in the middle of their finest work? And with so many depending upon them? How is that even possible? The whole notion seemed unreal and impossible. It must not be true.

"No, it is not true," I said, pulling myself up for another look, but without the strength. I sat back down and muttered incoherently. "Not possible. It's just… Uahh.. It's just not…"

Most of the men on the trolley had already poured into the bedroom, and nobody believed the very evidence before them. Hands rose to faces. Long inhales, uncertain exhales, heads shook and bobbed.

Terrible shock filled the room. Terrible and dreadful shock.

I wanted to smash the alarm clock by the bed because it kept ticking as if nothing had happened.

Twelve O' One.

Twelve O' Two.

Twelve O' Three.

Why doesn't it stop? The man is gone, for heaven's sake!

Miss Lorena had finally entered the bedroom with Levi and Adelaide. The small room had filled to over thirty people by now. Some came; some went. I was able to stand and greet her, but I had no words except, "He's gone. Just gone. From the crash."

W.F. Frazier called for meetings the very next day, as if we had any interest in business. But for him, something had to be done about the poor state of contracts and over-leveraged assets. It was a bad combination, he said, and one that desperately needed an answer. Even at a time like this.

"I honestly don't know if we'll come out of this," he lamented with shaking hands. "Meek was the life of this outfit. He closed the contracts. People liked him. And people do business with people they like." Frazier lifted a hand to me. "Clark, you're a likeable fellow. And you brought in those government contracts from your friends in Washington."

"Yes, but remember most of those have no congressional appropriation yet. That Lincoln Monument project has cleared the House, but it's still a ways off. I don't know—"

"Can you speed it along?"

"Maybe, but you know the Senate is still comparing our marble samples with those from Vermont and Georgia. That alone takes months."

W.F. threw up his hands. "Of course we'll come out on top. Our statuary golden vein is the whitest and handsomest, and cannot be duplicated in the world. So we'll come out on top."

"Of course," I said. "But it still takes time."

"We don't have time," W.F. growled.

"What do you mean," I asked.

"We have four bonds coming due next year. They are underwritten at a million dollars each. And we have to pay them in full. And then there are others to follow in 1914. I'm not even going to talk about 1916."

That thought struck me. I knew the Lincoln deal was only worth about one million to the Colorado-Yule Company, and it was the biggest in the works. The post offices, the court houses, the state buildings, and municipal offices in the backlog might add up to another million. That meant we were two million short. And that didn't count the forty-three-thousand dollars a month in wages. You couldn't raise that kind of capital through investors like J.T. Martin, even if you had spent five days next to them in a creaky farm wagon, and the next two years fighting

223

government prosecutors eager to hang your granddaddy. My old friend William Jackson Palmer was dead of a riding accident. His banker, Governor Peabody was retired and enjoying grandchildren in Steamboat Springs. President Roosevelt was tapped. Andrew Carnegie might be an option, but I didn't know him well – not well enough to float a million-dollar marble deal. Maybe the Mellon brothers. Those were all distant contacts I had not developed in years. Marble had been a retreat from all that – business deals, back-slapping, handshaking with brandy and cigars, late nights, and shaky partnerships.

I was out of that world.

How was I to come back? And did I even want to?

Nope. Not a chance.

I drifted into wonderment at why I had never taken the distinguished title of J.H. Clark over the less influential Jeremiah Clark. Wouldn't it have lifted my business acumen to greater levels? Initials like R.C. and J.T. and W.F seemed to do that naturally, as if some unnamed marvels lay stored up behind them. I pondered the successes and failures of the Black Jack Mine, and how Cripple Creek could have been just the beginning if only I had used J.H. instead. I certainly could have–

"Are you still with us?" W.F. snapped his fingers. "Jeremiah?"

"Oh, yes. Just considering financial options. I can get some new contacts. I'm sure. " Ooo, what about Charles Tutt and Spencer Penrose, I thought. They were still in the hunt for new investments, especially since the Utah copper mines were producing at a rate of $200,000 a month. Maybe I could–

"Come on, Clark. Stay with us. We need a new leader. What do you think of J.F. Manning?"

J.F. Hmm, you see now?

That's what I was just thinking. Those initials work. But still. "No, I like Mortimer Mathews." I said. "What do you think?"

W.F. grimaced. "Mathews? Uahh. Maybe."

"Let's bring Mathews out from Cincinnati for a trial run." I offered. "He's out here about every three months anyway. I think he likes the place. He's always cheerful and happy to be here. So he might come permanently and take the reins."

"What about you, Jeremiah?" W.F. countered. "What about you taking the reins?"

"Nope, not me. I'm out of that." Or at least I hoped I was. No, Mortimer Mathews was my pick. Let him suffer the sleepless nights and hand-wringing aggravation. I was out, and happy to be. Plus, I had more interesting thoughts to occupy my sleepless nights.

So we decided to bring him in. But that would take some time.

One week later, W.F stopped by the baby headstone rubbing beds with worry on his eyes and maybe the very evidence of tears. Of course you could not carry on a conversation in the mill. Not anywhere in the mill, and especially not around the rubbing beds or gang saws. I practically lost my hearing every time I went in. It only returned after an hour in the open air with a fly rod in my hands. I had to raise my voice just to hear myself think.

"What's the buzz, Frazier?"

"Clark, it's worse than I thought."

"What?" I asked, laying a hand on W.F, who could barely hold off the emotion.

"I got a look at the ledgers. We're going to have to stop payroll."

My heart fell. I had had an ugly hunch the contracts might freeze until the awful news cleared and new leadership calmed fears. That's how these things happen. It is the most dreadful panic and fear for a time. Every financial consideration halts until emotions settle. Problem is, men's livelihoods are at stake. Their families. Their lives. Eight-hundred men and their families depended upon those financial considerations. Contracts couldn't just freeze up. But evidently they did. But I could not let the men linger in uncertainty.

Fortunately, I had an idea.

Chapter Twenty-Four

I JUMPED OFF THE Denver & Rio Grande at the Midland Terminal in Cripple Creek and stepped out onto Bennett Avenue with high expectations. What had the city become in my six-year absence? Still a booming gold camp? Or a cultured metropolis like Paris?

Or maybe neither. First off, where were all the citizens? It was high noon; there should be two thousand citizens on this very street at this very time of day. There should be carnival barkers, peddlers and prospectors, teamsters and freighters, high fashion, men gone bust and men gotten richer than John D. Rockefeller. There should be drunks puking and busting up stuff, and the fervent faithful converting them into soldiers for the Salvation Army. Bennett Avenue had it all.

So where were they?

I walked from the Midland terminal at the east end of town all the way to the jailhouse at the west end, and did not have occasion to tip my hat or shake a hand. The place was a ghost town. Johnny Nolan's Saloon was boarded up. The Lonely Lode Saloon had changed hands and was renamed, but then closed. The Palace Hotel shuttered. Only the Imperial Hotel remained open.

Dust devils now blew over Bennett Avenue where hundreds of hungry men once trod. Windswept alleys filled with newspaper and trash. Creaky shutters banged on busted windows covered in oilpaper. Signs hung from single rusty nails. And an occasional wild donkey brayed in some back alley, evidently having the city to himself.

This wasn't Cripple Creek. And it wasn't Bennett Avenue.

I knew some of the mines were still open. The Cresson Mine, The Ajax, and Portland to name a few. But I did not expect this.

"Old-timer!" I hailed across the wind-blown street. "Old-timer, is there some big to-do outside the city? Maybe down in Victor? Or Gillett? Where is everyone?"

"Is that you, Jeremiah Clark?" the old man grunted and then headed for me. He didn't even look for oncoming wagons. "It is! Jeremiah Clark of the Black Jack Mine!"

I shook his hand but hung my head. "Well, you know I went bust up there." My eyes instinctively turned east to the Independence Hills and searched for the Black Jack headframe. My gut fluttered with nostalgia sickness. It was still standing, but I'd heard news that they shut the mine down. A lot of headframes remained. About two hundred, I'd guess. Probably all just catching dust devils now. All except the Cresson and a few others hearty enough to keep shifts.

The old man said, "Bust, huh? I did not know that. All I know'd was that you was gone one day. Somebody said yer wife died o' pneumonia, and you went lunatic crazy on account of the loss. We all thought you was up in that Glenwood Springs sanitarium with ol' Doc Holiday's ghost. Either dead or in a state of fixation. Nobody knew."

"I was danged close. I'll admit that." I huffed. "There was a time when I could have gone either way. That was a bad deal. I went bust at the Black Jack Mine, and then Patricia passed, and then my boys headed out for New York City. I was bad off."

"So, you didn't go lunatic crazy?"

"Not quite. I went to Marble, Colorado. And I found something up there."

"Gold?" the old man lifted an eyebrow.

"I don't know just yet. But I'm workin' it."

"You don't know. Okay." The man edged in closer and looked me over. He was clean and well-kept, but not in the highest spirits. "Brother, can you spare a dime? I'm hard up, you see. No shifts at the

Joe Dandy Mine, or the Doctor Jackpot. I check every day but–"

"Sure I can," I said, and dug out a twenty dollar gold piece. It was last week's pay, and about half what I had on me. But the man needed it. I knew this man. He was a mucker up at the Black Jack for a time, my own employee but I never knew his name. I guessed I was too preoccupied to learn it, and the sting of that realization now struck me. I remembered he showed up for work every day, on time, eager for a good ten-hour day. Never caused trouble. He made me rich, back in the day. Him and seven hundred men like him. Now he was roaming the dusty streets of a ghost town with wild donkeys as companions, and no shifts. I figured I owed this man.

I wondered if the anarchist and the unionist knew him, or had any hint of the devastation they left behind. My guess was, they had never even spoken to him. Never shook his hand. They never tested whether their works improved the man's life or brought it to ruination and misery. They just moved on and plied their social experiment at the next town.

It also sounded pretty close to what I had done.

"Come with me, old man. I'll pay you to haul some boxes back to Marble. Once we're there, I'll buy you a suit and give you a job where you can rest a little before you retire. This is no place for a man of your worth."

The old man chuckled, "Worth? I ain't no good. No good to nobody no more."

I laid a hand on his shoulder. "The kingdom of heaven is like a treasure hidden in the field, which a man found and hid again; and from joy over it he goes and sells all that he has and buys that field." I turned to the man. "You are the man I hope to be some day. Come with me."

The electric High-Line trolley was still running. But it was no longer five cents. The cost had jumped to eight, and me and the old man were the only passengers. I remembered when you couldn't get a seat and had to stand on the running boards and hang on. It still cost you a nickel, and you had to wonder if you might round a corner and fly over a two hundred foot cliff. But we all did it.

"We're going up to Victor. Independence, actually. I have an old miner's shack up there. Or at least I hope I still do."

"You gonna open a gold mine?" the man inquired. "Cuz you know… you could split-check lease any one of them derelict mines up there for a dollar a day. I can show you ten mines what still got color. I know the veins. I know every mile of them drifts and stopes."

I didn't answer. Mostly because the thought had not occurred to me in so long.

That was someone else's song.

"We could muck out a few ton and see what we can get. Maybe twenty cents. Twenty cents a ton. Or twenty-two. The Golden Cycle in Colorado City is paying twenty-two, or at least they used to. We could cart a few ton down thar. Look yonder." He pointed into the hillside. "Thar's beasts to be had. We could cart a few ton down thar. I could show you."

"I got other ideas. But I'll consider it." We sat quietly, clicking along the little track through wind-blown Anaconda and over toward Victor. The trolley climbed mountains, and flew into valleys, repeating that ten or twelve times to my delight.

I turned to the man. "Tell me about water."

"It's up to ten cents a bucket. Used to be five. That's a crying shame. But ya gotta wash."

"I mean in the mines," I clarified.

"Aw, they're all flooded. 'Cept them that got tunnels. Drainage tunnels, ya know."

"How come?" I asked.

"Too deep. You know they gotta dig two-thousand feet fer the gold. The Anaconda is three-thousand foot now. Almost down to Colorado Springs. Deep-wise, that is. You know what I mean."

"So why do they need drainage?"

"Cuz they fill up with water, is why. You must know that. Wasn't the Black Jack a thousand-footer?"

"Sixteen-hundred. But we never collected water. I don't know why."

"Well most do," the old man asserted. "And you got to drain 'em. That's tunnels."

"What's the biggest drainage company?" I asked. We had only about two miles until we hit the Independence townsite, up on the hillside next to Victor. I was afraid of what I'd see. How many of the twelve hundred men still remained? Was the Independence Mine still operating? How about the Vindicator? I didn't know.

What about Altman, that union stronghold up higher on the hill? Was it still trafficking in the souls of men? Or was it a long-forgotten pesthole, already stricken from the history books? The Western Federation of Miners was deported and gone, but its carcass might still remain, and its fangs might still be poisonous. I was afraid to look.

The old man pondered the question. "Biggest one? Roosevelt Deep Drainage Tunnel is the biggest. But they got a new one called the Carlton. The Carlton Tunnel, that is. But the Roosevelt... she's the big 'un.'"

"The Roosevelt, huh?"

"You must have read about it. The Roosevelt just flooded in March. They got to go deeper."

"So there's money in tunnels?" I asked.

"Big money! But you got to have heavy equipment and a thousand men for that kind of work. You can't just start up a tunnel bidnez with a mule and a coupla hard fellas. That's big business these days. Not like the old days."

The 'old days' the man spoke of was less than twenty years back. And I was one of those hard fellows with a mule and little ambition. That's all it took back in the old days. But I guessed things were different now. After all, it was 1912, a new century with everything mechanized. You couldn't do anything with a mule and few hard fellows anymore. Not like the old days. Not like the Black Jack days when Sam Whitman and me was double-jacking eighteen hours a day, coming up with fistfuls of high-grade ore every fifty feet, and hollering, "We're millionaires now!"

I almost cried.

But the little trolley squeaked to a stop at the Independence depot. "Here we are," I said.

And I almost cried again.

Everything was gone. Every sound. Every man. Like a snake that shucked its skin and crawled off somewheres else. The Vindicator hoist and headframe at the top of the hill lay silent. The old wooden Independence was derelict – the sheave wheel was crooked, and the cable lay slack. Even the iron-clad Theresa was closed down. Nothing moved. None of the familiar sounds filled the hillside – the thundering stamp mills, the squeaking conveyer belts, dynamite explosions, hammer and bit, men hollering when they lost a finger or an eye, nothing. No railcars collected ore from sorting house chutes, and no tailings piled higher. No billowing black smoke from the stamp mills and crushers. No waste rock spilling over the cribbing and holding up buggy traffic. Nothing but weeds and a few angry crows.

The old man touched my elbow. "You got pinkeye, son? Cuz you keep–"

I exhaled. "The Black Jack Mine was everything I ever wanted."

"Ahh, leave off, son. You busted out is all. It happened to every good man up here. 'Cept Penrose and Tutt. And old Stratton. They'z all busted out now." He looked around the silent scenes of halted industry where fragile fortunes crumbled and blew in winter breezes, and nature worked to reclaim lost territory.

"I just wanted a business. A company. An honest company. Not for riches. Not to be somebody. Just to build something lasting, that's all. But it's gone now. Busted out. I'm feeling a bit like you; no good to nobody no more."

The old man huffed. "Guess we're a pair." We stood mute on the Independence hillside, letting the August sun warm our faces, and the crows squawk overhead, and letting nature reclaim its territory.

I finally pointed up the hill. "Cabin's yonder. Hope it's still there."

And it was. Barely. Yes, it was still standing, but water had eroded the foundation badly, tilting the entire structure by some noticeable degree. I remembered it a little crooked, but not like this. Fortunately, what I was looking for was still there.

"Tear that ceiling out. I'll show you something you've never seen before!"

"The ceiling?" he asked.

"Yup."

Me and the old man climbed onto shredded wheat crates and tore the ceiling off. It was just painted burlap, so it came right off. I stood wondering why I had not thought to employ the burlap on the inside walls also, instead of layers of newspapers pasted one over another. Or even laying burlap over the newsprint, and then a nice layer of boiled linseed oil and lamp black on top of that. That's the formula used in Missoura for a hundred years, and it worked marvels on wind and weather. So why newsprint out here? Had I forgotten my own hearth and heritage? Some things you just cannot cypher out.

Tearing off the painted burlap filled my eyes and mouth with dust and rat turds. The old man toppled off his box and coughed up a gut. But he got right back up there went at it again. There were slats over the ceiling joists, and boxes on the slats. "Nice! All still there," I said. "Just where I put them."

"What is 'em, Chief?"

"You said Roosevelt Tunnel, right?"

"That's right, boss. Roosevelt 's the big 'un. Whatcha got?"

What I had was stacks of tunnel stocks. Boxes of them. Bought when they were ten for a penny. Now they were probably twenty dollars each.

"Look at this gold leaf!" the old man gushed. "This is genuine! Dang, son, you got yer gold mine right here. How many you got?"

"Let's look." Turns out, there were fifty-two boxes. Two-thousand certificates to a box. That was just about right for what I needed. "Now, they ain't all Roosevelt, but I reckon the other tunnels got investors too. This is what I come out here for."

"Whatcha goin' ta do with 'em, Chief?"

"Cart 'em down to the Colorado Springs and see what they'll fetch. You say thar's beasts to be had?"

"What then, boss? Start a gold mine?"

"I'm done chasing the vein."

"Then what?"

"Back to Marble. Want to join me? And before I forget… what's your name?"

Chapter Twenty-Five

I COULD TELL A lot about people just by the pieces they picked up, touched, and admired in my little marble shop on Park Street. If you exhaled to the point of bending over at the cherubs and angels, you might be the artistic type. Or if your smile turned up at the ground squirrels and babies by the riverside, you might just be the earthly and sensual type. Was snow-white marble your choice? Or spidery blue marble? Everything you touched told me something, and I watched everyone.

"Why hello, Lorena," Mortimer Mathews announced, coming into the shop and going straight for the angular cityscapes on discarded marble billets. I only carved those for Denver folk and the occasional Eastern traveler who stumbled into Marble on a Glidden Automobilist Tour. His choice didn't thrill me. But just then Mortimer turned to admire the blue marble broken heart statue, polished with 2,800-grit emery cloth for one-hundred and sixty hours, or until my fingers bled, whichever came first. There might be hope for him yet.

"Give me a minute, Mister Mathews. I'm a little busy just now." What I didn't tell him was that I was busy observing him. Plus, I already had an idea what he came in for. And I needed time to adjust my mind to it. Still, I wanted to see which marble works appealed to his nature. I could get a good bearing on his temperament just from that. And I wasn't entirely settled on the man's footings. Who was this man, really?

I had to know, because the next hour probably depended upon it.

But why? Hadn't I already put my moronic little plan into motion? Hadn't I committed the last two decades to it? And devoted the last measures of an empty heart? Wasn't 'The Big Stupid Plan' my only mental occupation for which I had turned over my independence and self-worth, and became subservient to its effecting?

Sure. But maybe God had a different plan, and maybe I didn't know it yet. There was that possibility. Maybe it wasn't all long shots and blue marble.

"I like the delicate white crystal," he called out. "Not the milky stone. Not the blue stuff. The mill doesn't use any of that." He moved on. "Did you hear about the new investor? At the mill?"

Suddenly I was no longer busy. "New investor?"

Mortimer put down a 'Wheels of Industry' carving. "It seems the Colorado-Yule has a benevolent tradesman. An employee. He saved the company."

"Saved the company from what?" I asked, puzzled by the oddity. What could the company possibly need saving from? A meteor?

"Receivership. For now... The man laid down a substantial sum, covered payroll for the next twelve months, then went back to work. That's why I'm in from Cincinnati. You didn't hear?"

I felt so ignorant. "What is Receivership?"

"Well," Mortimer lifted a finger to his lips, which lent him the air of both company executive and statesman. "A Receiver is a court-appointed man who sells off assets and distributes them to the shareholders. You know... to the investors just before a company is dissolved." He walked up close. "But I didn't come here to talk business. I actually had—"

I nearly dropped the rose press. "Dissolved? Sells off assets?" That was not possible. The city of Marble was forever, and the Colorado-Yule was its assurance of that. This was our home and one we all would defend with every passion within us. So how could anyone even think of selling off assets? Or dissolving anything? This wasn't some 'get rich and get out' kind of place. Colonel Meek would not have it. I knew him. And I knew every citizen in Marble. Not a soul would consider such a ridiculous notion. It would not be a topic of conversation by any right-minded citizen I knew.

Sure, you might read such rubbish in Sylvia Smith's Marble City Times. But Frank Frost would not allow a single line of such talk in the Marble Booster. It made absolutely no earthly sense.

The Marble Booster always had uplifting words like, "Don't you fret; the only way this town can fail would be for anarchists to take over and cause men to want marble as much as a starved dog wants ice cream soda. Cheer up folks! A year from now, if things go the way they're headed, we'll double our population. And you'll get eight full pages of the finest news in the Crystal River Basin."

Mortimer rubbed his forehead and cringed at the rows of bottles and crocks surrounding the shop. "Lorena, let's take a walk. I'm getting a raging headache." He glanced up at the rose oil and beeswax mixtures I had put together, which filled the shop with its unique aromas.

We slipped into the fresh air for a walk.

I rarely walked any further on Park than West 3rd. I'm not sure why, maybe because most of the lots were empty. The 25 by 75 foot parcels sat waiting for new businesses and homes as the company sought new contracts and demand for space increased. Everyone knew that wouldn't be long. In the meantime, every tree on the lots were cut and hauled off for firewood. We crossed Carbonate Creek, hit Center Street, and headed up to Main where all the good citizens mingled. Gentlemen escorted women to their shops and appointments. Silver-headed canes, silk top hats, and polished patent leather. I could sit and watch all day. Main Street in Marble on a Saturday afternoon was a pure vision. A vision of prosperity and promise.

I turned to Mortimer. "You mentioned a tradesman. A benefactor?"

"Oh he's of no concern." Mortimer said. "Just an employee."

"But there was a payroll shortage? And this man—"

"Yes, he covered it." Mortimer paused, "and selected me as the new acting president of the Colorado-Yule Marble Company. I am now the new president, taking the late Colonel Meek's duties and responsibilities."

He turned to me with some affection. "And I was wondering if you—"

"Mortimer! Watch out!" I pointed at two children disturbing the peace, running in between the gentlemen and ladies on the plankway. Upon closer study, I learned it was Levi chasing Adelaide up Main Street. She hoisted a cup of ice cream aloft, and he a spoon. She maintained about one stride of lead over him, giggling and shrieking. He threatened to lick her lips when he caught up.

Just then a hand snatched Levi by the hair. A scolding woman informed him. "Young man, you must be sixteen years old to escort ladies on this boardwalk. That is the city ordinance."

Levi whined. "Ma'am, this is my wife, and she is in the family way. I will be a father soon."

The Battle Axe reluctantly released his hair and said, "Then she should be indoors. This behavior is unseemly." She tidied her hands, having done her civic duty for the peace and tranquility of the city, and stepped back into the Marble City Drugstore. Once inside, Levi smiled and wagged his head, which set Adelaide afoot again. The two scampered across the Carbonate Creek bridge and into the haze of road construction.

I smiled. "Just like his father."

Mortimer shook his head. "Cincinnati is different. You've got your steel mills and coal mills. It's a big city. But we have culture and society. And it's butter upon bacon out there! There are dignitaries and politicians. Men of means, and ladies of leisure. You might like it, Lorena. Have you ever tried a raspberry sorbet? Or worn a cashmere sweater?"

I angled my head for a last look at the kids, then gritted. "I still don't understand why anyone would even talk about this Receivership thing. Until today, I didn't even know such a thing could happen. And I still don't believe it. Don't companies last forever? Why dissolve them? And did anyone even consider what Colonel Meek might say to such a notion?"

"Channing F. Meek was a good man," Mortimer explained, "but

he leveraged the company far beyond its capacity to produce. He overestimated the demand for marble. Companies dissolve all the time, especially when they have fragile profitability–"

I shook my head. "But the whole world wants marble, don't they?"

"It would seem not." Mortimer paused. "I'll be restructuring the company for profitability. Bring in new contracts. Calling in old promises." He inhaled cautiously. "And cutting workforce as needed. But don't worry; everything will be okay for Marble. I will be returning to Cincinnati next week to conduct my business. Have you ever been East, Lorena?"

"Who did you say that tradesman benefactor was?"

Mortimer hesitated. "He is secondary and incidental. The point is, we've still got far too many outstanding bonds, and too much capital investment for business that may never come. The mill is twice the size it should be. It's just too big for the business we're bringing in. Plus, those bonds are coming due next year and the years following. 1916 will be a whopper!"

"Can you fix it?" I asked, still seriously alarmed.

"I can fix the financial end. That's easy. But I lack the artistic craftsmanship this business is based on. I need a partner with hands on the marble. The actual marble." Mortimer took my hands and slid a finger over them. "We're industrialists, not artisans." What he didn't know was that it took a half-pint of beeswax and rose oil every day to keep those fingers smooth and feminine, like baby skin. Without it, the daily carving and polishing would practically turn me into a man. And I wanted to be all woman, all the time.

"What about the Italians? Isn't that why the company brought them over from the Old World?"

"True," Mortimer agreed. "But they could leave just as easily. We need investors closer to home." He turned my hands over and stroked them again. "With the same passions. The same interests." He kissed my hand. "Deep passions."

"Did this tradesman have a name?"

Mortimer became agitated. "Lorena, what is holding you here?"

He waved his hands at the mountains. "Trees? Lorena, I've been to society parties where the enterprises funded and run are decided solely by the wives in attendance. If you think the world is run by men, you have some surprises ahead! Women are the true captains of industry. And you could be one of them, for heaven's sake."

"Captain of industry." I smiled. "I can hardly keep my marble shop open."

"That's because it is undercapitalized and over-resourced. You're putting too much time into each piece. There are machines for most of what you do. You have to think like Samuel Colt. Machines could turn out twice as many carvings in a quarter of the time. I could introduce you to the companies that build such machines. They could take every ounce of human toil out of your work."

"Interesting perspective," I said, tilting my head out of his field of view. We continued east on Main Street to the Main Fork of Carbonate Creek, at the edge of town. All the lots there were staked but never occupied, and maybe never even considered. After all, it was four whole blocks from City Hall. Grass and bushes on all the lots were overgrown and untended. It was no wonder they were unoccupied. It even occurred to me to come out with a hand-scythe and trim them, if nothing more than for the tidy appearance of city. Did the wives in Eastern society do that?

Then I mused aloud, "I was just thinking this fellow must really love this place. You know… to put his own money into the company."

Mortimer added, "Or he's expecting a fat return. No doubt a greedy fellow."

"How much of the company did he buy?" I asked.

"I don't exactly know. Over half."

"So, he owns the place now?"

Mortimer lifted his eyes. "I suppose. He appointed me President, so I'm running the company, not him. My guess is he's just not a true businessman."

"Then how do you suppose he came up with the money."

Mortimer shrugged. "I don't ask questions. Inherited it? Borrowed it? Any number of ways, I suppose. I just think he's not a major factor in the success or failure of the Colorado-Yule Company – just an investor, I'd say. The real decisions are made at higher levels by men with years of business acumen. In Cincinnati and New York. Those are the new power centers. Colonel Channing Meek is gone, and we've got to manage things the way we see fit – from a sound business perspective, not by what locals think."

"What's his name," I asked. "The tradesman investor?"

Mortimer exhaled. "I'm trying to tell you that the man is inconsequential. And I'm hoping you'll recognize the new force of power. I was hoping you might come out and take a look at Cincinnati for yourself. Enjoy the society life. Mingle with the men and women who influence this country. Trust me; you will like it. It's about as intoxicating as fine wine. And just about as sweet."

"Excuse me for my ignorance, but what exactly are you asking?"

Mortimer took me by the hand. He knelt before me. "Miss Lorena, you and I have known each other for years. I come into Marble five times a year, at least. Every time, I stop by to see you, and we have fun, like at the Penny Hot Springs with Blanche. Remember the time we had?"

He paused and smiled. "I think we have a fair basis for an expanded relationship, beyond Hot Springs and walks in the mountains. I've asked you for your hand in marriage before but was not sure of your disposition to it. So I am back again, this time more determined to make you mine. I'm a man of means and an important part of the future of the Colorado-Yule Marble Company."

He kissed my hand.

"Miss Lorena, I'm asking you to marry me and go east to Cincinnati with me. Would you consider that?"

My heart skipped. Breath faltered.

This was real. Not some silly plan I'd invented in my youth, and had never seen the least evidence of reality.

I had to consider this.

"Mister Mathews, you are wise man, and I admire your opinions."

He looked expectantly.

"If I agree to consider your proposal," I began in uncertain territory that nearly gave me the shakes, "would you sit and listen to the silliest idea you have ever heard in your life, then council me on its merits? And would you talk me out of it if sound logic dictates?"

"I'll talk you straight out of it." He said smiling. "And straight into my heart."

Chapter Twenty-Six

"MISTER CLARK, YOU'VE LOST any chance you ever had with me!" I turned and huffed. But sometimes I had to wonder why I said the things I did. The man was always pleasant, never an unkind word. I don't know why, but sometimes I got a bug and said the most awful things. But then I was at my scripture reading spot on the Crystal River just wanting to be left alone. The spot was now twice as nice since the marble snow-slide wall went up to sixty-five feet. Sitting at the base of Mill Mountain under the elm trees next to the footbridge, I was not longer bothered by the big mill or its industrial hum. It was just rippling water in a canopy cocoon. This was my little place and everyone knew it. So what was he doing here?

"I had a chance with you?" he beamed, bouncing from one foot to foot in the chilly morning.

"Probably not. Doesn't the Bible say it's easier for a rich man to go through the eye of a needle than a camel to enter the kingdom of heaven?" The light had not quite peaked over Sheep Mountain, so I read by firelight to the rhythms of churning water. With some chocolate and a little peace and quiet, I could do this all day.

Mr. Clark threw a stick on the fire. "It's the other way around."

I lifted a cross eye. "What?"

"It's the other way around. It's easier for a camel to go through the eye of a needle than for a rich man to enter the kingdom of heaven."

"Whatever you say, Reverend Clark. I guess you know everything." Right there! That's exactly what I meant. It's no wonder men can't figure us out; half the time we don't know what we're saying either. Why not just, Oh you're right, Mr. Clark, and laugh with him? And invite him to my fire? I guarantee it would be a trial for any female to give full attention to the scriptures with a specimen like that next to her. But no, I had to run him off.

But he was jovial. "It also says, with God all things are possible. Hey, want to catch some rainbow's? Maybe a big brownie? I know a honey hole. We'll have breakfast!"

"Already ate. Are we going to have to call you Colonel Clark now? Now that you own the Colorado-Yule?"

"That's an idea!" Mister Clark said with eager eyes. He extended his hands in a grand framing gesture. "I'll have it engraved on my title plaque where I still work: the baby headstone rubbing stones."

"You own the place, right? You bought the majority shares. You paid off two bonds and got payroll out just in time for the men to keep their jobs. Aren't you taking over Colonel Meek's office?"

"You mean Mortimer Mathew's office? Of course not. I'm just a baby headstone polisher. The lowest position we got. Mortimer is still—"

"Oh, you poor thing." I wagged my head and mocked, "I don't know anything; I'm just a baby headstone polisher?" Okay, I'll admit, sometimes I don't know when the kettle's full.

Mister Clark stopped bouncing. "Hmmph."

I lifted the Bible up in front of my face. "Guess it's time to run along."

But he didn't run along. "What is bothering you? And why can't I ever be good enough? First I'm a no-account drifter – a transient, and then I'm your brother's killer."

That earned him a cold hard slap. But he took it without reaction.

"And then I'm an evil rich man. Can I ever be good enough for you?"

"Why don't you marry Blanche? I know you love her."
"You're a child."

Another stiff slap.

The boyish charm Mister Clark came over the footbridge with was rapidly washing down the Crystal River. He stood silent, tightening his lips and favoring his cheek, then clucked his tongue.

"I think I'll leave you now. I'm sorry to bother you."

"Suit yourself. I have my scriptures."

"I'm going back to Kansas," he announced. "I'm going to look up that little girl named Monkeyface and learn her real name. You probably don't remember." He pulled out the old daguerreotype with the name etched onto it. The one he showed me at this very scripture reading spot three years ago. He sniffed and admired it. "I want to find her."

A lightning bolt struck me. I dropped the Bible and fought off a hot flash.

He had my attention now.

"Maybe she's married. Maybe dead. Maybe a committed librarian. But I'll find her." He paused and frowned. "I don't know why I'm telling you; I just thought you should know."

He touched his hat and headed for the footbridge.

Thunder bolts don't always leave you speechless and immobile. Sometimes they make you jump up and grab somebody by the coat and plead, "Please stay. I want to catch rainbow's and have breakfast with you. I'm sorry; don't go. Plus, I need to tell you—"

"I'm sorry, Miss Lorena. I'm leaving." He pulled loose and started again. The train whistle across the river blew. I did the only thing I could think.

I threw myself down on his leg. "No! No! No! Don't go."

But he only dragged me a step or two before turning with a frown. "The train leaves in three minutes. You gotta let me go."

"No, no, Mister Clark," I said, looking up at him. "I am so sorry. I've been a childish brat. Please don't go. I really do need to tell you something." I had promised God a half-dozen times, and each time failed on my promise. The Lord wasn't exactly mad, but liked to remind me from time to time, especially while meditating in the Word of God and prayer. Lately it had gotten a little annoying. I guessed this was the last time.

"The truth is, Mister Clark I knew you–"

"Can I get my leg back?"

"If you promise not to leave," I said, still gripping his feet. He reluctantly promised and returned to the fireside. It would be a quarter hour before light came streaming over the mountain, which meant I could hide my anxiety in the shadows for a short time. But still, Mister Clark didn't give me much hiding room next to the little fire. He edged up close enough to smell him.

The fact was, I wanted to touch his hair and push my fingers into his scalp like a wanton woman. And drag my fingernails over tightened shoulders, and push my fingertips into each little crease between muscles, where the shoulders meet breasts, where the breasts touch the stomach and gut. I wanted all of him. And I always had.

I swallowed hard and settled for his hand instead. "The truth is, I knew you before you came into the store with Levi, six years ago."

"Knew me? What are you talking about?"

I buried my head. "Don't make me tell. Please?"

"Well you can't just say a thing like 'I knew you' and then not tell. What do you mean?"

"Please don't make me. I can't–"

"Alright, then I'm leaving." He stood up and started for the bridge again. "I've got about one minute to get over to that depot."

I lifted my eyes. "What if you reject me?"

That stopped him. "Reject you for what?" he asked.

"I'll tell you. But you have to promise to listen and not leave me." I placed my hands on his cheeks and pulled him close. "I feel so bad at how I've treated you."

He turned and put a few more sticks on the fire. "Okay. I can take the next train."

"Should we catch brownies first?"

"Are you going to tell this? I've already missed my train."

I paced the riverbank for thoughts. And expected a disaster. The moment he learned my lunatic story he would reject me. He would stand straight up and walk over that bridge and never return. This would be the last day I would ever see him, or touch him, or admire him from a distance with his playful little son, Levi. This would be the last time he waved a threadbare immigrant hat on a cold autumn morning, and wished me good tidings for the day, and smiled and skipped past me backwards to the mill, and fell into a ditch but rose up with a smile and a wave. He would never again climb up the sixty-five foot snow slide wall and wave at me on Sunday mornings, and almost slip off, and reach for his hat as it fluttered to the bottom.

He would leave the moment my plan came out of my stupid mouth.

"Mister Clark…" I faltered and cried. "I can't. I'm so stupid. You won't like me."

He sat confused, with hands open and head shaking. But he waved me back to the fire and tapped on the oak stump. I guess he wanted to hear this. A clean handkerchief greeted me.

I cleared my eyes and tried again. "Do you remember Crystal City?"

"Of course, we bunked there fifteen months – me and Levi. The day we arrived here in Marble that sheriff gave us no other option. Except to head back on the next train. They had that NO CREEEKERS sign up at the depot back then. If you ever lived in Cripple Creek, or had any dealings with anybody from Cripple Creek, you were out. It was either Crystal City or the next train."

"Why didn't you take the next train?"

"Well…" Mr. Clark shrugged. "I don't know."

"Umm, I sort of talked to that sheriff–"

He stood up. "What?"

"Umm, well, let's just say I was so happy you picked Crystal City when you left the marble shop that day. I would have been heartsick if you had gotten back on that train. So I kind of slipped over there and talked to Big Jim, the Sheriff."

Mr. Clark shook dumbstruck.

"Remember me in the marble shop that day? Every breath in me wanted you. I knew about the NO CREEKERS sign, and I knew you had a choice so I sort-of told Big Jim the best one." I breathed so free, because it was out now. Or at least it was coming out. Oh God, give me strength… and please don't let him be mad.

"Miss Lorena, you're making no sense." He shook his head. "But I get the feeling there's more."

"I wanted you closer than Crystal City. It is so far up there. But at least you didn't leave. But still Crystal City is six whole miles away, and up that rugged wagon road which I refuse to travel. That is why you ended up in Quarry Town. It took me nearly two years to convince Colonel Meek to put you on a quarry crew."

Mister Clark stood erect. "What!"

I had his attention now.

"Colonel Meek was serious about that NO CREEKERS thing. Good, bad or indifferent, there would be no Cripple Creekers in Marble. That was the law. But I worked on him for months. I don't think his wife liked it, but I poured the man's honey. I sweet-talked investors. I carved monuments for shows. I carved salesman samples. It's a wonder my shop survived. Plus, I did all his photographic promotions. Remember that one at the quarry when we met next? I did twenty of those, just so I could ask him again and again. Colonel Meek said, 'Miss Lorena, your obsession has gone on long enough. You're a beautiful woman with ten strapping men in line for you. I would marry you myself if not for my lovely and devoted wife. You must let this man go.' But I kept asking."

"Asking for what?"

"That you and Levi could come into Quarry Town. I argued that the NO CREEKERS sign applied to Marble, not Quarry Town. But Colonel Meek didn't see it that way, on account of it all being Colorado-Yule property. But he finally assented reluctantly, maybe just to get me out of his shadow. Of course once you were there, I did more of the photographic sessions just to see you. You didn't even notice until that day we met again."

"I don't remember those."

"Remember the day we picked up the cracked stone in Glenwood Springs? And you had to rent that awful swimsuit, and Blanche decided you were a Greek god, and she wanted you that very day? I picked you and Levi for that assignment; Colonel Meek just shook his head and agreed."

Mister Clark began dipping his hands in the water and washing his face. "I'm..." he shook in disbelief. "I... You..."

"Remember the Denver Post Office trip? And the burlap sack of cash?"

He stuttered. "That was–"

"Yes, me again. I convinced Colonel Meek to let me go, and I convinced the Denver Stock Yards to go with marble. Even though they backed out later."

Mister Clark protested. "No, no, sister! I organized that. I remember–"

"Yes, but I did some underground work a month before you ever talked to them. They were ready. I hand-crafted the miniatures six months in advance of the Denver trip. Who can resist those cute little marble miniatures? I put three-hundred hours into them. And I prayed over every one. Lord, give Mister Clark your favor. I polished every one and thought of you. That was my sole occupation for a month. The shop produced nothing until they were complete. I nearly lost it. But I didn't."

Mister Clark squinted into the distant mountains, looking for the first rays to break over. He smiled. "I must say, those miniatures did the deal. I don't believe we would have gotten it otherwise. I still remember the looks on their faces when you pulled them out and arranged them on the desk. It was a vision. The whole plan suddenly took form before our eyes. Even I could see it in a new way." He shook his head. "So that was your doing? I am impressed."

"Mister Clark, I wanted you to know that I'm sorry for what happened at the funeral. I was a fiendish devil, and I am so sorry."

"You had good cause," he said, frowning sadly. "I am so sorry for Thomas."

I took his face in my embrace. We were so close I could have kissed him. "I am sorry too." His newly shaved skin allowed my fingers to find the little creases in the cheek and jaw. Handling marble put experience into my fingers. I felt everything. I had polished every form of the stone, for every kind of customer, for hundreds of hours, and knew the intimate touch of every piece. My fingers fit his face naturally, and found the essence of his being like they had a thousand times in my dreams.

Mister Clark did not pull away, but said, "I was gone after that incident. Plumb gone."

"I know you were. And I am so sorry." I stroked his hair and turned his face back to me. "I was distraught. Lost. And heartsick. Sometimes I just don't—"

"But I thought we had a thing."

"Which is why…" I inhaled long and hard to say, "Please don't be mad…" I held his jaw firm. Mister Clark nodded with equal parts curiosity and disbelief.

"I wrote your Uncle in New York."

The disbelief turned to shock. "You did what?" He broke away and strode into the river rock next to the rushing water, and spun back around. "You wrote Uncle Olin?"

"Your sons, Caleb and Micah told me—"

"Those little—"

"Don't be mad. Please? I didn't know what else to do. I was desperate! I had to do something. You were gone from my life and it was my fault. I just wanted you back again. Plus, it turns out you can write a letter to the White House, and the President will answer. And if you're a pleasant citizen, he will correspond with you. Mister Roosevelt is a very curious soul. His questions didn't end with—"

"Roosevelt too? Gosh, Lorena! How did you… How many letters—"

I thought a while. "Twenty-eight. Over nine months. We were pen pals. I explained marble qualities – you know, crystal structures, hardness, stress fractures, how to find cracks, cutting techniques, extraction, vegetable matter pressed into seams, which seams are okay, and which to avoid. I sent samples of good marble and bad so he could see the difference. Teddy Roosevelt is a real outdoorsman; his appetite could not be satisfied. Plus, he wanted to believe in you."

"You mentioned me?"

"In every letter. T.R's curiosity did not end with marble. So he knows everything."

"Everything what?"

I drew hard breath, and those hard feelings came right back. "Mister Clark, Please don't make me tell. I can't. I'm..."

The worry must have fallen onto my lips because I had to cover my mouth and then my eyes. What if I told him, and he just walked over that footbridge? And he took the train, and never came back. What would happen then? Would I close up and shrink into a nervous mute? A lunatic? A sanitarium stiff with blank eyes and drooling spittle? Probably not, but that's all I could think of. So I forced myself to speak.

"Umm, I sort-of persuaded T.R. to—"

Mister Clark objected. "No! That Lincoln Memorial contract was my idea. Actually, it was Uncle Olin's. He wanted a memorial to Bloody Bill Anderson, but T.R. said that wouldn't hunt with the Yankees. Not after the man scalped and murdered two dozen federals at Centralia – all for just cause I understand – but still a sore subject with the Yankee invaders. So I suggested a memorial to Abraham Lincoln instead. That's how it happened."

I nodded. "I understand. But you came back with the contract. T.R. gave it to you."

"The promise of a contract. It's still not closed, but my confidence is high. So you're saying—"

"I hope you're not mad. But I wanted you back... so that I could tell you one more thing." And then I turned my head. "But that's when Levi started asking about his brothers in New York. And maybe joining them. And you all could live in Long Island with Olin. I panicked and started petitioning Colonel Meek to put Levi on the drafting crew."

"You can't just do that!"

"Oh, Jeremiah... Levi has such potential. Have you seen his drawings? There is life in them. I swear to God. An overflowing spirit, a living water that moves the soul. He didn't belong on the rubbing beds. He's a tender lad, not like you. He didn't have the childhood you had. He's a gifted boy."

"Yes, but—"

"Okay, here's what I mean. Levi once pencil-sketched me while making breakfast, still in my silky night laces because he had to be at work soon. I stood there flipping Johnnie cakes and frying eggs while he confided in me – the whole time drawing on a scrap of paper or cardboard or something, like he does. I didn't think anything of it at the time, until he handed the drawing over. That sketch alarmed me so bad I dropped the lard bucket and put on a proper dress."

Mister Clark's eyebrows went up. "Really? I'd like to see that!"

"Don't even ask."

"Yeah, but do you still have it, cuz–"

"Shut up; I'm trying to tell you something. Gosh."

Mr. Clark stopped misbehaving long enough to listen.

"Levi has exceptional talent and he got on the drafting crew because of it. But I sort-of helped. I felt so selfish, I just wanted you back, and I wanted you to like Marble – to like what we have built here, and to like Colonel Meek and his little enclave in the mountains, and to want to make this a home for Levi and Adelaide, and for you… and me. New York is no place for a child. Levi should be here in Marble with fresh air and Christian values."

"I can't argue that." Mister Clark pulled his fishing rod out of the brush where he stashed it. He tied a fly and whizzed it over the water four times until it landed softly in a little pool and floated around a log and down the river. Sunlight crashed over Sheep Mountain and onto the riverbank. Downy Cottonwood lighted into the river valley under the elm canopy, and warm breezes went through my hair. The hat came off, and my light blonde hair fell out in waves.

Mister Clark noticed.

My heart took healing from the view down river, and wanted to sit by the fire and eat biscuits and trout, and laugh, and test Mister Clark about camels and needles, and hold his hand and smell his hair. I wanted to touch him. And sit and admire him. By noon, the hot summer would tempt us to spread out a bed of aspen leaves and doze and forget whatever lay beyond that sixty-five-foot wall. Chipmunks would chatter in the Ponderosa pines where chickadees nested and chirped, but our eyes would close and warm river breezes wash over us.

I could lay here all day, just looking at him. His presence was chocolate enough.

But the Lord whispered, "Don't get comfortable. You haven't told him everything."

Sometimes I just wanted to say, Oh be quiet, Lord; you don't know everything. You don't know what he would say. The bucolic scene in my mind changed to Mister Clark taking a handcar down to Redstone like before, after hearing the truth, and swearing, never again. That woman is nuts.

But I pushed the fears behind me.

"I liked the little copper wedding ring you made me," I said. "Back when Levi interviewed." I pulled it from my dress pocket and put it on.

Then I bedded and banked coals for Mister Clark's trout. He also liked to stash a tin of biscuit flour in the aspens. So I pulled it out and made dough. Two trout filets were soon on the coals, followed by the biscuit dough.

"The stupidest thing I ever did," I continued, with Mister Clark still in a state of disbelief and probably wondering what came next, "was work the telephone office when Myrtle Linda had the flu, and I knew snow slides were imminent. Everyone knew. All you had to do was look up at those fifty-foot cornices hanging over the ridgeline of Mill Mountain. Colonel Meek knew, and he should have closed the mill but he didn't. So I manned the telephone offices."

"That was a little crazy."

"But nobody thought the mill would be crushed like it was. The worst anyone could imagine was a few caved-in roofs. Total wreckage wasn't even imaginable. Of course, that was before the marble wall." I pointed yonder at the massive avalanche wall, erected only one year earlier – fifteen feet thick at the base, and now sixty-five feet tall.

"I expected you and Levi to come over and force me to come home, and I'd bake pies for you, and we would have a sing-along because I know your favorite song, and I would sing for you, and you would fall sleepy by the fire and I would sit next to you with a book. I never thought the whole thing would be in ruins."

"You were almost killed." he paused. "Wait... you know my

favorite song?"

"But you saved me." I said.

Mister Clark nodded. "And then almost died."

"Did you know that I nursed you?"

"No, I did not. I remember dreaming in delirium. I was on pillows of cotton. Drifting, dreaming. Happy and delirious dreams, I guess. It was nice. Nicer than one might imagine, in the death throes of pneumonia with only a quarter of a lung holding you to this world. It was nice. I do remember that. I felt warm and loved. And I felt like it wasn't time to go into eternity – that there was something here for me, something unfinished, something to come back to, and that I should figure out how to live. So I did. I lived again." He shook his head at the absurdity, and then turned to me. "How did you nurse me?"

I blushed. "You don't need to know."

"But I want to."

"Sorry, Jeremiah. There are some things I will not say. So don't ask."

"Like the pencil sketch?" he teased.

"Oh, shut up!" I shoved him and hid my face. "But I sang to you. Your favorite song."

"Which one?"

"You know."

Mister Clark served up the trout and biscuits. I wondered how a man could cook so well. Did mothers teach those things? Or did men figure things out for themselves? I watched his efficient moves over the fire, squatting and spinning, nursing a hot finger, and finally dishing up a little riverside meal as delightful as any boarding house could manage. The man was handy. And not a bit tiring to watch.

He finally said, "I don't love Blanche. Maybe she thinks I do, but I don't. I never have."

"I had to let Blanche try, you know."

"Why?"

"Remember the Glenwood Hot Springs? At least she had the etiquette to ask back then. And I said yes, even though it nearly ruined my heart. But I figured if you loved her, then it didn't matter what else I had to say."

"What else do you have to say?"

I inhaled hard again, and breathed out between salted trout and biscuit. "I have to say that both Olin and J.T. made marriage proposals. You should know that. They are genuine men, and they both stirred me in their own ways. But I turned them around and persuaded them both to invest in the Colorado-Yule. Which they both did, as you know. And Buford. They all invested in you. Not the Colorado-Yule. You. I guess you know that. But, Mortimer Mathews... I'm afraid you'll fire him."

"Why would I do that? Mathews is a good man."

"Umm... because he also wants to marry me. I'm afraid you'll just fire—"

"I'm not like that. Mortimer Mathews is a capable manager and—"

"Jeremiah, I have more to say."

"I figured," he said.

Oh gosh, Lord. This is it.

I reached into my purse and slid out a silken pouch I had carried for twenty-five years. It was faded and frayed, stretched and stitched, and patched and pampered. I marveled to see it in one piece. Actually, I had not pulled it out in two years. My broken marble heart could not bear it, cracked and spidered in flinty blue such as it was, broken and discarded on the ash heap of ruined dreams – a state of ruination. The little silken sleeve was forgotten.

But I knew exactly what the pouch contained. It contained my last hope in life. My failing pulse and lifeblood. The very last reason for living. A stupid and shallow reason by all human reckoning, but it was my reason. My reason for living.

Mister Clark asked falteringly, "What do you have there?" But he knew. The man wasn't senseless. His own body betrayed the shallow question. It could no longer carry him erect. And by my best calculations, he could no longer talk.

He knew. And I knew that he knew.

I unwrapped the little sleeve and pulled an old tin daguerreotype from it. The image was as brilliant as the day it was struck, but fuzzy about the edges, with thumb prints permanently imprinted by a hasty photographer who had simply wanted his three cents from a young customer and to move onto more lucrative sittings. For that price you only got the two-by-three-inch tintype. And this photographer needed every customer.

Even an eleven-year-old customer. With three cents to spend.

On the bottom was scribed the odd word, Monkeyface.

I handed the image to Mister Clark who managed to arise and take it, although he shook so bad that it escaped his grasp for a half-second before being snapped up again.

"Jeremiah, do you recognize that skinny boy? And the little girl who loved him so?"

Jeremiah touched the image and could not breathe. He only huffed in short sequences, eyelids fluttering and head bobbing. Tears formed and fell. Then he cried and sobbed and lay his head on my breast, but could not so much as lift his disabled arms. He could have toppled into the river and washed downstream like a leaf.

I propped him up. "I love you, Jeremiah. You are good enough for me. You always will be."

I touched his face, still fixed on the image of us as happy children who played together in Leavenworth City, Kansas.

I did not remind him that the smile on the boy's face was just after he had tricked me into hanging upside down from a tree limb so my dress would fall over my head and he could sneak a look at my under-bloomers. But even so, I was happy too.

The mischievous boy was my hero and idol in Leavenworth. He had faced his fears in a strange land far from his home and mother. I was eleven; he as fifteen, and he could do anything – a giant, a hero, a real man. I dreamed of this giant man every night since, and smiled at the mere thought of him.

"I have loved you my whole life," I added. "I just met you a little too late. You belonged to Patricia."

I stroked his cheek and hair, and placed my face next to his, pressing my breasts into him. I breathed in his fragrance and breath. Two became one breath. He breathed in mine, and I his. I wrapped my hands around his, which still clutched the image as if it too was his only reason for living.

Our lips met for that one kiss I had waited for since Kansas.

"Jeremiah," I said softly. "I am Monkeyface, and I have waited for you, my love."

Epilogue

ONE WONDERS IF COLONEL Channing Frank Meek had jumped a minute earlier and survived the trolley accident of August 10, 1912 if Marble, Colorado could be producing quality stone on an industrial scale to this day. The truth is, the Colorado-Yule Marble Company and the city of Marble, Colorado never really survived his passing. The company fell into a string of human tragedies, natural disasters, and financial woes that brought an undignified end to Colonel Meek's grand vision.

Trouble began almost immediately after Meek's death with another trolley death, followed by a mill fire the next year. Mortimer Mathews perhaps sensing financial ruin resigned, leaving J.F. Manning at the helm. The company had issued $3.5 million in bonds that all came due in 1916. The inability to pay put the Colorado-Yule in a state of default and eventual receivership. Even the million-dollar Lincoln Memorial contract could not pull it out of a bad fix. Mortimer Mathews stepped back in and attempted reorganization, but was unable to raise enough capital to cover obligations.

The Great War in Europe drew all skilled Italian and Austrian workers back to their native soil. Demand for marble as building materials dropped to unsustainable levels during war years.

By 1917, the Colorado-Yule Marble Company shuttered operations.

Every employee was gone.

And then the mill practically burned to the ground.

A contract for the Tomb of the Unknowns finally came through during the Great Depression, but it was not enough to return the company to any profitable form. Skeletal crews quarried and finished marble on a reduced level until Carbonate Creek overflowed its banks in 1941 and washed out nearly every building on Main Street. The Second World War followed within months. When it ended, like evil bookends to an already beaten community, Carbonate Creek overflowed again, taking almost everything else.

The mill was never rebuilt.

Studious visitors to Marble today soon ask a dizzying string of questions like, where exactly was the finishing mill and how big was it? The books say a quarter mile in length, but I can't see it. And what about that sixty-five-foot avalanche wall? Where is it now? I see a few blocks by the Crystal River, but no giant wall. How about the big turntable? I couldn't find it at the east end of the old mill site. And I'm confused by the position of Carbonate Creek. Shouldn't it be running a few blocks east of its present course? What about Quarry Town up on the mountain? Where's that? And the most puzzling question of all, where was Main Street? There's nothing left.

That is the legacy of a once-grand utopia beset by disaster and bad luck.

It was a blowing ghost town for decades.

But still, the town of Marble remains as a pleasant tourist destination today. It's not all gone. Beaver Lake remains, and the lodge next to it. The Crystal City Mill remains, and so does the old church and schoolhouse. The quarry is still there, and still producing on a small scale. Marble shops and museums remain, and a thriving vacation rental community remains. You can still walk Park Street under downy cottonwoods, and gaze up at towering Colorado mountains all around you.

Plus, the finest marble artisans in the world still pilgrimage to the origin of the hardest and highest quality statuary marble found anywhere in the world, Marble, Colorado.